and
its Role
in
Asian
Communism

A Novel by
Colin Cotterill

Copyright © Colin Cotterill, 2005
First Published 2005

Published by
DCO Books
Proglen Trading Co., Ltd.
Bangkok Thailand
http://ebooks.dco.co.th

ISBN 978-1500750404

Preface

I'm telling you this story on account of it being personal, on account of us spending this morning at the cemetery, and on account of there ain't no-one else that wants to tell it. So if you care to hear it, looks like you and me's stuck with each other.

I don't say I can tell it as good as it should be told, and I ain't gonna win no No Bell prize, less they got a special section for books that don't got no grammar in them. But it's important it gets told. That's my opinion anyway.

I guess it all started in 1970, before I was born. There's folks wish I wasn't born at all, but it's too late now and I don't want to get on to that.

If you never heard of Indiana, then you sure as hell never would of heard of Mattfield. But this is where the story started. Back then there was a factory here. It sort of give folks a reason for living in Mattfield. Once the plant was gone there weren't a reason no more, and anyone needing work just left. It's kind of quiet now. Fact there's just me.

But this story ain't about now, it's about then. The young guys at the factory, them that couldn't get out of it, was all doing their patriotic duty in Vietnam. Most of 'em had their patriotic duties splattered across some rice field by the Viet Cong. While they was off getting themselves killed, the factory took on women and other second rate people to fill the gaps. Them years saw some odd characters on the shop floor. A lot of 'em couldn't of got work minding street poles nowhere else.

But I'm gonna tell you about two people that was about as different from each other as a lobster and a bank. The only thing they had in common was they was both outsiders, and they got kind of squeezed together by fate.

I'll tell you about what happened to these two. I'll try make it sound like a real story, you know, throw in a few jokes and make you feel like you was there too. I'm new at all this. Here goes.

1

A pink 63 Chevy pulled up inside a shadow in front of the factory. The driver kicked open the stuck passenger door, got out, hitched up her glittery skirt, and peed on the dust. When she was done, she stayed squatting and looked up at the black walls and the meshed-over windows.

There was two lights over the factory sign. One of 'em was throbbing like a hangover. Their job was to announce to the world that this was, 'ROUNDLY'S POOL AND BILLIARD BALL COMPANY CORP. Established 1928'. She should care less. The paint on the sign was peeling and it was kind of embarrassed by all the attention.

Squatting there with her bare ass sticking out she looked one hell of a queer sight. If she'd been that five year old kid beside a rice field in the middle of Laos, no one would of minded. It was all pretty darn normal when she was a kid. You took your bath in the rain hole with the buffalo. You et the scraps that was left for you. And you stuck out your fanny and peed wherever the mood took you.

But there was different rules in Indiana and Ohio and Pennsylvania, and all them other shit holes she'd drifted through over the past sixteen years. All that drifting was slowly rubbing away the memories of what her home had been like. She didn't have that many to start with: her one and only cloth skirt that she'd scrubbed so many times there was only hope holding it together, the sun roasting her bony back when she gathered the squeaky rice, the mosquitoes chewing away at her when she slept on the bare bamboo slats, and the old witch snoring beside her. There was only about that much left.

And time, the same time that was rubbing away the memories, was making them memories feel a lot better than they deserved to be. Cause if she compared them with what she was now, they wasn't so damn bad.

She sighed, climbed into the back seat, and tried to get some kind of sleep over the next three hours. There weren't nothing to dream about.

"Another frigging factory".

2

Six blocks south there was a room. It smelled of cremated hamburger cause that's what burned there earlier and smells didn't have nowhere to go. Sounds? Well, there was the ticking of a clock, the wheezing of a busted cistern, the pings of dumb insects butting the light bulb outside, and fat Waldo's watery snoring.

It was some time after three and the quietest time the room ever had. The late drunks and ragers and sex maniacs in the rooms around was all unconscious at last. The wife slappers was slapping other men's wives in their dreams. The bratty kids was smiling sweet like they'd never made no one miserable.

It'd be another 200 minutes before the morning sounds woke up; the throat clearing and screaming, the slamming, crashing, rocking and rolling, motors roaring, glasses smashing, Crispies snap, crackle and popping, coffee bubbling, and miserable babies warbling. Course, that was all other folks' business, but in a stack of apartments thin as cardboard you minded other peoples' business like it or not.

Waldo was busy dreaming about Mexico again.

He's dancing on a sombrero. His old fat legs are going at it like bee wings. You can't hardly see 'em. There ain't no music far as he can hear but he sure is making a mess of that old sombrero. It don't seem odd to him he'd be dancing on it. Hell, it's Mexico. They all dance on their hats in Mexico, right? Least that's what he thought.

But then the dream camera pulls back and all around him is this circle of mean looking Mexican hombres with black moustaches under their noses The more he dances, the more he mashes up that sorry sombrero, and fluffs of material start settling on them black mo's. The Mexicans sure don't like that, and one by one they draw these razor knives and

3

…and that was when Waldo pulled the dream emergency cord and bailed out before it was too late.

He was back in his room swimming in sweat. Why did all his Mexico dreams end up like that? He wiped his shiny black face with the pillow. It was still early but there wasn't no way he was going back into that there dream alone. No way. He couldn't work it out. All his awake Mexico dreams was so happy, but his sleeping ones was blacker'n midnight. It didn't figure.

He walked slowly across to the bathroom. He stood himself under the water rose and turned the tap on. Water come out. It's true. That wasn't such a normal thing in Waldo's place. It only happened if you got in there early enough. The brownish water washed away the sweat and the nightmare, and left him feeling as good as he was likely to feel all day.

But he didn't care about nothing. He wouldn't have to put up with all the crap much longer. Two more months and Mexico wouldn't be a dream no more. Two more months.

3

Feet shuffled past the pink 63 Chevy, through the gate and into Roundly's. Waldo's feet was among 'em. All the boots made sounds, but the people in them didn't. There was some unwrit rule you had to be as miserable as sin before the siren sounded. These was folks that resented their lives being interrupted by work. They ignored each other till they was forced to be workmates.

Waldo looked at faces he'd been seeing all his life. They'd started off as little round red faces, then went through being pimply, then smooth, then hairy, till they ended up miserable, no-hope faces walking to Roundly's like they was walking to reckoning day. He remembered his grandma telling him how every time you smile at someone and they don't smile back, a bird drops out the sky.

Thirty-eight years ago he tried to smile at everyone in the morning but them faces stayed sour as unwashed milk cartons. So thirty-eight years ago he stopped smiling too. There was too few birds in the sky as it was.

After 7 you might get the odd grin. That's when folk's engines kicked in like old VW vans on cold mornings. Once they started being sociable there was the chance of a conversation or two. But don't you go confusing 'sociable' with 'friendly'. Weren't really no-one on friendly terms at Roundly's. Best buddies arriving at the plant together was likely to be knifing each other by the third week. It was just that kind of place. Some said it was the ball fumes.

Waldo got more bad feeling than most. It wasn't cause he was a nasty person. He was probably the nicest guy at Roundly's. It wasn't cause he was black. He'd been around so long, most people had forgot what color he was (and we'll get on to colour later). Only young punks passing through town tried the 'nigger' thing on him. But they didn't last long at Roundly's. No-one with the initiative to be racist could survive the mind-numbing work at that damn factory.

Waldo had been there since his 27th birthday. He'd done every job in the plant. He knew the habits of every bit of machinery and, you can't take it away from the guy, he could tell you the weight of a pool ball just by looking at it. With all his experience and patience, old Mr. Roundly's alcoholic daughter had no hesitation, or choice, but to name him Quality Control Officer (that's QCO). A position he'd held for seventeen years.

Well, I guess from what you've heard so far, you'd of worked out that the word 'quality' and the word 'Roundly's' ain't exactly kissing cousins. Wasn't nobody in Mattfield could have took the responsibility of being QCO as serious as Waldo did. He didn't let you get away with nothing shoddy. Roundly's probably lasted as long as it did thanks to Waldo. But it didn't make him the most popular guy there. Why would you want to make a billiard ball round when you get paid the same for making it egg-shaped?

Waldo wasn't nothing if he wasn't dedicated. Roundly's owed him a lot. But there comes a time for all men great and small to reach the end of their careers, and Waldo was two months away from making the workers at Roundly's real happy.

-o-

Waldo carried his belly over to his locker like he was a few days away from giving birth to a medicine ball. He'd had the gut for so long he couldn't imagine being without it. But recently he'd started to notice something about his health. He didn't have none. He'd eaten junk all his life and turned into a big piece of junk himself. He couldn't breath good cause of the lard around his lungs. He was tuckered out just walking the six blocks to work. But he was gonna get in shape for his retirement, starting real soon.

Stage one was diet. Into his locker he put two very long peanut butter and honey sandwiches - baguettes they call 'em - six bananas, four Snickers bars and two cans of Coke. The bananas was his idea. He figured once he got used to them, he could cut down, maybe even leave out the Snickers. The honey was Jessie Jackson's idea. In his wilder, less knowledgeable days, Waldo would of plastered jelly on his sandwich. But he heard the reverend on the wireless once saying that jelly was just fruit coloring soaked in sugar for a month. He convinced half the black mid-west that this was another white plot to incapacitate the colored masses.

So, Waldo, not wanting to be incapacitated for Judgement Day, switched to honey.Honey was after all 100% pure natural sugar with no artificial flavoring or additives. It did concern him for some time that it was pretty much just bee sick, but that was an obstacle he managed to climb over.

He took the industrial goggles and gloves out of the locker and locked it.

"Two more months," he said under his breath. "61 days, 9 1/2 hours, 33 minutes and it'll all be over." He wondered what the people at the resort in Lerdo de Tejada was doing right that minute. Probably not even up yet. Probably sleep to 7:30 or something crazy like that. Go burro-back riding before breakfast. What a life. Them burros was so close he could almost smell them.

But it turned out to be B.O. Bulokavic standing behind him.

"Move your fat arse Waldo."

"Sure, B.O."

On Mondays Bulokavic didn't stink so bad as other days. Rumour had it he even took a shower at weekends, least got close enough to soap to make a difference. Sure if you couldn't get closer 'n handshaking distance on a Monday, you never would all week. He had himself a wife at home. You're probably asking yourself how she could of stood all that stinking. Tell the truth she didn'tknow he smelt bad on account of her not having a nose. Serious.

Seems she got caught in her papa's lawn mower when she was a littl'un. It mashed her head up something horrible. They hurried her off to the hospital in South Bend and the doctors there did a pretty worthy job of stitching her back together. But there weren't nothing they could do about her nose. They reckon the chickens must of got it. So they just plugged the hole and sent her home.

She come out of it looking okay, if you don't think noses are important for looks. At high school she noticed B.O. He was a good-looking boy and she couldn't understand why the girls stayed away from him. She figured B.O was his initials. Getting wed suited the both of them. At the ceremony, B.O. read a poem he'd writ. The line everyone recalls went;

'Between her eyes and headin south, ain't nothin till you reach her mouth."

It was real pretty that. But I'm letting myself get side slapped here. This book ain't about B.O. It's about Waldo. Good story though, eh?

4

When he got in from work that evening, there was a cranky mood in there waiting for him. It was like someone had been pumping bad feeling in through the air vents. That's what he thought at first till he realized he probably fetched it in with him. He wasn't of a mind to do nothing but sit and grumble.

"Aretha, honey. You wouldn't believe what the management's brought me to train up. This little China girl with no more fire in her than an icy pole. She don't give a shoot about quality control. I don't get the feeling she'll be around long enough to finish the training. You know what she said to me today?"

Aretha didn't answer on account of Aretha being dead. I don't mean she was dead and he was there talking to the body or nothing weird like that. She'd been dead and buried some fifteen years. But that didn't stop him talking to her. Just cause she was dead didn't mean he couldn't talk to her, right? Just cut down on the answering time was all.

"She said, 'Them's balls. Why don't you just roll 'em? If they roll straight, that's quality ain't it? If they don't roll straight you just quality control the little suckers out of there.' Jees, Reet. You see what I mean? She'd have balls rolling around all over the plant if I didn't stop her. I tried to explain to her about weight, and balance, and torque, and sheen and all that stuff, and you know what she said? You won't believe this, Reet honey. You'll laugh when I tell you. I was too bellypunched to laugh myself. She said, 'Hell, they's only balls.'

'Only balls.' Them's the very words come out of her mouth. Jees."

He was feeling better now. Talking things over with Aretha always made him feel better. She was the only one that really understood how he felt about stuff. All that moaning had made him hungry as a dump dog.

First he went off and took a shower. Well, tell the truth he just boogied around under a drip barely wet enough to rinse the soap off. But if it weren't for his shimmy in the shower, he wouldn't of got no exercise at all.

He put on his red flannel pajamas even though it wasn't barely dark outside, and went to his favourite place in the apartment, the kitchen. He transferred the top two aluminum trays from the freezer to the snack oven and set the dial to 'rapid defrost and bake'. He emptied a liter of Coke into a pitcher and carried it to the living room. "White for fish. Red for meat. Dark brown for TV dinners."

He sat and waited patiently for the ding but he still counted the rapid defrost seconds in his head. He was so good at it he was already there at the oven door with his mitt when the sound come. He carried the two trays to the table and peeled back the tops. The beautiful smell was carried up in the steam and he hoovered it up his nose. It smelled just like real food. It usually looked and tasted like something less so he liked to stretch out the smelling as long as he could. He always felt sorry for B.O's wife that she couldn't appreciate the scent of a good TV dinner.

And, thank heaven for ketchup and mustard. He didn't know where he'd be without 'em. The paint and plaster of food. There weren't no meal construction faults that couldn't be put right with generous helpings of ketchup and mustard. It made his meals all taste the same but he'd gotten used to that taste a while back.

"So anyway," he went on like he'd only just left the conversation. "I went over to tell Desire. 'Desire', I say, 'that little girl in there, she can't be no QCO. She ain't got the aptitude. She got no interest in pool balls. Man, it's like it's just a job to her.'

And you know what Desire says back to me? She says, 'Waldo, (and I'll cut out the 'f' words for you, Reet) If the

Pacers get on a losing streak and bomb one game after the next, (she's always comparing the real world to basketball) you don't see Slick Leonard come on TV and say his boys ain't no good. He says, "I take full responsibility. It's my fault them old boys can't play worth a shit, not theirs. I here on by tender my resignation."

"So Waldo you old trainer you, if you can't train her up, if you ain't man enough for the job, I'll have to find me someone who is. But don't blame the nip. She's got her elementary school certificate, and that's about five years more schooling than most of you other morons got. You understand that?"

Hell, Reet. That Desire. Ever since she got interviewed on Indiana Tonight, she thinks she's something else. Well, I got half a mind to tell the bitch that she ain't. You know how it is, don't you, Reet. When Waldo got half a mind, ain't nobody can sleep easy."

With all the words coming out and all the food going in, that was one hell of a busy mouth on the face of Waldo Monk. There's old faces like balloons that get shrunk and wrinkled when the air gets out of them. And there's others that swell up and kind of grow, you know? Waldo's was an expanding balloon face. The type where all the features got bigger; the eyes got rounder, the lips got fuller, and the nose blew up like a bubble of licorice gum.

That was the face Waldo ended up with after sixty five years of stuffing junk into it. He wore his gray hair so short it was easy to forget he had any, and he never did find the secret of growing any type of whiskers. His body was kind of made up of put-together balls, like a snowman, but black. He had round everything; arms, belly, thighs, even his fingers and toes was starting to look like something they produced at the factory. He was a round guy.

But he wouldn't be round for much longer. Once the diet started to kick in he knew he'd be on the beach at Lerdo de Tejada with his Bermuda shorts, playing beach volleyball with the spinster chicks. Only one pitcher of Coke tonight in spite of urges otherwise. Only two TV dinners. And the *piece of resistance*, an apple with his ice cream. They'd probably brand him a health fanatic, but it'd be worth the effort.

5

"Well excuse me, miss, but I don't think you need to be talking like that."

She give him the evil stare. "Like what?"

"You know, using the 'f' word."

"The 'f' …? Shit. You some kind of friggin' preacher or something?"

"Don't have to be no preacher to know what's right and what ain't."

"Shoot. 'Fuck' don't mean nothin. It's just a noun you know, like 'rather'. Fucking great just means 'rather great', right? Don't mean 'sex' or nothing."

"It's vulgar."

She laughed in his face. He noticed she had nice teeth. He'd never seen inside her mouth before.

"Vulgar? Where'd you get a word like that, man? They use the fucking 'f' word around here like breathing. If there ain't a 'fuck' in the sentence nobody understands it."

"Them's men, and they got no class. You're a lady and when you use the 'f' word you sound cheap. It ain't necessary."

He got to see her teeth again.

"A lady? That's a friggin' good one. I ain't never been accused of that before."

"If it means the same as 'rather', then use 'rather' why don'cha?"

"Fuck."

"You're saying it deliberate now. I don't wanna listen no more."

"You ain't got no choice, pal. You're training me, remember? You gotta listen to my filthy mouth for two months. And I'll say any fucking thing I want. Thank you." She walked off, still with that big rude smile on her face.

It was true. He was training her. Some hope. No one said he had to like her, and that was just as well, cause he didn't. She was unrespectful, and ignorant. It riled him that Desire was giving his job, a job he'd taken seventeen years to fine tune, to this little girl with no ambition. And they'd given him just two months to turn the sow's ear into a silk purse.

By lunchtime she was still a sow's ear, and if anything she was even less silky than when he'd started working on her. When the lunch horn sounded, she didn't bother to eat nothing, just crawled onto a stack of packing cases and went to sleep.

Waldo watched her curl up like a plastic playing card on a hot grill. She all but vanished. Bore no relation to a body. She was just some thrown-out overall in the corner. He fathomed that his right leg had to weigh more'n she did. Didn't seem fair that; one person having too much of everything while another got nothing. Couldn't be no QCO in heaven.

Couldn't of been no QCO when they built Roundly's neither. It was a big biscuit box with little windows so far up the walls you couldn't see nothing but the pearly gates. Least you would of been able to if they'd ever cleaned them windows. They was so greasy you needed to have the lights on, even on sunny days.

The ceiling was about high enough you could stand old Liberty up inside and her torch wouldn't even scare the rafter-pigeons that shat all over the plant. All that upward space didn't serve no purpose other than to make heating a waste of time in winter. All the ball making went on down on the ground.

It's funny, everybody in the world probably handled at least one pool, or billiard, or snooker ball in their lives.But you ask 'em how the things is made and I bet you they wouldn't have the first idea. Bet you don't even know. If this was one of them well-researched serious novels, I reckon we could spend a couple of chapters explaining it all, round about here. But this ain't that kind of book and I never worked there, so I got no idea how the hell they make the frigging things.

6

By the end of the first week, Waldo knew he was wasting his breath. The girl did the work okay but he couldn't get her real motivated. She didn't have no ambition, no hankering to carve out a career in pool ball manufacturing. It was such a waste. She'd been handed a golden opportunity on a golden plate and she couldn't see nothing but balls.

"I tell you Reet, young people today. They got no appreciation for stuff our generation would of been grateful for. You know how it was, Aretha honey. When we was young we was begging for work. Twenty of us fighting for one position. You recall how happy you was when they took you on at the sewerage works? Ten dollars a month plus overtime. That was real money in them days. And you got to keep the boots and snorkel.

He sat watching I Dream of Genie. He had no choice other than watching cause there wasn't no sound. He just sat and guessed what skinny old Major Nelson was moaning about and laughed. His guessing was probably funnier than the script anyway. He knew if Major Nelson was any kind of red blooded military man and he had Barbara Eden half dressed giving out wishes …Well, it was frustrating to see was all. He could of got the sound fixed but he was saving for Mexico.

He'd been saving for Mexico for ten years now. The company had an account he'd been paying into. The interest it built up would pay the final month's installment so really he saved money that way too.

'A Retirement You Could Find Only in Your Dreams.' He'd memorized all the advertising slogans.

'Lerdo de Tejada, Your Last Resort'.

'American Class at Mexican Prices'

'End it all with Us.'

'We'll Fill you Full of Beans'.

'Sunshine 24 Hours a Day.'

It'd been a sunny day indeed when he met the agent guy at McDonalds. It was the guy's day off but he just happened to have the photos with him. All them happy old folk playing croquet, and ballroom dancing, and riding donkeys along the beach. The guy worked for the company, but he'd already paid the down payment to go there himself. If that don't give you confidence, what would?

He was a likeable guy. He was an ex-lawyer so Waldo knew he could trust him. But even without his scholarly background, Waldo would still probably of trusted him cause Waldo pretty much trusted everyone. He was already dreaming about retirement under the hot Mexican sun even before the second Big Mac went down.

Another stroke of luck was that the guy had all the papers, the brochures and the contracts outside in his pickup. The pamphlet was real professional, all color and big words. There was more pictures and recommendations from satisfied retirees. They had ex-schoolteachers there, engineers, TV personalities. Waldo couldn't be certain, and the lawyer guy weren't giving nothing away, but one old biddy in the photos looked a lot like Marlene Deitrich. The lawyer just winked at Waldo when he asked. Marlene Deitrich. Man it had to be a hell of a place.

He signed right there in the truck, filled in the form, and handed over a small 'trust' deposit. He'd been paying off every month since for the past ten years. He got regular updates; the new tennis courts, the hiring of a chef from the actual France, and a Xeroxed sheet of useful Spanish phrases he hadn't quite memorized yet.

He'd learned some. 'Hola,' that was like 'hi'. Then there was 'yo tengo hambre'. That meant 'I'm hungry'. He figured that'd be the one he'd use most so he learned it first.

Course there'd had to be sacrifices through all this saving. There'd been no vacations. Plenty of overtime. He hadn't bought nothing new in all that time. If something broke down, he'd get it fixed. If it broke again, it could stay broke, like the TV.

So that's why Barbara wasn't saying nothing. But it was okay. He could talk to Aretha without no distractions.

"So what can I do, Reet? How can I convince the kid? If you and me'd had kids, they'd of had values. We would of had some good kids, you and me, Reet. I'd of been a good pappa. You'd of been a great momma."

He come over all nostalgic again. Getting old was making him soft on the inside as well as out. He got a lump in his throat and he couldn't swallow the hunk of Hershey bar he'd been chewing on. Him and Aretha hadn't had no kids on account of her problem. Her pipes was all messed up. That weren't the technical term for it, but whatever it was, she'd spent more time in the hospital than some of them doctors. She must of ended up real puzzling inside, all mismatched and wrong placed. There was so much plastic inside her she sure as hell disappointed the worms at the cemetery.

Waldo only upset himself more by thinking about it. She'd been gone fifteen years already but he still saw her. Still talked with her. Still loved her like no woman before or since. But man he wished she was there loving him back.

7

"Miss, could you come over here please."

"Miss? You talking to me?"

"Yes'm. I want to .. need to talk to you a while before we go in."

Waldo had ambushed China on her way out of the ladies' change room. He'd been not really training her for nine days now, and come to the conclusion he needed to work on stimulating her mind. He played Aretha's old Dale Carnegie tapes the night before, 'Think Positively to Turn Your Life Around'. He figured, if China was stimulated mentally, she might take more of an interest in calibrating eight-balls. Cause right now she didn't see nothing exciting in it at all.

"Yes, miss. Could you sit down here please." He directed her to the desk in the interview room, closed the door and sat opposite.

"You gonna call me 'miss' now are you?"

"It's polite."

"Shit. What you wanna be polite for?"

"A few good manners go a long way. Ain't no reason we shouldn't be polite to each other. We gotta be together seven more weeks."

"Hell. Just call me China like all the other morons here."

"That ain't your name, and it ain't polite."

"You got some fucking fixation with politeness or what?"

"I told you already it ain't necessary to use that word."

"Fixation?"

"You know the one I mean."

"Oh, the other 'f' word. The one that makes me sound cheap. Sorry. I forgot." Waldo, looked down at his pen that was doing all his agitating for him between his fingers.

"Is it everyone in the world you hate, or just me?" He guessed that must of come out of his own mouth. She blushed.

"Whachyousay?"

"Miss. I ain't got nothing 'gainst you, or 'gainst Chinese people, or 'gainst women. So I don't see why you gotta fight me. I ain't done nothing to you. The world's a lot easier to take if you're nice to people. Being nasty don't get you no place."

She stood up like she was shot out of a mortar.

"I don't remember seeing nothing about mindless gabbing when I read the contract. So I don't think I gotta listen to this crap. Miss China here got balls to roll. If'n you'll excuse me."

She didn't wait for an answer. She walked out on him and slammed the door. Waldo wasn't no expert on counseling, but he had a feeling his first motivation talk didn't go too good.

8

To be the QCO at Roundly's you had to have a working knowledge of each facet of the pool ball production process. China was spending three days at each of the twelve stations in the plant. But it didn't take her half a day to master the skills she needed in each one. It wasn't that hard. Any moron could do it. Except maybe the ones they hired at Roundly's.

If she could of been bothered, she could of recommended stuff to improve the system and increase their output too. But she couldn't be bothered. She knew she wouldn't be around long enough to pick up her end-of-year bonus, or reap the fruits of any wasted effort she put into the place.

By lunchtime she was so moody she didn't even head for the cartons. She was pissed at the fat man, but she was more pissed at herself for letting it get to her. He didn't mean no harm. He was just some dumb ass, small-minded hick whose whole life rotated round this shitty factory. Weren't his fault.

She walked over to where he sat on a sack reading the paper and eating a long sandwich. She crouched down in front of him in a way Waldo couldn't of crouched in a million years.

"Lao," she said.

"I beg your pardon?"

"I ain't Chinese. I'm Lao …from Laos." She pronounced the 's' at the end so he'd understand it. He thought about it for a bit. His sandwich hovered in front of his mouth like one of them spaceships waiting to dock.

"The country?"

"Yeah," she laughed. "The country." The sandwich spaceship still hung there, susceptible to attacks from alien raiding parties.

"Landlocked."

"You what?"

"Laos. It ain't got no coast. Surrounded by Vietnam, Cambodia, China and Thailand."

She made them little eyes as round as they'd go.

"That's right. How the f ... how the *rather* you know that?"

"Me and Aretha got atlases and maps and stuff. I like to look things up when I read them in the papers. When they talk about our boys in Nam, I like to see where they're talking about."

He finally took a bite of his baguette. She made eye contact with him for the first time that week. It looked like she was gonna get into a conversation, but it only looked like it.

"Right." She stood up. "Just so's you know I ain't Chinese." And off she walks.

Waldo was all ready to get into that conversation they didn't have. He already had questions queued up to ask. But he was too slow. By the time they'd worked their way up to his mouth, she was over there curled up on her packing cases.

9

At 3am the same pink Chevy pulled up in front of Roundly's. She wondered about driving straight into the building. But they made factories tougher in them days so there wasn't much hope of knocking the frigging place down.

She banged her head on the steering wheel a couple of times, not hard enough to knock herself out, but enough to beat out the unhappiness. It didn't work. She climbed between the two front seats into the back. The rear seat was her living and sleeping room. The front seat was just for driving.

She pulled her shiny cocktail dress off over her head and looked at it bunched up on her lap. The crap they give her to wear. She didn't know what they'd dress her in from one night to the next. Jesus knows what vermin there was frigging around inside it, or what diseases they'd give her.

She leaned forward and flicked on the dumb little ceiling lamp. It hardly give out enough light to see herself in the driving mirror. Compared to the assorted lady farm animals working at Roundly's, hers was the body of a child. She'd seen ten-year-olds with bigger tits. She was twenty-four, but folks that could be bothered, guessed anywhere from fourteen to fifty.

She saw herself having a grumpy Asian grocery store face. No one had ever called her pretty so that must of meant she wasn't. Her eyes wasn't as squinty as some, and her naturally wavy hair was unnaturally streaked brown. Being Asian give her the shits. But she still had to fight often to defend it. She wondered if she wouldn't have gotten so hateful if she didn't look the way she did. That big soft nigger was right. She was nasty.

As always she'd have to wait for the factory change room to open before she could get herself a shower. Thank God the caretaker opened up early so she could get in and get cleaned up before them shoefaced sows got to work. Them women looked at her like Vietnam was her fault. She looked at 'em back like it was too. There wasn't much dialogue. When it come, they spoke at her like she was deaf and stupid. It didn't matter none. It never mattered.

So, with three hours to go till opening time, she put on her factory overalls, rolled down the windows and got some sleep.

10

"You live in that Chevy?"

"What business that of yours?" She bit her lip. She'd kind of promised herself she wouldn't attack the old guy no more. Now, first chance she gets and she snaps at him. "Yeah. For now."

"Can't be comfortable." Waldo was at his locker fumbling.

"Somewhere to sleep." She pretended to be fumbling at hers too, 'cept there weren't nothing in it.

"Saves money I guess."

"Saves belittling." She said it easy without thinking about it. Waldo looked at her. She wasn't nothing special to him. But she wasn't nothing to hate neither. Being black, he'd had his unfair share of bigotry in his lifetime. But being big and black, most folks waited for him to walk on by before they said something. It ain't easy to get your teeth into race-hating someone who's bigger than what you are.

But this little thing here, she would of just soaked it up. He heard 'em talk about her around the shop floor. People can be real nasty. He'd like to parachute some of 'em into North Vietnam and see if they got the balls to say their shit there.

He pulled out the back-up 'B' sandwich from his locker. It was carefully wrapped in aluminum foil. He tossed it into her hands like a Pass the Parcel prize when the music stops. She caught it and looked at him all surprised.

"You can either eat it, or give it away," he told her. "But don't you let me see you throw it out. Aretha always said there's six million people starving to death in the world. Wasting a sandwich is like killing some little kid in India. I mean, she said the first part. The part about India I made up myself. It's like okay to add bits."

"You bought this for me?"

"Nope. I made it myself." He bloated up with pride, if that was possible.

11

"So you know what she did?" Waldo was in the kitchen fixing baguettes.

Now I guess some of you real hard-assed book readers out there been saying as how it ain't culturally likely that some factory guy in Indiana would be eating baguettes. Maybe even some of you didn't get this far cause you was so disgusted by it. Too bad you couldn't wait for the explanation.

The French bread come to Mattfield thanks to Aretha herself. Her sister in New Orleans, whose name I can't recall right off, had a friend who was on her way to Canada to start up a little French bakery. So Aretha's sister told this lady who had the name Sendrine on account of her being French, to stop over in Indiana to break the bus journey some. She was gonna stop at Waldo and Aretha's place for a night or two.

Sendrine was a fine looking, big boned woman who spoke English with a funny accent. Aretha had left the sewerage and was at that time working as a housekeeper for the town clerk. Mattfield wasn't never important enough for a mayor, so town clerk was as fancy as you could get. To cut a long story short, Sendrine got introduced to the clerk, and they had a baby together, then got married and set up Mattfield's only bread shop. You ain't never seen two people so caught up on each other.

The daughter, who inherited her mother's big bones and her father's moustache took over the business when her parents went off to France. She also kept up the family tradition of delivering three courtesy French loaves to Waldo in gratitude for bringing her mother and father together.

"I'll tell you what she didn't do. She didn't eat it. Not right off." Waldo was still there in the kitchen despite all this side-tracking. He was being adventurous with his sandwich making. He'd bought some processed cheese and onions and mustard and he was experimenting with the right combinations. He even put margarine on the bread. You get fancy like that when you're cooking for someone else as well as yourself.

"She walked off with it like it was a little baby cradled in her arms. She looked at it real sad. I thought maybe she didn't like peanut butter or something." He took a bite of the latest experiment. Two-thirds onions.

"Then she unwrapped it real slow and looked at it. I was getting uneasy by this stage, Reet. I just wanted her to eat the darn thing. Then, at last she took a bite, smiled, and ploughed into it like she hadn't eaten for a year. That made me feel real good, watching her enjoy my sandwich, so I thought I'd give her another one tomorrow."

It still wasn't quite right. He doubled the mustard and tried it without cheese. This sandwich-making thing wasn't as easy as he figured.

12

At lunchtime on the following Friday, B.O, Planks and Ribs flocked around Waldo in the coffee break.

"Waldo, we been talking," said B.O. Being Friday, it was his least sweet point of the week. He could of stopped a charging rhino just by holding up his armpits at it.

"What you been talking about, B.O?"

"'Bout you leaving next month and all. And me and the boys reckon, given you been like a fixture round here, the place'll be kind of empty without you." Waldo raised one of his eyebrows.

"B.O, you been smoking some of that Acapulco Gold they's talking about?"

"Come on Waldo. Sure, we give you a hard time here at work, but it ain't nothing personal. You supposed to trash the QCO. That's tradition. Don't mean we don't like you."

"Sure fooled me."

"Look, man, we'll show you. We planned a surprise, farewell night for you next weekend." Waldo was shocked.

"I ain't leaving till next month."

"We know that, Waldo, but given that next Friday's payday, Saturday could be the only day we got any money before you go." Waldo looked at the boys for some evidence that this was all a joke. He didn't see none.

"Well, boys, I don't know what to say. Thanks, I guess."

"OK. Hot diggety we'll have a good time."

Waldo watched them walk off talking about what a good time they was all gonna have. It didn't fit none. He was sure they was all glad to see the back of him. He would of understood things a lot better if he'd been at the secret meeting that morning.

Desire, arriving at her office direct from one of her gin breakfasts, called a couple of the boys in. She told them, as the old guy had been with Roundly's for longer than anyone, she wanted them to organize a little going away party. Something she wouldn't have to attend herself.

When they protested, she offered a financial contribution to the festivities. Being full of gin, she probably offered a little more than she should of. That put a completely different light on things as far as the boys was concerned. They set about planning the evening. Too bad they had to invite Waldo but they didn't really have no choice, did they?

13

She was finding the fish and potato baguette hard going, but she never complained. She was thinking about the fat man's woman. She'd asked him when he handed over her lunch.

"How come you don't get your old lady to make your sandwiches for you?"

"Aretha passed away fifteen years ago."

"OK. That's a good reason."

A lot of folks would of said, "I'm sorry." at a time like that but she weren't one of 'em. If she'd killed her it might of been appropriate. But it weren't her fault, so why apologize? As she sat on her cartons working on the sandwich, she imagined what it would be like to be married to someone. She wondered if her husband would still be talking about her fifteen years after she croaked.

The big guy was always "Aretha this'n" and "Aretha that'n", so she figured she had to be alive. It was kind'a sad and pathetic, and lovely in a way. But none of her business.

14

"I'm going out tonight, Reet. Bet that surprised you. The guys at the plant are taking me to some classy joint over near the state line." He had to yell to compete with the people in the next apartment. They was screaming at each other in Spanish. He'd been listening real close but he hadn't been able to pick up a 'hola' or a 'yo tengo hambre' in amongst all the yelling.

He was always sure the neighbours was killing each other when they had one of their scenes. But it turned out that was just how they communicated. They was always real lovey-dovey at the supermarket. He figured plates smashing against the walls had a different meaning wherever it was they come from.

Waldo was wearing his best shirt. It was one of them Hawaiian reversibles you didn't have to tuck into your pants. It had big mother-frigging hyacinths all over it that made him look more like a flower arrangement than a guy going out for a good time. He figured it'd help divert peoples' attention away from his weight, but it didn't.

15

They parked their trucks in the lot and herded together for confidence as they walked on over to the pink florescent frontage of the Inn Diana Butterfly. They was clearly out of their paddock. This was class. A couple of the guys already wished they'd worn ties.

A man built like a seven-foot pigeon stood in front of the door. He was wearing a white suit and a black lace tie and looked how Colonel Sanders would of looked if he'd started taking steroids when he was three years old. His little beard was braided. Man this was classy. A goddam doorman and all.

"Good evening gentlemen. Do you have a reservation?" He said it with a face so straight you could of leveled cement with it. The herd stood before him, silent. "Do you speak English?"

"Hell, yeah," said B.O.

"We're from Indiana," added Sweet Potato. They all nodded their agreement.

"We ain't got no reservation but," said Waldo.

"No reservation eh?" The Colonel seemed mighty perturbed by this news. He tutted and shook his head real slow and the boys was starting to get disappointed. "Well, you look like nice enough guys. Why don't I go see if I can find you a table. Don't you go away now." He turned and went inside and the herd stood its ground, not daring to move.

"Hell, we might be lucky," Shithead whispered. "Might of known we'd have to book for a high class joint like this." The Colonel was back in no time.

"It ain't gonna be easy, guys. If I had some …ehr, incentive for the Maitre D' I could maybe …" He raised his eyebrows and winked. The herd looked at him, waiting for the end of the sentence.

"I mean, if I could offer him a little something …" He looked one by one at the faces of the collective genius of Roundly's. It was like staring into abandoned igloos. Subtlety had no place there. "You guys wanna give me a couple of bucks to find you a table?"

"Sure, buddy. Why didn't you say?"

"Right."

They give him a couple of bucks. Two's a couple. He knew he should have been more specific. These guys didn't work on the space program. He knew that much. He took the two bucks and led the gentlemen inside. A farm lass crammed into a bunny uniform took over from the doorman. She told 'em to follow her and headed off into the blackness. Her tail was flashing with little Christmas tree lights. What service. What class.

The boys formed a chain cause they couldn't see nothing, and Brylcream in front kept as close to the tail as was humanly possible. It led them to a low lounge suite made of black vinyl set out in a square around a heavy wooden coffee table. There was one of them luminous wax lamps as its centrepiece. That was a little too sophisticated for some tastes, especially cause if you looked at it squirming around too close, it tended to make you throw up. But they still appreciated the ambiance.

They was in a room about the size of an infield, and once their eyes got used to the dark, they could see twenty or so other lounge suites laid out in grids along and across the room. There was a few guys at one table, and some sad old bastard alone at another. Apart from them, the place seemed deserted.

There was tasteful sketches of naked women with butterfly wings painted with luminous paint around the black walls, and assorted liquor signs, but they was the only other source of light. The music was so loud you had to lean right in your buddy's ear and yell your guts out for him to hear anything.

A real sexy girl in a black mini dress and shoes like oilrig platforms staggered over to their table to take their order. At first she leaned over B.O. to ask, but even on a Saturday night, bathed in Brut for Men, there was no mistaking B.O's natural odor cologne. She moved over to Ribs instead. From close up he noticed she was a whole lot older than she was pretending to be. Ribs ordered eight beers and she didn't bother to write it down. They all watched her aft sway off towards the bar. Man, this was class.

They'd come just in time to catch the first show. Sweet Potato had told them what to expect. The girls at the Butterfly sure wasn't no slags. They was artistes. Professional dancers and singers who just worked at the place to help out the owner who was an old Broadway show guy. Sweet Potato's brother had learned all this from the manager's hairdresser.

When the girls finished their acts, if they took a shine to some guy in the audience, they might come down and charm him with their conversation, maybe even let him crack a feel. Of course he'd have to buy 'em a drink. Singing's thirsty work.

There was stories that once in a blue moon, some guy would get real lucky and the girl would go out with him to his truck and, you know. But he'd have to be some kind of Robert Redford to score with one of these classy ladies. They're used to rich guys up there in Broadway.

All of a sudden, one corner of the room that was in shadow when they come in, got all lit up. There was all kinds of spots and strobes and floodlights making a fuss of this little eight foot stage. A grease ball in a striped jacket was sitting at a fancy organ and the taped stuff went quiet and the grease ball started to play something. Live. Just like that. He didn't even read no music, just played out of his head. Boy, was this something or what?

And a singer walked up on the stage. She was a dream. The Roundly's boys' tongues unrolled out of their mouths like red carpets at the Oscars. They'd never seen a celebrity up close before. Two of the boys swore it was Diana Ross. Even took bets on it. On account of him being black and everything, they had to take Waldo's word that it wasn't her.

She had legs so long they must of reached half way to Michigan if she laid down. She wore one of them haute couture PVC hot pant outfits. Could of been the same material as the lounge suites. She was saving her voice. That was obvious. Hell, if you can make a million dollars on album sales, you sure don't want to tire it out helping out an old friend in Indiana. She was definitely holding back, but, man she looked good.

The boys hooted and clapped their palms raw when she finished her set, and she must of really taken a liking to Ribs, because before you could say, "Can I have your autograph?" she was there beside him sipping on a Bacardi Coke and kneading away at his bony old thigh. None of them could believe Rib's luck. They was all in shock.

The singers kept on coming and as the night got older, more guests arrived and the place started to get raucous. Guys was whistling and yelling stuff at the new singers. They wasn't showing no respect to the artistes at all. They might as well of been twenty cent whores at a barn dance. The boys seriously considered going on over to teach them goons a lesson, but they was some big old goons so they let 'em be. Lucky for them.

The boys now had four singers sitting with them. It showed that class women didn't respect goons. The ladies knew gentlemen when they saw 'em. Waldo was right about Diana Ross. Her real name turned out to be Bubbles. It seemed Bubbles must of saw something in Ribs that his wife didn't, cause she just fell head over heels in love with the guy. It was all so romantic he borrowed the truck keys from B.O. and him and Bubbles went off for a little canoodle.

They all felt proud and kind of jealous. It got them all thinking too. If a pop star like Bubbles could fall for Ribs, there had to be love dust in the air that night. Wasn't a one of them without a chance of some romance of their own. Excepting for Waldo that was. He was enjoying the night, kind of. Well, it was his night so he had to. But he wasn't really sharing the enthusiasm the boys showed for these girls.

For one thing he was a music lover. They'd been there two hours and he hadn't heard none yet. If the singers was holding back to save their voices like Sweetpea suggested, they was holding so far back as to suggest they couldn't sing at all. Course, that was just his opinion.

The grease ball announced the final singer of the troupe.

"All the way from Pay Jing China, the top chanteuse in the charts over there, brought to Indiana at great expense for a limited season …Miss Wanita Wong."

An Asian beauty in a kimono split to the waist to reveal a hint of leather panties, hair blooming with plastic orchids, climbed up to the stage on stilettos with little flashing lights. She was a sight. If there'd been a travel agent in the place, every guy there would of booked himself a flight to Pay Jing China. She had one heck of a chest packed into that old kimono and every time she swayed back and forth, her pretty legs come into view.

Her singing wasn't much, but hell, this weren't even her language. She was probably great in Chinese. But, man she was a picture. Even Waldo couldn't take his eyes off her. They was pinging and ponging out like table tennis balls. The other guys elbowed each other and chuckled.

The Chinese babe must of noticed Waldo staring cause she looked over in his direction and even dropped the microphone. Probably didn't have black guys in China. If possible, her singing got worse after that. She lost her rhythm completely but Waldo was fascinated.

Ribs and Bubbles come back from the truck, Ribs with a smile on his chops like the bottom half of a supper plate.

Bubbles had to prepare for her next set after the Chinese so she went off to the ladies' room and they never saw her close up again. Seems her fiancée turned up at one of the other tables.

The girl with the orange Afro wig whispered something in Sweetpea's ear and he grabbed the keys from the table and led her off outside. It was a hell of a romantic night. Waldo went over and sat in front of the stage where he could study the Chinese girl. She grinned at him and he fell back like a big sea lion clapping its flippers. The boys was glad he'd found himself some romance too, although they knew that being old and colored he wasn't likely to get much more than a look.

So imagine their shock when Wanita Wong finished her set and went down to talk to the old guy. Maybe she was just being charitable, they thought. But no. It was clear them two hit it off real big. They wasn't talking more than two minutes when Waldo stood up and followed her out back.

"He ain't got a car man," B.O. said, all jealous and irritated.

"She's a star," Doddy reminded him. "She'll have a room. Maybe even one of them caravan things." The others nodded and B.O spat on the carpet. What a send off this was for the fat guy.

16

They was sitting on two Chevron oil drums out back beyond the latrines.

"Shoot." She said. "How the *rather* d'ya know it was me? I got more make up on me than a Cherokee war party."

"You're my trainee, girl. I been watching you real close, making sure you don't do nothing stupid. I know how you move. How you sound. But most important, I know how you smile. It don't happen that often, but when it does there ain't nobody can smile pretty like my trainee."

She looked down and smiled embarrassed at her shoes. They blinked back at her.

"I nearly shit myself when I saw you guys out there. Whatcha gonna do?"

"Do?"

"Yeah, you gonna tell them at Roundly's?"

"Tell 'em what?"

"That I'm a singer."

"A singer?" He drew his big lips back from his teeth and laughed a deep chesty laugh. She jumped down from the barrel, put her hands on her hips and waited for the laughing to stop.

"You hear something funny, old man?"

"Well, I know what I didn't hear, girl. I sure as hell didn't hear no singers in that there butterfly dungeon."

It was suddenly like steel shutters dropped down over her mood. The butterfly turned hostile.

"Well, fuck you, nigger. They say you black mothers got some rhythm but you obviously wouldn't know talent if it walked up and bit your fat arse." Somehow, a tear managed to find its way out of all that mascara and run a little trail through the cheap makeup.

"I got more talent in my left tit than them whores in there got in their entire bodies. Screw them."

Waldo watched the little renegade tear rolling its way towards her chin. It weren't no bigger than a ladybug but it sure carried a lot of weight. It made him feel as sad as he'd felt since he lost Aretha. Felt like he had an ironing board in his chest. He didn't know what to say to make her feel better. There was more tears following the first one now and she spoke through the sobbing like a child telling how it got beat up at school.

"I ain't one of them hookers, Waldo. They only come here to turn tricks man, you know that. They only get up on that stage so they can show their bits. Ain't one of them could carry a tune if you put wheels on it.

"OK. I ain't no Gloria Gaynor. Not yet anyway. But voices like that don't just come. You gotta work on 'em. I know I got it. Gotta get my lungs bigger, that's all." To emphasize her point, she used both hands to hitch up the foam she was using as a chest that evening. The tears was spraying out all over the place and making a hell of a mess of her paintwork.

Waldo realized he'd read the girl wrong. This wasn't acting. When he first saw her up on the stage he assumed she was a hooker like all of 'em. Didn't worry or surprise him none. It was her life. It surprised him more that she wasn't. Dressed up like Wanita Wong there, she could of made a better living than the Inn Diana and Roundly's combined. He wondered why she didn't.

17

It was a week since the visit to the Butterfly. It was all everyone could talk about. Sure they boasted about the girls, and the ambiance and everything, but mainly they talked about the arrest.

You see, once the boys had helped the singers out with a few bucks, when it come to paying the bill at the end of the night, even with Desire's generous contribution, they was forty bucks short. Seems they miscalculated by not adding something called a 'service charge'. None of them ever heard of a service charge and didn't understand what service it was for. But there it was on the check large as life.

It seemed like the cops had been called out to the Butterfly before. The sheriff and the bouncer was on a first name basis. Even though the boys was drunker'n skunks, the cop let 'em follow his car across the county to the lock up. There they was all allowed one call each to try and round up enough money to pay the bill and the bail.

It probably couldn't be said the wives and girlfriends was too pleased to be woke up at 3 am to bail their fellas out of jail cause they couldn't pay the bill at a fancy whore house. Them girls wouldn't never let it rest. That was the night Ribs' and Doddy's marriages started rolling downhill without brakes. Lot of silences at home for the longest while.

Even though it was supposed to be Waldo's night, he ended up paying more than any of 'em. When they invited him, they knew he was a soft touch when it come to money. Wasn't many in the factory didn't owe him this or that amount they never intended to pay back. He'd had one or two Cokes in the Butterfly and didn't have to pay for no fondles, but he handed over most of the deficit, and the cost of the wax lamp no one remembered busting.

-o-

The relationship between Waldo and China was weird there for a while. It didn't make 'em any better friends right off, but it sure made 'em lesser enemies. They probably already liked each other by then but didn't know it yet. The sandwiches had brought them together. She never said 'thank you', but she never refused neither. She ate 'em too, even when they was odd tasting, like when Waldo experimented with curry.

18

It took longer at Roundly's than other places for the first attempt at sampling Chinese meat. The aspiring rapist was a nineteen-year old machinist name of Kirk Workington.

He knew she parked out front of Roundly's, and turned up there after three a.m. He'd watched her undress in the back seat a couple of times. It'd got him real excited, mainly cause her body looked a lot like his younger brother's. His brother weren't having none of it, and he figured the chink would be more accommodating.

"Hell, she'd be grateful to a white boy for showing interest in her."

He lurked there in the shadows one morning and waited for her to be in her underwear before the attack. The only weapon he needed was his old fella. That should scare her enough. Show her he meant business. He got it poking out of his jeans like the figurehead on a Viking long boat before throwing open the back door of the Chevy and hurling himself inside.

He hadn't never seen a knife that long before. When he retold the tale later, he left out some parts, like how she took hold of his figurehead in her left hand and held the blade tight up against his balls with her right.

He was froze there, especially when she said, "You want 'em on or off?" You ain't never seen a figurehead sink so quick. He didn't dare move a muscle cause he really wanted 'em on, and he knew she wouldn't think twice about having 'em off. He could feel the cool steel against his sack and he was sure he'd be singing soprano in the church choir till he was sixty.

Kirk was one big old farm boy, but when you got a little China lady with a knife holding on to your cock, it really don't matter how big you is. If you could save your personal belongings, you'd take whatever chance you was given. She only give him one.

"Here's the deal," she said. "I imagine you wanna have children some day. If that's the case, I don't wanna ever see you around me, or around this car again, anytime." He nodded gently so as not to disturb the knife. "Wait, I ain't finished. If anyone else comes here and tries this, first I'm gonna slice theirs off, then I'm gonna come looking for you and slice yours off, cause I'll assume you recommended my tasty Chinese ass to someone else. You understand what I'm saying, you sorry looking redneck?" He nodded again.

As soon as she let his old fella be and lifted the knife, he was out of that car and halfway home before she could say, "Have a nice day." Old mamma Workington sure had her work cut out on wash day, getting the stain out the seat of his underpants. China didn't have no more trouble with the boys from Roundly's after that.

19

I been kind'a slow in telling you China's name I guess. But that ain't by accident. You see, most places she went she was China, or Nip, or worse. Whatever they felt like calling her. Wasn't too many people went to the trouble of asking her real name. Bet you was quite happy with her being called China. Having an Asian in the factory in them days was something like buying a goldfish. You could call it whatever you wanted.

"You got a name?"

Waldo knew she'd got a name cause he saw it on her job application. Just didn't seem right using it without permission. She'd never said, "Call me …" whatever. But today, out of the blue, she'd said "Thanks" for the sandwich, and sat down beside him to eat it. Once he'd gotten over the shock, he asked her her name.

"What you wanna know for?"

"Do you sooner I call you China?"

"No I don't sooner." She looked into his big ostrich egg eyes to see if he was making fun of her. She didn't see no mockery.

"Saifon"

He thought about it.

"That sure is a pretty name. What's it mean?"

"What's it mean?"

She thought back all them years to when she first found out it meant something. It was the only thing that was hers in them days. The only thing she'd bought to America. She treasured it because of that, but it hadn't crossed her mind it was anything other than a name. When the old Lao lady at the centre told her what it meant, it was something like magic.

It was like the story they'd told her about the little country boy who was given a birthday present by a rich widow just before she died. It was the only present he'd ever had and he treasured it and protected it all his life. Even though he was so poor he couldn't afford no coal to keep warm, he refused to burn the present.

On his deathbed, his grandson saw the box with its dirty ribbon and asked him what it was. The old man told him it was a birthday present he'd gotten when he was child. The little boy asked him;

"What's inside it grandpa?" The old man looked surprised.

"Inside? You think there might be something inside?"

That's the way she felt when she found out her name had a meaning, and it was such a pretty meaning.

"Raindrop," she said.

"That sure is pretty."

"Yeah."

20

Two days later they was sitting eating their baguettes together and she asked him a question. It was the first question she'd asked him about him.

"You like being black?"

"Don't know. I ain't never been black."

He was quick to answer so she knew he'd already thought about it a lot.

"No?"

"No."

"Then what color you being now?"

"Burnt sienna."

"You what?"

"I'm burnt sienna." She stared across at him.

"And who in hell's name told you you're burnt …"

"Sienna. Ain't nobody told me. I looked it up."

"You looked up your color? Where the …*rather* can you do a thing like that?"

"At the hardware store."

"You're messing with my brain now, fat man."

"No ma'm, Saifon." She liked how that name sounded coming out of some other mouth. "At the hardware store they got color charts for paint. You can see what color you really are. I'm too light for dark chocolate and too dark for coffee. But you stand me in front of a field of old siennas that got 'emselves burnt down, and I'd be invisible."

"Why would you go to all the trouble of looking up something like that?"

"I just wanted to know."

"Why?"

"How come you never ask me this many questions about pool balls?"

"Why?"

He rehearsed his answer to himself before he spoke.

"Well, there's people call me black, right? But it ain't really talking about color. It's a word they use to describe my race. Except, black got a lot of other meanings too, like dirty, like sinister, you know? Them civil rights brothers stand up and tell us we gotta be proud of being black. But I ain't black so why should I be proud of being it?"

"You sooner be proud of being burnt sarsaparilla?"

"No. Well, yeah, kinda. It ain't easy to explain. I just wanna put 'em straight you know? I got this perfect world planned out. First we get to be proud of being black, and the people who ain't quite black enough say, 'hey, what am I gonna be proud of?' So they break away and make a brown group. But in that brown group you got all different browns, you know? So they all break away and make a coffee group and a burnt sienna group. But the burnt sienna group got frizzy hair or they got straight hair."

Saifon knew there had to be a point somewhere at the end of all this. She waited patiently, chewing on her sweet corn and beet baguette.

"So, where do we get to? The 'being proud' groups keep dividing and splitting cause they realize they got differences. And at the very end, we got millions of groups with one person in 'em. And each of them one-person groups is real proud of themselves. But it ain't cause of their 'sameness' no more, they're proud cause they're different, they're unique.

"Can you imagine how difficult it'd be to hate people on account of their one-person group? Can you hear 'em? 'I can't stand you dark pink, bald, green-eyed, long-legged, nine-toed, bad-breathed, small-butt people.' Think how exhausting that would be."

"Wow."

"It's like if they call you, excuse me, if they call you yella, you can put 'em straight and tell 'em what you really are."

"What am I?"

"Well, hell I don't know. You have to go and look it up at the hardware store."

She looked up at the greasy windows, but she could still see the light.

"You know Waldo, I'm gonna *rather* well do just that. Being called black don't seem too bad to me, but yella, man I hate that. They say yella through their teeth like it's something you catch. Ain't nothing yella about me."

"All right."

"What time is it?"

"Ten of one."

"Should just be opening when I get there."

"Where you going?"

"Hardware store."

"We start work in ten minutes."

"*Rather* you, Mr. Trainer. Old Desire says to me, 'Do everything Waldo here tells you to.' And Waldo just told me to go to the hardware store to look up my color. So here I go." She stood up, dusted the breadcrumbs off her front, and headed out to her truck.

"Wait I ...didn't mean n ..."

21

"So she comes back about an hour later and tells me she's magnolia white. Hell, Reet, that ain't even yella. You know? She's a shade of white. She's whiter than any of them pinkies at Roundly's. Can you believe that? She was so happy."

Waldo had emptied everything outa the closet, and was going through his clothes. He figured it was time to select his wardrobe for Mexico. Raking deep into that closet was like one of them archaeology digs. He dug through the layers like he was digging through time. He hadn't been in there for so long, the nostalgia rating was almost as high as the mothballs.

First thing he come across was his old Indiana Pacers sweatshirt. He used to wear that thing all the time. Him and that shirt was inseparable. There was only one thing could stop him wearing it, and that was himself. He grew out of it. The hundred and seventy pounds he'd put on over the past six years was more than that sweatshirt could hold.

Then there was the nylon jacket he'd wore at the hospital the night Aretha went to meet her maker. It was the last thing she'd seen him wearing. He hadn't worn it since. There was some fossilized paper tissues in one of the pockets and a bus ticket from South Bend.

The deeper he dug, the smaller the clothes got. He couldn't believe he ever wore the T-shirt with 'Jelly Roll Morton' embroidered across the front of it. But he had. Both of 'em was wearing the same T-shirt, if you know what I mean. Him and Aretha was together at the show. They'd saved up for five months to go and listen to Jelly Roll and his Coloured Jazz Orchestra at the Tokio in South Bend.It was supposed to be a sitting show but the bouncers couldn't control the impulses of the audience. After the band's second number, every ass cheek in the house was off its seat and jiggling.

"Reet. You recall what we did after that show?" He blushed just thinking about it. Him and Aretha down the back of the bus depot. He put his hand on his belly. "Don't reckon I could manage tricks like that no more." But he smiled at the memory. Him and Aretha sure was an active couple in them days.

Way at the back of the shelf behind the clothes, there was a box of bullets. There weren't a gun no more to put them bullets in. That was probably still covered in rust at the bottom of Lake Michegan. There was only one bullet missing outa the box, but that's all it had took to do the job. He still couldn't bring himself to ask forgiveness for the one evil thing he'd done.

There weren't a thing in that wardrobe Waldo could use in Mexico. But it turned out that didn't matter none.

22

The two guys in suits might as well of had 'cops' written on their backs. Always seemed odd to Saifon that cops would study their asses off to get out of uniform, then all walk around in the same suits.

She'd been watching Ribs making a mess of the lacquer dips. He'd only been working on it two years so it wasn't surprising he hadn't quite mastered it yet. It was a process that involved using his eyes and his hands at the same time. Didn't seem to be much communication going on between the two. She looked over his shoulder at what was going on at the far end of the plant.

The two suits had surrounded Desire. She seemed to like the attention. She called Waldo over and the cops escorted him to an alcove in among the loaded boxes. She was too far to hear what they was saying, but they sure said something to shock old Waldo. It was like they'd found his valve and let some of the air out. He kind of collapsed onto the cases. One of the cops put his hand on the old guy's shoulder and nodded. The other one slipped a cue ball in his pocket cause he thought no one was watching.

When they'd finished doing whatever damage it was they'd come to do, they walked out without stopping by Desire's office. Once they'd gone, the excitement went with 'em. Weren't no attention spans in Roundly's long enough to think on about Waldo. Saifon saw him get to his feet and stagger out the back door. She looked back at Ribs.

"Ribs, what color's that ball you're holding?"

"Color?"

"Yeah. You know. Is it blue or red or what?"

"Shoot, China. I don't rightly know."

"You're color blind, ain't you?"

"Hell no. I can see white real good."

"S'what I figured. You been lacquering here for two years, and nobody noticed you can't tell the colors apart. I love this factory. I think it's time you got promoted to packing."

"Gee, China. You think so? Thanks."

She left him smiling at his good fortune at being promoted to a job that paid a dollar a month less, and went out back to find Waldo. He was hiding behind the trash. She went over to him.

"I was …" He looked up at her surprised and she could see he was crying. It embarrassed her. He wiped his eyes with his big old hanky. "Sorry, I'll ask you later." She turned to go, then turned back. "Hell, no I won't. What you crying for Waldo? What them pigs want with you?"

"Nothing," he blubbered.

"Nah. I seen nothing before, and it don't look nothing like this." He blew his nose so loud, some folks inside thought it was the lunch horn. "I ain't leaving here till you tell me. I ain't being nosy. I know it helps to talk about stuff."

He thought it over for a minute or so, and she was right. It would help to talk.

"Lerdo de Tejada. It's in Mexico." She crouched down in front of him. He wrestled his nose with the hanky. "I been saving for ten years to go to a pretty little retirement village on the coast there. I met this guy in McDonalds, see, and … Shit. It's a long story."

"Give me the ending."

"It was … I can't believe it." He started to bawl again. She looked away.

"It was what, Waldo?"

"It was …a scam. Some old biddy hired a private dick to go down there and check the place out for her. There weren't nothing there but goddam sugar cane. No one ever heard of the Lerdo de Tejada Retirement Village. The old biddy called the cops. They traced the address, staked out the post office box and the bank, and rounded up this gang of con men. Seems there was over a hundred old fools out there paying them money for a dream."

"Oh Jees." She had her face in her palms and peeked out through her fingers.

"I was so sure it was above board, Saifon. The guy was an attorney even. If you can't trust a lawyer, who can you trust?"

"Right."

"The gang spent most of the money on the high life. Cops said I might get something back but I shouldn't hold my breath. It could take years."

Saifon didn't think she needed to tell him how dumb he was, cause she figured he must know that himself already. But she wasn't sure what else to say. The guy's life savings and his dream was all sitting in a lock-up in the state capital. Ain't much you can say to cheer a guy up in a situation like that.

"You really screwed up, Waldo."

"Tell me about it."

23

If it ain't no different from pre-retirement, retirement ain't nothing to look forward to. If all you got to dream about is dribbling showers, screaming neighbours, and silent TV dinners, you might as well not dream at all. And if you ain't got dreams, what's the point of being alive?

It probably ain't easy to imagine how it felt when Waldo's world fell in on top of him. He didn't have nothing in his present, now he didn't have nothing in his future. That, for a guy so alone and so desperate, was the end of all hope.

That's what was going on in old Waldo's head that night as he lay in bed. He hadn't been able to bring himself to tell Aretha about what happened. Fact that he'd only ever kept one thing from her made this secret hurt a lot more than it should of. Weren't no way he was gonna fall asleep with all them Mexicans in the dream waiting to mock him.

He even skipped supper that night. Wasn't hungry for the first time in sixty five years. Disappointment was a great killer of appetite. Anyhow, if you're planning on doing away with yourself, it seemed like a terrible waste of food, if you know what I mean.

Waldo didn't figure anyone'd miss him. He could go away someplace, pretend he was going to Mexico, and throw himself in the sea instead. No, that wouldn't work. Weren't enough rocks in America to stop Waldo Monk floating. And there couldn't be no blood. He couldn't stand the sight of blood, specially his own. So that counted out shooting, jumping, wrist-slashing and train tracks.

Didn't leave much did it? Only one thing really. And he knew what that was and where to get it. Instead of sleeping, he planned his suicide down to the last detail. Odd thing was it made him feel better. By morning he was wide-awake and ready for work. He didn't hate his God-awful apartment no more cause he knew he wouldn't have to spend another week there.

24

She was watching for Waldo in the Chevy wing mirror. When he went past on the morning misery shuffle, she opened the car door in front of him. Either he didn't see it, or he was in a mood to walk into doors that day.

"Sorry Waldo," she said. But of course she wasn't sorry. She'd been plotting. Last night at the Butterfly while she was getting pawed by a bunch of miners from Michigan, she hatched a plan to rescue Waldo from his depression. Course then, she didn't know he was planning to drink enough Elliots Solvent to dissolve a dozen billiard balls. She just thought she'd cheer him up some.

"Oh, hi, Saifon." She joined him on the shuffle to the gate.

"Waldo, I was wondering if you could give me some advice."

"Eh?"

"Advice. I was wanting some."

"Advice?" She noticed how he'd forgot his mind someplace.

"Yeah. I been thinking on how the cooling system on them balls straight out'a the kiln ain't even, you know? And maybe that's why so many balls get out of shape. What do you think, Waldo?"

"What? Oh sure, Saifon. We can talk about it at lunchtime. See you later." He walked on through the 'employees - male' entrance and left her stranded in front of 'employees - female' wondering if he'd heard her. This was pool ball talk. She was showing an interest. If that didn't get him excited she didn't know what would. He was in a bad way.

"Move your ass sister." She was causing a traffic jam of big industrial-sized factory gals. "Ain't they got no doors in China?"

She was too concerned about Waldo to swear at 'em.

"No."

-o-

It was about eleven when she saw him look around all shifty and smuggle something out back. She'd been watching him real close all morning. It suddenly hit her like a truck what he must of been planning. She ploughed through the sample trays. There was balls bouncing around all over the damn place. She high-tailed out through the back door like the Laotian sprint champion of the world.

The old guy was back at his trash pile. He was holding this plastic quart bottle full of something colorless up to his lips.

You seen flies, and you seen cows. And you know that no matter how much of a head of steam that fly gets up, he ain't gonna move that cow none by flying at him. Well, you'd of thought the same laws of size would of applied with Saifon and Waldo. But you'd be wrong.

She ran over and threw herself at the old man mountain, and even though she didn't weigh no more than his nose, she toppled him over sideways into the dirt, and slapped the bottle away from him. He kind of bounced some. It knocked the wind out'a the old guy, and she was worried he wasn't gonna find none to replace it. He was coughing and spluttering and his eyes was bugging out.

"What …what in heck's name you think you're at girl?" She was over sniffing at the bottle. She raised her eyebrows and sat cross-legged on the ground.

"Sprite?"

"7-Up"

"Shit." She laughed. "I thought you was …Ah. Never mind." Waldo was breathing heavy but at least he was breathing.

"What?"

"Nothing."

"I seen nothing and it sure don't feel like this."

She smiled.

"Why'd you go and put 7-Up in a bottle the same size as one of them Elliot's Solvent containers?"

"I …I was (He was practicing. Seeing how much he could swallow in one go.) …thirsty."

"Shoot. I thought you was gonna do away with yourself." She laughed cause it was funny. He laughed cause it wasn't.

"And you wanted to stop me?"

"Yeah. Well."

They say once an old bull elephant rolls onto its back, it can't never get itself back on its feet again. Waldo couldn't get himself into a sitting position. She had to help roll him onto his front so he could get his knees underneath himself and rock back into a kneel.

"Waldo, you gotta lose some of this weight."

"Nah. It's just that I ain't been on the ground for a while. I'm outa practice." She smiled that nice smile of hers. They knelt face to face. "Saifon, that was the kindest thing anyone's done for me in a long time. I thank you."

"Ah. Shut up."

25

"What're you planning to do Waldo?" Desire asked him.

It had been three days since his suicide practice and although Waldo was still depressed, he didn't see such a pressing need to leave the planet no more. Just the thought that there was someone cared about him was enough to reconsider. Him and Saifon was getting along okay.

But in two weeks he'd be out of there and into a big empty.

"Do?"

"When you finish here."

"Hm." He saw himself emptying his locker, stepping out of the employees - male door, and falling head first into that big old empty. "Don't rightly know, Desire."

She'd called him into her office at 3PM on the Friday before he was due to leave. She'd slept off her gin hangover through lunch, and was running on coffee till she could get herself back to a bar.

Waldo figured there had to be people better suited to running a factory. Her pa had been such a hard-working sober little guy it was hard to believe this big lush was really his.

There was two of 'em worked in the office; Desire and an eighty-year old accountant, Walt. Walt's only claim to fame was in confounding medical science. Even though he hadn't had no hair since he was thirty, he still managed to suffer from chronic dandruff . That's why they called him Snowy behind his back.

Walt kept the Roundly books, like he had since he was sixteen, with a pencil. It annoyed the hell out of the external auditors but it did allow Desire to be creative. Fact was, the factory had been slipping down a slidy slope for years. They hadn't had no new customers since 1968. They relied entirely on the old faithful Desire's pa (and his pa before him) brought to the business. When them old geezers passed away and their kin sold off the companies, Roundly's profits started to get humble.

Desire drank a good deal of what was left. She was tall, and rubbery and red. Now, I can't think of nothing else that's tall, and rubbery, and red, so I can't help your imagination none. She wore clothes unsuitable for a female that wasn't sixteen years of age, and she'd waved that number goodbye some forty years hence. She was a mess was Desire.

She usually talked to Waldo like he was a trained seal.

"Sit, Waldo."

"Yes, Ma'am." He sat.

"I'm gonna talk to you in confidence now, cause you been here since my daddy's time, and I know you'll understand what I got to say."

She sat down at her desk and her little cotton frock rode up her big ugly thighs. He diverted his eyes. "You know, Waldo, that my daddy's first concern was always that he do right by his employees. 'A happy worker is a successful factory.' That was his motto, Waldo.

"Yes, ma'am."

"Well, Waldo, them days are gone."

"Ma'am?"

"Waldo, you're probably thinking that, seeing as you've given a large chunk of your adult life to this company, you will be getting a generous bonus and a small monthly pension. Am I right?"

"That's what I been thinking, Desire."

"Well, we ain't gonna pay it." Waldo did this expression he did that made most of his head look like eyeballs. "Don't you look at me like that, Waldo. I think you'll find I am entirely within my rights."

"Desire, I got me a contract. You can't …"

"And if you read that contract, you'd know what I'm talking about. Tell him, Walt." She crossed her legs. Man, that wasn't a pretty sight.

"Waldo."

"Walt."

Walt had a voice like Cary Grant, except for some times when his teeth fell out in the middle of a sentence.

"I have here a copy of your Roundly's contract, Waldo. Desire's right. The contract you signed didn't actually commit the company to any post-employment payments."

"But it says …"

"What it says is that Mr. Roundly would pay you a bonus and pension after twenty years of employment with the company. It does not however say that he would be paying it on behalf of the company. This was a contract between you and Mr. Roundly. When he passed away, the contract became null and void."

"It ain't worth the paper it's written on," Desire turned the screw. "I checked it with a big law firm in South Bend."

Waldo was struggling.

"Desire, I been working here thirty-eight years."

"We didn't give you no salary?"

"Well, sure you did, but …"

"Right then. Hell, Waldo. There's a war going on. You ain't gonna haggle for money when the country's in a recession are you?"

It hadn't occurred to him the country was in debt. But it didn't seem right he had to give up his bonus to pay it off. Sure, he didn't pay into no retirement fund at Roundly's. No one ever had. But, when Mr. Roundly was alive, he paid out the bonus with a big smile on his face. No question.

Waldo got this feeling. It was hard to describe. To most of us it would have been familiar. We get mad all the time, over nothing usually. But big Waldo didn't get mad, so he wasn't sure what the feeling was. He couldn't explain the craving he had to climb over Desire's desk and club her to death with her own telephone.

"It ain't fair, Desire, …Walt."

Desire was flying.

"Fair Waldo? Fair? I been more than fair. Didn't I increase your salary when I took over this factory? Didn't I pay out for new plumbing for the men's bathroom? Shit. Didn't I pay for your farewell party a few weeks back, out of my own purse?"

"You paid for that?"

"You're darn right I did. And what gratitude do I get? Here you are blaming me for some contractual error my senile old daddy made, me a single woman with barely two cents to her name." Waldo hung his head.

"Yeah. You're right Desire. I'm sorry."

"And so you should be."

26

"She said what?" Waldo and Saifon was fighting their ways through two stewed beef baguettes. They was tasty, but hard work. "What gratitude did she get? That frigging drunk whore."

"It ain't easy Saifon, a single woman running a big factory like this."

"She ain't running shit. You and Snowy the accountant run Roundly's and you know it. Half the time she don't know what you're making here. Shoot. Ain't you mad Waldo?"

"You know? I got this feeling when I was in there. It come on me all of a sudden, like heartburn. It scared me some cause I wanted to hurt someone. It passed."

"You ever hurt anyone, Waldo?" He hesitated for a bit.

"Not deliberate." He felt a pang of guilt for saying that.

It was Saturday lunchtime. It would of been overtime day if Roundly's had ever had a union. A lot of things would of been different if Roundly's had a union. Waldo wouldn't of been robbed of his bonus for one. But Mr. Roundly and Mattfield had always been against that kind of thing.

Unions meant organization. Organization meant regimentation. Regimentation meant communism, and our brave boys was over there in Nam fighting to keep communism away from these shores. Sure wouldn't be right to encourage it in the factory.

-o-

Roundly's was burnt to the ground the following day. It was Sunday. Waldo and the other eight people in the chapel heard the scream of Bill Pocock's fire engine. They figured he was letting his son Scott play with the siren again.

Preacher Le Saux was always taxing the minds of his congregation, so when he asked,

"Anyone here smell the smoke?" they thought it was one of them spiritual questions. They thought he was referring to the 'smoke of lust' from the 'tobacco of sin', that kind of thing. So they answered together;

"We smell it. We smell it." Even though they didn't smell no actual smoke.

"No, I'm serious. Can you smell it?"

"We smell it. We smell it."

They was getting quite worked up now and the preacher was frustrated he couldn't make 'em understand that he really smelt smoke. He walked down amongst the flock.

"No. Listen. Hold your noses up and sniff." They held their noses up and broke off into spontaneous rapture.

"I smell your smoke, Lord."

"Puff on that sinful cigarette, sweet Jesus."

It was Waldo first made the connection between the spiritual smoke and the smoke that came floating in through the missing panes in the window.

"That really is smoke," he said.

"I smell it O' Lord. I smell it," said sister Floretta.

"Hold up, Floretta," that really is real smoke." He went over to the door and walked outside.

Eight blocks east, the Roundly's building belched black smoke up into the blue sky. There was flames of purple fire licking out through the windows. The grease and the bird nests all made the place real combustible. It was asking to get burnt down.

Waldo and the congregation stood behind the chapel, watching it burn. Wasn't one of 'em considered running on down there with a pail. Being Sunday, there wouldn't be no one in the plant. There weren't even a watchman. Desire had been too tight-assed to hire one. Funny thing was, even though the entire town depended on Roundly's for its income, there weren't one single person went to help put out the fire, other than Bill. But that was his job.

Some folks dragged their easy chairs into the garden and popped open a can or two. But no one went down there to get a closer look. I guess they was fearful they'd be blamed for setting the fire. A lot of 'em had thought about it. Anyway, the view was fine from most places cause Roundly's was in a dell, and the houses rose up away from it. There wasn't no homes close by, cause that was Roundly land, the land Mr. Roundly had put aside for extensions. There was real loud pops and cracks and stuff exploding, and the breeze brought up hints of just how frigging hot the fire had gotten.

By the time the real fire engines arrived from South Bend, Roundly's was already deceased. From outside, the big black walls didn't look much different. But the inside was gutted.

Waldo, sister Floretta, and preacher Le Saux had found a good spot on the chapel roof to watch the brave South Bend fire officers fight the smoldering embers. The preacher, apart from being an inspiration, was also a collector of town gossip. He looked at Waldo. Waldo looked at him.

"They're gonna blame you for this you know, Waldo."

"Me? Why would they wanna blame me, reverend?"

"Vengeance."

"Gainst Roundlys?"

"Gainst Desire in particular."

"You hear about that already, preacher? Heck. Vengeance ain't something I'm noted for. You know that."

"I know it, Waldo. But the investigators ain't gonna know it. Just you be careful."

"Yes, sir."

27

Normally, the police would let the insurance assessors do the preliminary investigation in cases of fire, and the owner would be the chief suspect. But in the case of Desire Roundly, there wouldn't be no external assessment, and she wouldn't be a suspect at all. She didn't have no insurance. She hadn't kept up the policy. Apart from the value of the land, she lost every damn thing she had in the fire.

The police crossed her name off the list. She wasn't guilty of arson, but she sure was guilty of stupidity. Can't arrest no one for that but. Most folks in Mattfield would of been in jail if you could.

That left Waldo Monk's name at the top of their list. Him and the chink. She hadn't shown up on Monday for the meeting in the ashes. They figured she'd heard about the fire, and didn't bother coming in. The others was all there to make conflicting statements and collect one of the round flapjackpool balls as a momento.

They had some darn fool idea they'd be getting the two weeks pay they was due, but after a half-hour of Desire ranting and bawling, they knew they was screwed. The cops set up a table under one old singed tree and collected facts. Weren't no question it was deliberate. There was the remains of three gas cans by the back gate. The forensics guy from the state capital knew straight away it was a crime.

28

They called Waldo into the regional police headquarters two days later and sat him at a desk. There was two detectives. They was different detectives to the two that told him about Mexico, but they was wearing the same suits. One of 'em was hazel, even though these was the days before hazel detectives was fashionable. I guess they bought him in cause the suspect was burnt sienna. Kind'a color coordination. He was trying his darnedest to look tough.

"We know you done it, Monk."

"What'd I do, officer?"

"You tell us."

Clever exchanges like this was too much for an uncomplicated guy like Waldo.

"Gee." He scratched his head. "I don't rightly know, sir."

The other detective was extreme white, like stewed bones. He leaned over to Waldo and asked,

"Why'd you burn down Roundly's?"

"Sir, I don't have no good reason to burn the place down."

"That ain't what we heard."

"We heard you had a fight with the owner the day before."

"Officer, I don't reckon I ever had a fight with no one in my life. It ain't my way." The cops looked real disappointed.

"Where was you at the time of the conflagration, Waldo?"

Man, he got a look on his face like this was the twenty-thousand dollar question on Jeopardy. They could see him struggling with it.

"The fire, Waldo. Where was you when the fire started?"

"When we smelled the smoke I was in the Chapel of the Holy Lamb of Bethlehem, sir. It was Sunday."

"How long had you been in there?"

"Got there at five, like I always do.

"Five?"

"I'm the chapel clerk. I set up."

The interview went on like that for another twenty minutes or so, them asking, Waldo answering. When he'd gone, the cops sat at the desk like they was interrogating each other. If the truth was to be told, it hadn't been much of an interview. Soon as they saw the fat guy, they knew there weren't no way he could of snuck down to Roundly's with three cans of kerosene, without being seen. He didn't have no car neither.

The forensics people said the fire was lit about eight AM. Waldo had seven witnesses swearing to God on High that he was in the chapel then. It was peculiar that no one saw no one outside the factory. You'd think someone would of been out in the street by then. Old girls walking their dogs. Sunday joggers. But this is Mattfield we're talking about.

The cops was still looking for the chink, but there weren't no address for her. No one had seen the pink Chevy since the girl left work at three on the Saturday afternoon. The home address and references she'd given Roundly's didn't check out. She'd lied about all of it. But lying didn't necessarily make her a fire starter.

There was a hundred things more important for the police department to be doing than chasing smoke. That drive to solve cases you see on the movies don't happen in real life. Actual cops are only too happy to admit when they're clueless. In general, a criminal has to be real dumb to get himself caught. Fortunately for the police, there's a hell of a lot of dumb criminals around to make 'em look good. The Roundly's arsonist wasn't dumb.

Them two cops looked at each other. The extreme white one asked, "Any thoughts on what we do next?"

"Go get a beer and a pizza?"

"I mean Roundly's."

"You see anyone really gives a shit?"

29

So, that was the end of the Roundly's case, and the start of the end of Mattfield. Folks started moving away almost immediately. With no factory there wasn't no income. No income meant no spending. No spending meant no point in the stores staying open. Sendrine's girl shut up the bakery and completed her ma's cut-short mission to Canada.

Three months after the fire, Mattfield was already something of a ghost town. Christmas had come and went but folks was holding on to their money. Fact was, the only person there with money coming in, if you don't count alimony, was Waldo. Course he didn't know he had money coming in. Since they'd uncovered the Lerdo de Tejada scam, a lot of the old folks had passed away from the shock. That wasn't good luck for the old folk in question, but it was for Waldo.

The cops had found a bunch of money in the con-men's account and made some more by selling off their cars and stuff. The court ordered that the proceeds get shared equally between the victims. So, one day, this pretty gal from the South Bend Justice Department turned up on Waldo's door step and told him,

"Mr, Monk, I'm going to make you a happy man today." She giggled and wiggled some.

Now, there's some dirty old men with less manners than Waldo, would of taken advantage of an offer like that. But Waldo just invited her in and give her an apple. In return, she give him $3,783. 32 cents. That was a lot in them days. Of course it was a cheque, but they're every bit as good as money.

It wasn't just luck. It was divine providence. The Sunday before at the chapel, he'd asked his Maker what the hell he was gonna do with no job and no bread. The Sabbath services had become, what you'd call, 'intimate' since the fire. There was just him and Preacher Le Saux. Even Sister Floretta had packed her cats and headed off west to her sister's.

As Preacher Le Saux didn't have a lot to keep him occupied them days, he found himself answering questions he wasn't asked.

"What am I gonna do, Lord?"

"I think you oughta ..."

"Hold on, Preacher. I'm talking to the Lord here."

"I was just gonna make a suggestion, Waldo."

"I'm sorry Lord. Where was I? Oh, yeah. If'n you got any suggestions as to how I can stay alive through these troubled times, I'm ready to hear you."

"You know Waldo? You got a few dollars saved up. (That was Preacher Le Saux talking, not the Lord.) I think you oughta head south and leach off Aretha's family in Baton Rouge."

Waldo opened his eyes and glared at the preacher, then he got back to God.

"Well Lord, what you think of that idea?"

And in a sign clearer than a Las Vegas neon, the ground shook, and a goddamned candle fell off the altar. Preacher Le Saux dropped to his knees and joined Waldo in prayer.

The contractors had finally gotten round to bringing down the unsafe walls of Roundly's with a ball and chain. They was all agnostics so they didn't worry none about Sabbath retribution, just overtime.

"I hear you tumbling down the walls of Jericho, Lord. I hear." Then he whispered to Preacher Le Saux so's He couldn't hear. "What d'you suppose that means, Preacher?"

What followed turned out to be Preacher Le Saux's final interpretation of spiritual signs before his transfer back to Boston, and the transvestite scandal. But he did a good job.

"Waldo, the bringing down of the walls signifies the bringing down of your limitations. The prison ofRoundly's has been destroyed. Your soul is liberated." He put his palm against Waldo's forehead. "The falling of the candle signifies that a small orange person will fall surprisingly into your life. (It was a small orange candle), and together you will flee the crumbled masonry of your respective histories."

It sounded like Preacher Le Saux was just making it up at the time, but Waldo come to think back on that prophesy a hundred times after his airplane ride. He wished he could of gotten back in touch with the preacher and told him how his interpretation had been right on, apart from the "orange person" thing. It should of been a magnolia white candle.

30

It was so damn quiet in Waldo's apartment he'd gone out and bought one of them transistor radios and put it on loud so's he could think. The electric store had everything on sale. They was almost giving it all away before they shut up shop.

He'd played all his records so many times the needle was blunter'n a thumb and he couldn't get a replacement cause they stopped making that model in 1942.

There weren't even no neighbours' screams to whine about.

"There's only me, the Dacostas, skinny Blue and his wife, and that scary guy with the lips, Reet. All the others are moved out already. I don't reckon there'll be more than a dozen folks in the whole of Mattfield by next Christmas."

He'd almost drowned himself in the shower that morning there was so much darned water coming out the spout. He'd gotten dressed and walked around town, and seen folks loading up their trucks with mountains of bad furniture tied on with stolen Roundly's packing thread.

He'd come back with the newspaper, made himself a pot of coffee, and reached for the cookie jar. Weren't nothing in it. He knew that but his hand sometimes had a mind of its own. In the months since Roundly's got toasted, Waldo had gone cold turkey on sweet stuff.

For the first time after fifteen Arethaless years, he'd started eating food that didn't come in aluminum. He had more fruit in the kitchen than Tarzan. He'd been doing a lot of walking too.

One night, and this is a secret, when he was out and no one was watching, …he ran. You probably wouldn't of recognized it as running. He kind'a toppled himself forward and his legs had to move faster to get under him again. There was a couple of scary seconds where he wasn't sure he could stop. If he hadn't gotten hold of the street lamp when he did, he could of ended up in Texas.

He took his coffee over and stood in front of Aretha's full-length, half-width mirror. He couldn't see no difference in his shape, but he sure felt better. He wasn't so out of breath no more. He slept pretty good too. Maybe there was something to this health food. It was times like this he regretted not being in Mexico. He had his health, he had money, but he didn't have no place to go. Nothing tickled his fancy like Lerdo de Tejada.

It was weird, retiring. When you're working full-time, you cram all your housework and homework, and hobbies and shit into late evenings and weekends. But when you don't go to work no more, all them things sort'a expand and fill up more time. Ten before-retirement minutes and a hundred after-retirement minutes is the same thing. It's like crossing into the Twilight Zone. He'd been afraid he'd get bored but he couldn't find the time to be.

31

One evening he was sittinglooking up words from the newspaper in Aretha's Webster's. The doorbell didn't ring cause it wasn't connected. But he knew the sound of it not ringing real good. It was only a little click but there weren't nothing wrong with Waldo's ears.

He was shocked when he opened the door and found Saifon outside stabbing at the bell, trying to get a ring out of it.

"Saifon. Son of a gun."

"Hiya, Waldo." If he hadn't been blocking up the doorway she would of went inside. The guy with the lips was standing out in the hall. He had a habit of kind of mashing them old lips together and drooling. It scared a lot of people. "You gonna let me in?"

"Sure …sure." But he wasn't. Sure, I mean. Waldo didn't get many visitors carrying a suitcase. He rolled out of the way and she went in. She was wearing heels, and a skirt so short he could see what she had for breakfast. They stood looking at each other. She hadn't put her suitcase down. Waldo coughed.

"How'd you find me?"

"Asked some guy on the bus. He knew you."

"The bus? What happened to your car?"

"Sold it. That's why I'm dressed like a hooker."

"It is?"

"You'd be surprised how much more guys pay for a piece of shit on wheels if they think they might get some tail."

"How much you get for the Chevy?"

"Eight hundred bucks."

"Jees. What'ja tell the guy?" They was still standing facing each other like gunfighters.

"That I needed the money for a down payment on an apartment in the area. I might of give him the idea he could come calling after I moved in. He took me to the bus depot to pick up my suitcase. I guess he's still waiting."

"You wanna put that down?"

"Yeah. Thanks. Roundly's sure looks a lot flatter'n I remember it." She sat down on the sofa.

"They thought I did it." He sat on the easy chair. "The cops called me in for questioning. But preacher Le Saux told 'em I was in the chapel."

"You wouldn't do nothing like that, Waldo. You're the world's last nice guy. You should be in a museum." He did one of them burnt sienna guy blushes, and she laughed. "It's true. You're the only person I can remember who's been nice to me without wanting nothing back." He didn't like hearing about himself too much.

"Give it a rest, girl. What you come back here for anyway?"

"Two things really. First thing is that Desire owes me two week's pay." Waldo grinned.

"Saifon, you got more likelihood of getting pigs out of a mamma cow's rear end. She ain't paying no one."

"She'll pay me."

"Admire your confidence, but I seen bigger things than you try to get money out'a that woman."

"She'll pay me."

"Good luck. What's the other reason?"

"For coming back?"

"Yup."

She looked down at his rug.

"I want you to be my daddy, Waldo."

32

The Elk's Mouth Bat and Grill was a place out on the highway with more class than Mattfield was used to. It relied on highway traffic and put a couple too many cents on the drinks to keep out the dregs of society. That was probably why the place didn't do a lot of business.

The owner, Elk, was a stubborn son of a bitch who never admitted he was wrong. When the sign people called him up to tell him he'd spelt the name of the bar wrong on the paper, he cursed 'em out and told them he should know how to spell the name of his own goddam bar, and they should just get on with making it, and shut the hell up. That's how the The Elk's Mouth Bar and Grill got to be called The Elk's Mouth Bat and Grill. Most folks was used to it now.

Weren't never any of the Roundly's morons in there, except for two. One was Snowy the accountant. The other was his boss, Desire. Desire? That's a laugh. There weren't never nothing 'desirous' about the woman. She'd been soaking her insides with gin since she was fourteen, so you can imagine. Her nose was the shape and colour of a button tomato. Elk and the short order cook called her Rudolph, not to her nose of course.

But she sure helped keep The Elk's Mouth open. Elk was more'n happy to help her spend her old man's money. The only reason he didn't date her was cause he feared she'd stop spending and start drinking for free. That would of wiped him out. And there wouldn't be 'special' nights like tonight.

She'd booked a table at the back, like anyone else might of wanted it. He laid on one hell of a feast and wasn't charging her the full hog. If things went well tonight, he figured he could afford the jukebox he'd dreamed of. Tonight they was all hoping she could sell off the land that used to be under Roundly's factory.

Desire had never really forgiven the Japs for Pearl Harbor even though she'd been in a gin coma when it happened. But she'd sure read about it after. She figured any country sneaky enough to creep in and blow up a navy without telling no one, wasn't to be trusted in business. So she didn't have no conscience at all about lying to the Jap auto people when they wrote and inquired about her land.

She'd told 'em the people of Mattfield would be delighted to have a Toyota Plant in their midst, and relish the opportunity of culturally integrating with the three hundred Japanese technicians that'd come with it. She sent 'em fifty-year old studies of the site that was done before the surrounding land started sliding. Most of the houses was a yard closer to the plant than when they was built. Them Toyota people wouldn't have to walk to work, just ride their houses down there.

Desire didn't see it was her place to tell the nips that. They'd find out soon enough. Desire saw herself as a mature business woman. It hadn't taken her long to run Roundly's into the ground. But she blamed the world downturn in pool playing, not herself. The factory had been rooted in the past. This was her chance to get some collateral and set herself up in a more seventies kind of business. She was planning to go technical. She had her heart set on typewriters.

There was a danged foolish notion going around at the time that computers would be taking over from the sturdy typewriter. She was one of the few people at the time who could see how soon that fad would die out. Shit, how the hell could normal folks afford one of them big brain boxes or be smart enough to use it? Yet everyone was talking about how businesses was all gonna get computerated. Typewriter companies would panic sell and switch to computers.

That's where Desire come in. If someone had a little capital they could stock up on typewriters and bide their time till the computer frenzy fizzled itself out. It was so obvious she couldn't understand how no one else had thought of it. But foresight was what showed the difference between a gambler and a lady entrepreneur.

Japan was her chance. She had a high power meeting tonight with Miss Ajinomoto, the ex-ecutive secretary of the ex-ecutive director of Toyota. As Desire's house was kind'a neglected, and her office was kind'a burnt down, the Elk's Mouth was the only place she could meet and give a good impression.

When the Jap arrived, Desire had already gotten through half a bottle of gin for Dutch courage. She was at her most charming. Miss Ajinomoto was right on time and she bowed when Desire introduced herself. She was a little woman in a grey suit and her hair was all piled up on her head like a soft black ice cream cone swirl. She wore a load of makeup and thick glasses that made her eyes look bigger than they probably was.

Desire yelled at her, "DO YOU SPEAK ENGLISH?"

Miss Ajinomoto yelled back, "YES, A RITTLE BIT."

There was only two other customers in The Mouth and they was both at the bar. One was a big old guy in a rug. If it had been green it would of looked like a tuft of grass. He smiled a near perfect set of dentures at the two broads as they walked past and wondered why they was yelling at each other.

Elk had set up the rear table real pretty, silver service and all. Miss Ajinomoto touched the tablecloth like she'd never seen one before.

"This is most rubbery."

"It is? I'm sorry."

"No, rubbery is good. Is like, your face is rubbery too." Desire was gonna smack her one till she realized the woman had a speech defect.

"OK, I get it. Thanks." Elk brought over a plate of entrée spring rolls he'd defrosted specially in honor of this visit.He leaned over the Jap.

"Have a roll. They're Asian." Desire was delighted when the visitor took a bite and smiled.

"You see? Authentic Asian cuisine. All the Toyota staff could come and eat here. Home away from home. Except you probably don't have homes, right? What do you people live in over there?"

"Wooden huts."

"Really? How fascinating. America must be a real eye-opener for you." She blushed. "No offence intended."

Apart from that accidental 'eye' insult, the rest of the evening went real good. Desire crossed over into the gin zone and got more difficult to understand. But she thought the nip was warming to her. Elk had done 'em a steak for main course and Desire taught the woman how to use cutlery. She was a quick learner. Even her English had gotten better the more beer she drank.

By dessert they was best buddies. Desire knew all the bullshit had paid off when Miss Ajinomoto leaned over to her and said,

"Desire, I have to make the decision." She lowered her voice. "My boss don't speak no English so I gotta make recommendations for the guy." (See what I mean about how good her English had gotten?) But I'm supposed to pretend it's a committee decision. I'll be honest with you. I've been to see five other plots of land already and there ain't much difference between any of 'em. It's good that you've got all these empty houses here, and I like you, but ..."

"But what?" Desire was close to a deal. She could taste it. Lady entrepreneurs had a tongue for an opening.

"I ...I'm too embarrassed to say."

"Aji, you can tell me. We're friends, ain't we?"

"I have brought dishonor on my ancestors. One of the land owners made me an offer."

"What kind of offer?"

"He knew that my decision was final, so he offered me ...an incentive to choose his land."

Here it came. Desire'd been right. They were shifty little people. But she'd expected it. Business was business.

"We're talking money here, right?"

"I'm so ashamed, but I have twelve starving people in my family. What he offered could keep them alive for ten years. I could never earn …"

"I understand. I'm a woman ain't I? Just cause I'm a serious business person, don't mean I ain't got womanly feelings. How much did he offer?"

Miss Ajinomoto held up two fingers. Desire was pleasantly surprised. She splashed some Coke on top of a half glass of gin and sort'a puffed herself up.

"You know, girl? I'm gonna make your day. I'm gonna top that offer, and I got cash right here." She reached in her bag and came out with five fifty dollar bills. Miss Ajinomoto looked disappointed.

"I guess I didn't make myself clear enough. He didn't offer me two hundred. His bid was two grand."

Desire almost fell off her chair and off the end of the earth at the same time.

"Two thousand fucking bucks? Are you out of your tiny yella mind?" The guys at the bar looked over. Miss Ajinomoto almost lost it for a second but got her composure back. She opened the briefcase at her feet and took a bit of paper out.

"Of course, you're right. I was shocked at the size of his offer too. That's why I have no choice but to give him this." She put the paper down on the table. All Desire could focus on was the word Toyota at the top, and all them zeros after the number at the bottom. All I need is his signature at the bottom of this and I can go back to Japan with two thousand bucks in my pocket."

She stood. "I can see I've offended you by talking about money. I'm very sorry. Allow me to pay for this derightful meal."

"Hold your horses sister. You sit your little fanny right back down there where it come from. When you going back to Japan?"

"Tomorrow morning. Early." She sat down like she'd been told.

Desire rustled around in that bag of hers and come out with the car keys. She stood up kind'a shakily.

"You wait there. Don't you think about leaving." And she staggered out of the Bat and Grill leaving a grinning Asian all by herself. She sat politely at her table and sipped at her beer.

-o-

"Hi, baby." She looked up. The guy with the grass on his head was standing over her.

"I been to Bangkok." She was in too good a mood to let this sorry creature spoil her night.

"Wow. Really? I used to be a hooker there." He was a bit stunned at her honesty but it confirmed what he knew about oriental chicks. He smiled and went to sit down. "Till I got the disease."

"Disease?" He froze where he was.

"Yeah. Man that thing just spread and spread. Made one hell of a mess of me, down there. But the doctor gives me these special pads, you know? To mop up the puss. And if I burst the blisters regular, I can still perform pretty good. You wann'a sit down?"

"No. I just come over to say hi."

"OK. Hi. Bye."

"See you around."

-o-

Desire was back twenty-five minutes later. She was sweating and shaking. But that could of been from not having a drink for twenty-five minutes. She seemed relieved to see the Jap still sitting there.

"I was afraid you'd gone. I didn't see no car outside."

"No, I ehr, parked down at the police office and walked up. The company don't like me parking outside bars. You know what I mean?"

"Yeah." She signaled over to Elk to bring another bottle and she put a big brown paper bag on the table. She wasn't a woman who was used to moving fast, that was obvious. She slumped down on the chair and fanned herself with her hand. "Shit I gotta start having sex again. I'm out'a shape."

She'd gotten home, raided her cash stash and made it back in some kind of a record time. But given the number of zeros she'd saw on that contract, two thousand dollars wasn't that much of a sacrifice. Never look a gift horse in the mouth, her dad always said. She never really understood what it meant, but it seemed fitting in this case.

"There's two grand in that bag. The bills ain't pretty but money's money. That's what I say. You can count it if you want. And here," she stuck two fingers down her cleavage and found a rolled up bill. "...is another twenty bucks to take my offer over his. I think that pretty well seals the deal. Right?"

They shook hands on it and toasted it with a couple of drinks while Miss Ajinomoto filled in some details on the contract. The director had signed the thing already so the whole deal was done before 10 PM.

-0-

Desire was feeling mighty proud of herself. After the nip had left she ordered drinks for everyone in the house. That was her and Elk and a little drunk guy with a Davy Crockett hat. She sat at the bar on her favourite stool and enjoyed the adrenaline surge from her first major business negotiation. She was a natural.

She read through her copy of the contract with Mr. Kamikaze's signature on the bottom. It sure was a nice contract. She hadn't noticed before how Toyata had the same logo as Holiday Inn. Maybe they was partners.

33

"Man, I'm bushed."

"You wanna beer, Waldo?"

"No, thanks. But I could kill a Minute Maid orange juice."

"I'll fix it. How'd it go?"

"Pretty good. A lot of folks left already, but I got addresses for them. The one's that was still here couldn't believe what they was seeing."

"But you did tell 'em not to thank Desire personal if they saw her?"

"I told 'em. But you know, Saifon, none of us can imagine her being modest, let alone generous."

"That's what she told me to tell everyone. She said she felt bad about everyone losing their jobs and she wanted to pay 'em up. But she didn't want no one embarrassing her with outward signs of gratitude."

"You see, honey? You dig deep enough and you'll find goodness in every one of God's creatures. Even Desire."

"Right." She handed him the glass of juice and watched it disappear down his throat in one swallow.

"Waldo, I gotta go."

"Go?"

"Soon as the passport gets here. I got enough money now to do what I gotta do." He leaned up against the sink unit and the pipes creaked all the way to the ground floor.

"This place has kind'a got used to your being here."

She'd been at Waldo's place for two weeks while they was waiting for a sleazy lawyer guy to do the paperwork. All you need is money to turn the illegal into legal in the good old US of A. It was a remarkable country in them days. Course, there ain't no corruption no more.

She'd been sleeping on his sofa. It was luxury compared to her pink Chevy. She knew he didn't want her there at first. But when she'd hit him with her idea, he was too stunned to kick her out. She really floored him that day she arrived.

-0-

"You want me to what?"

"Adopt me."

He grinned and looked around his room.

"This is Candid Camera, right?"

"I'm serious, Waldo." He could see she was.

"Ain't you ...I mean ain't you a bit old to be adopted, girl?"

"Now I am. But you ain't adopting me now. You adopted me fifteen years ago."

"I did?" They sat down opposite each other.

There was a lot went on that Waldo didn't get. He was okay with facts and figures that was lined up on one level. But he couldn't keep two levels running at the same time, you know what I mean? So stuff like sarcasm, and hidden meanings, and them cryptic crosswords was all mumbo jumbo to him. If him and Aretha adopted Saifon, he was sure he would of known about it.

"Come again."

"Waldo, let me give it to you straight. I need a passport. To get a passport I gotta have an address, and relatives and all that crap." She lowered her voice as if anyone outside the room gave a shit. "And I ain't got none."

"You ain't got relatives?"

"Not a one."

"Dang, Saifon. That's too bad."

"It sure is if you need paperwork."

"How did you get a driving license?"

"You look real close at the picture and you'll see some other scrawny Asian lady. Her license found its way into my possession. The cops never look that close."

"What about your folks? You got a ma, ain't you?"

"Hell, Waldo. Being as I'm here, you'd have to assume I had a ma. I just never got introduced to her."

"That's real sad, girl." He really meant it.

"Come on man. Let's cut out the sentimental shit. This is business we're talking here. There's this lawyer who was a regular at the Butterfly. I remember you got the greatest respect for lawyers, but this one's as crooked as lightning. He can do me the papers for a passport, but he says I gotta have an address that checks out. I ain't ever had one of them. I can pay you."

"Can'tya make it up?"

"He reckons they check. And if they find out I been lying, they can make it real hard for me to ever get one."

"What does the lawyer get out of this?"

"Money. A lot."

"Can you trust him?"

"No, but I don't have to pay him in advance. It's cash on delivery. Waldo, there's something else."

"What's that?"

"If I put down that I was a state orphan, cause that's what I was, they'll run a check. There's stuff back there I don't want them digging through. I'd have to explain a lot of stuff. But …"

"But what?"

"But if I had papers to show you was my daddy, they'd check you out, and not me. See what I mean?"

"I think I do."

"This sleazy lawyer guy can do it all. He can draw up adoption papers backdated to when I was at the home. I'll tell you all about that some day."

She was fishing a dry lake here. She didn't think there'd be a lot of hope. He didn't owe her nothing. Waldo looked down at his tits, first one, then the other.

"Look, Waldo. If you don' t want nothing to do with this I understand. I got no right to ask you really. If you want me to *rather* off, I'll *rather* off right now and there won't be no hard feelings. I mean that."

Waldo stared over at her. She looked like a matchstick puppet on his big fat sofa. She was so tiny. He imagined her slipping down the back of the cushions with the dimes. They'd find her in a year and wonder when they'd lost her.

"You want me to be your poppa?"

"Well, yeah. Kind'a.

He thought about all them times him and Aretha talked about having kids. They'd get into it, give 'em names and all. They'd spend hours talking about what they'd do with 'em, and for 'em.

Saifon could see Waldo was getting all misty-eyed. She figured she must of upset the guy somehow.

"Waldo, you okay?"

"I ain't never been a daddy before."

"It ain't like you got to take me to school or nothing. And I already been told about the birds and the flies and stuff." That made Waldo laugh.

"Miss Saifon." With a bit of effort and some grunting and heavy breathing, he got to his feet. He stood straight like he was about to make the most important announcement of his life. Maybe it was. "Me and Aretha would be honored to be your parents."

Saifon was amazed.

"You would?" She got up and give him a hug and a kiss. It weren't easy reaching his face. "Shit. Thank you, daddy." She felt kind'a strange cause she knew it wasn't just the papers she was getting. She was getting the feeling of being wanted, too.

34

So, that was it. That was how Aretha and Waldo finally got the kid they'd always dreamed of. She probably didn't look like they'd imagined her to, but Waldo considered himself lucky to be having any description of child at his age. It was a kind of miracle. He knew Aretha'd be thrilled.

Saifon's passport arrived registered mail on the Monday. When she told Waldo she'd be gone by the end of the week he felt cheated somehow. It was like he was losing a daughter. They was sitting watching the Beverly Hillbillies. Just watching it. Granny was stuck up a tree and there was this lion below her. Beverly Hills seemed like a dangerous place.

"Where you going then?" They watched another ten minutes of granny making friends with the lion and setting him on Jed just for the heck of it, before Saifon answered. It was one hell of an answer. (I'd better warn y'all now there's some depressing shit coming up that might just kill off any good mood you thought you was in. If you'd sooner not know, I guess you could skip the next couple of pages. But don't blame me if you get lost later.)

"Waldo, something real bad happened. I mean real bad. It happened when I was a little girl. I was bought up by some frigging old witch aunt in Laos who didn't want me. I guess, if the old witch was to be believed, my parents had gotten themselves shot. I don't remember 'em. When I was seven or eight years old, the aunt sold me."

"Jees, Saifon. They sell kids where you come from?"

"It ain't usual. I just got lucky."

She was talking to Waldo through the TV. Didn't take her eyes off it. I guess it was easier to tell Granny Clampett than telling Waldo. "Some guy drove me and some other girls the same age across into Thailand in the back of a truck.

A few days later and we was in the stinking hold of a tanker. Nowhere to pee or wash. No light. We was scared shitless, Waldo."

"I can't even imagine how terrible it must of been. This tanker, it's like a boat, right?"

"Yeah. A big empty son of a bitch. Every sound echoed around inside it like some big giant was clanking around. And that's how I got to America. Now, we gotta interrupt this exciting story for a cup of coffee. Stay tuned for further installments."

She went off to the kitchen and left Waldo sitting there all dumbfounded. What she'd told him was so far out, it might as well of been science fiction. He believed her sure enough, but he couldn't never put himself in her shoes. And he got a feeling this was only the start of one nasty story.

She come back with two coffees, handed one to Waldo and kept right on talking like she hadn't let up.

"So that's why I been saving, Waldo. That's why I been working two jobs to get the money together to do what I gotta do, and go where I gotta go."

"Where you gotta go, Saifon?"

"Back there."

"To Laos?"

"Yeah. Man, I make a mean cup of coffee."

"Why the hell you wanna go back there after what they done to you?"

"I wanna go back *because* of what they done."

Waldo tried to think of a fitting passage from the bible but nothing come to mind, so he made something up.

"Lord said, 'revenge maketh man as sinful as the original person what sinned in the first place …against the revenger'."

"Shit. Sinning's the last thing I'm worried about. If he ain't struck me down yet then I got away with it. I don't just want revenge. I want to be sure this shit ain't still happening.

When I got to New York, they fed us up and cleaned us and dressed us pretty. I remember they took us to this big … like, closed down theatre full of guys in suits. They paraded us up and down on the stage and they was bidding for us, like cows, Waldo. Like cows.

"The guy that got me handed over eleven hundred-dollar bills. That's eleven hundred bucks and that was fifteen years ago. That was a hell of a lot of money, and I bet you anything the trade's still going strong. I sure ain't seen nothing about it getting uncovered in the newspapers."

"Me neither."

"And if they'd busted the ring, it would have made news."

"Saifon, honey. We should tell the cops about this."

"Man, I been in contact with the cops. But you see I ain't got no proof. I can't recall where we landed, where they took me, where they sold me, nothing. All I remember was getting away and this cop taking me in his car. I couldn't tell no one what happened. They sent me to social services. I guess I was pretty fucked up by then. Excuse my mouth. Cause by the time they worked out what language I was talking and they found me a Lao social worker, I didn't wanna talk to no one. I was one evil little bitch in them days, although you wouldn't believe it when you see how sweet I turned out."

"I believe it."

"Thank you. They tried to force some learning down my throat but I wasn't having none of it. I did get into English, but. I could see that being real useful for me so I was the ace student in English class. That's why I speak English so good now.

"It wasn't till four years ago I got this hankering to close them kid smugglers down. I went looking for the cop that picked me up when I escaped. He'd retired already but he was interested in the story, and I guess he believed me. He told some pals that was still working. But there weren't nothing he could do without evidence.

"The old cop drove me around in his car, but I didn't see nothing I recognized. I gotta go back over it. Go back to the start. Retrace like every step. See if anything comes back to me. If them people are still trading little girls, I gotta do something about it. Know what I mean, Waldo?"

Waldo's head was spinning. I don't mean rotating. I mean he was real confused and shocked. Being a parent wasn't going to be a piece of cake at all.

"Saifon, what you're suggesting here ain't gonna be easy."

"No."

"And it ain't gonna be safe."

"I know."

"Fact is, there's a lot of money in this people smuggling business. Where there's money there's corruption, and where there's corruption, there's people who'll shoot you for a share of that money. You could get yourself killed."

Saifon smiled. Then there was the longest silence while Waldo lined up all the details and possibilities in his mind. She thought he'd wandered off the subject altogether till he finally said,

"So, I guess I'll go with you." She didn't see nothing funny about that joke.

"You what?"

"What kind of a daddy would I be if I let my only daughter go off and get herself killed?"

"Waldo, that's only on paper. You don't got no obligation."

"Aretha wouldn't never forgive me."

"She never met me. Waldo you …"

"No, my mind's made up."

"That's crazy, man. Shit. Where you gonna find the money to travel to Asia? I sure as hell can't pay for you."

Waldo went across to the desk, took his bankbook out of a drawer, and let her look at his last deposit.

"Damn, Waldo. You rob a bank or something?"

"It's from the Mexico sting. The cops salvaged it."

Her eyes rolled in desperation.

"Absolutely frigging not. I don't want no big ball of lard there with me. What frigging good would you be to me in a fight? And you can't frigging run. And how the frigging hell would I go about disguising a three hundred fifty pound nigger in a country where nobody's over three feet? You'd screw everything up."

He wasn't offended.

"That's okay. I know you're just talking like this to test my will."

"No. I'm talking like this cause I think I just heard the stupidest thing I ever heard. Get it out of your fool head. Ain't no way in the world you're coming to Laos. Jees."

35

"May I help you with that sir?"

The steward was one of them queens Waldo had read about. He hadn't never seen one in real life. Not less you count the farm boys that experiment on each other before they get married. He'd seen plenty of them.

"Waldo was certain this was a real one. He wasn't quite manly and he wore his hair too neat. But Waldo was a tolerant man.

"I can't do the sucker up."

The queen steward leaned over Waldo to help force the two ends of the seatbelt buckle to meet, and there was a whiff of lilac.

"If you could just breath in a little more, sir."

"I am breathing in, boy. But that don't make no difference on the outside."

"OK. Then I'm gonna have to squeeze you some." And he did, and the belt kind'a dissected his body like a wire through wet clay. As soon as his friend had left, Waldo undid the thing cause he didn't wanna be two little Waldo's.

Saifon was sitting in the aisle seat pretending to be asleep. She was still sulking. He told her she was gonna have to start talking to him again soon. But it hadn't happened yet. She'd get over it. If she really didn't want him there she could easy of run away and not told him. But she left her air ticket lying around so it was easy to call up and book the seat beside hers.

But Waldo was too excited about leaving the ground to get dragged into her mood. It flew, man. He couldn't believe how this big piece of old tin was able to lift him up and carry him away. The country below looked just like it did in Aretha's atlas. Except the states didn't have their names written across 'em. They must of made that bit up.

He felt like a little kid again. He'd surprised himself as much as he'd surprised Saifon when he said he'd come along. But hell this was gonna be fun.

"Sir, would you like something to drink?" Saifon's pretend sleep had turned into a real sleep beside him. The queen steward and his boyfriend had this trolley full of all kinds of neat stuff. Waldo ordered a Coke.

"Coming right up sir."

It made him feel real special when they called him 'sir'. He already had a soft spot for pansy boys. He reached into his pocket and wondered if he had enough change to pay for the Coke.

"You boys take American money?"

"Sir. You don't have to pay."

"I don't?"

"No, sir. Everything's free on board."

"Well, I be damned."

"Saifon woke up when they was over the Pacific. Waldo was there beside her, trying to open the window so's he could smell the sea air.

"What the hell you doing, Waldo?"

"Hi, Saifon. I guess this sucker's stuck."

"It don't open."

"No? That's too bad. They tell me sea air's real good for you." She laughed.

"You open that window and you wouldn't have no head to breath through."

"Hey. You're talking. I guess that means you forgive me."

"Shit no."

Yeah she'd forgiven him, but she wouldn't let him know it yet. It almost knocked her own goddamned head off when he followed her through the gate at Michigan airport. She asked him where he thought he was going and he told her he wanted to see the airplane. Then he followed her on the airplane and she knew he'd fooled her. She made this crazy scene but he just grinned at her. She was so happy inside it almost made her cry. So she shut her wet eyes and pretended to sleep.

She was mad at herself. In spite of all the cussing and the orneriness, inside she was still the scared little critter from the hold of the tanker. She was frightened about what she was about to get herself into. Waldo wasn't much use for nothing, but he was a size, and she needed something heavy to hold her down. Stop them belly butterflies from flying away with her.

She didn't rightly know what she was gonna do. She knew what province she was born in but she couldn't recall where her witch aunt lived. It was way out in the Boondocks. There wasn't no other kids, no town. Just her and her no-talking, no-loving aunt, and plenty of rice fields. All she had was a phone number in Bangkok.

Waldo looked back over his shoulder.

"You suppose David would let me have another Coke?"

"Who's David?"

"The steward."

"Well, ain't you been busy while I was asleep. I thought you give that shit up."

"Yeah. I did. But I never been out of America before, and I need something patriotic inside me. Who knows how long it'll be before I see Coca Cola again."

36

The big red sign at Don Muang Airport read, 'Coca Cola Welcomes You to Thailand' It was eight times bigger than the official sign. It probably had something to do with all them American boys passing through on their ways to getting killed in Nam.

Waldo and Saifon stood in the immigration queue holding their brand new passports. South Bend bus terminal was more sophisticated than Bangkok's airport in them days. There was a lot of chaos. Guys in tight uniforms with big guns, drowsy passengers not knowing what direction they was supposed to go, piles of lost bags with panties and socks spilling out of 'em.

When Waldo and Saifon both stepped up to the immigration officer's desk together, the guy yelled at 'em. Waldo had to step back over the red line he thought was just a floor decoration. When it was his turn, he felt bad he was forcing this poor little guy to do a job he obviously didn't like.

"You not military?"

"No, sir."

"Why you come here?" Waldo remembered his line.

"Transit to Malaysia." They come up with the Malaysia story because there weren't no fighting there. If he'd said 'Laos' they'd figure he was a spy or something. According to the papers, the US had been using Laos as a transit route to get to Vietnam.

The officer demanded to see his return ticket and his money, and he didn't make no secret of the fact he didn't like the big guy. Or maybe he just didn't like no one.

The drive into Bangkok City took longer than the flight. They spent more time stuck in traffic than they did moving. It was two in the afternoon and the sun baked 'em inside that old taxi like one of Waldo's TV dinners. There was this box affair in the front pretending to be an air conditioner, but the windows was jammed down. What was coming in was hot and sticky. Waldo still had that dumb grin on his face.

"What is it you find so goddamned pleasant about all this, Waldo?"

"Look, girl. We only just arrived, and I'm already sweating like a hog. A few weeks of this and I'll be Sidney Poitier."

"Who?"

"Darn it, Saifon. Don't you ever go to the movies?"

"No."

Twenty minutes after they left it, the airport was still there grinning at 'em in the rear-view mirror. Saifon was already feisty after the flight. She was surprised when her old language come out of her mouth.

"Driver, ain't there some quicker way than this?"

He smiled the first of his eight thousand smiles of the trip.

"This is the expressway, ma'am."

"Jesus. I'd hate to be on the frigging slowway."

It took 'em an hour and twenty minutes to get off the expressway and on to something that showed Saifon what 'slow' really meant.

All the stuff that got Saifon pissed about being stuck in traffic in one of the dirtiest cities in the world, turned Waldo into some happy black Buddha. He sucked in exhaust smoke from old wooden-bodied trucks like it was fresh air or something. He waved his thumb at every vibrating *tuk tuk* driver that pulled up alongside. (A *tuk tuk's* kinda like a golf cart but without the luxury.)

He'd been practicing his *wai*-ing since the tour company girls at the airport prayed at him. It weren't nothing religious or nothing. That's just how they say hi to each other over there. It's called a *wai*. Them girls at the airport *wai*'d hi and tried to convince poor Waldo to sign up for a Bangkok Sex Tour. He threw away the brochure but he hung on to the *wai*.

There he was *wai*-ing at all the confused pedestrians, and they didn't have no choice but to *wai* back. He got plenty of practice. There was crossings painted here and there across the roads but they didn't mean shit. Cars ignored 'em like they was just art to make the road prettier. So people clubbed together in little bands and launched off into traffic so's they could get across the road in one piece. There weren't no people bridges in them days.

Waldo noticed how everything was just that little bit smaller than back home. Sidewalks was narrower. Bus stops was shorter. Cars was dinkier. And of course the people was all Saifon-sized. Some of 'em was even tinier than she was. He felt like he was in this one episode of Land of the Giants where some giant kid had real people to play with like they was toys.

Nearly all the shops was joined together in rows, and opened out onto the street. It was like looking in on an ant farm, like all the rooms was sliced open and you could watch 'em living their lives without their noticing.

Some old guy sat in his underclothes in his hardware store reading a newspaper. A big lady in a cake shop was fanning herself with a pancake. Three un-moving girls with overdone make-up was sitting in a gold shop like cadavers in lipstick. A young couple sat out front of their sign-writing shop and laughed when their baby crashed his stroller into a dog. The dog didn't get the humor.

Waldo soaked it all up like one of them Kitchen Guzzler magic sponges. Saifon was that other ad; the spray for your sofa that stops spilled stuff from soaking in and leaving a stain. You know the one I mean? She didn't let nothing in at all. She grumbled and cussed all the way.

Dtui the driver looked at her in the mirror one time when they was stuck at a red light that didn't do no other colours.

"What you looking at?"

"Sorry, sister."

"No. You got something to say, you say it."

He looked up again and weighed up whether he was likely to make her any more pissed than she already was. It didn't seem possible so he spoke his mind.

"Well, I come from the north-east. The only reason it's Thailand and not Laos is cause it was easier to use the Mekhong as a border than putting down ropes. But you ask 'em all up there and they'll tell you they're Lao. So I got sisters that's Lao, and I got a wife that's Lao. And all my neighbors and friends and fiancées up there is Lao. And if I saw a photograph of you, I'd say you look just like them."

"So, what's your point?"

"So, it's only the look. You got a Lao nose on a Lao face on top of a Lao body. But there ain't nothing Lao about you."

"Good." She said 'good' but in truth it hurt.

"It's like some foreigner found this empty Lao body and climbed inside."

"And that's positive or negative?"

"I don't know. It must be confusing, sister."

She leaned back onto the hot seat and, for the hundredth time, wondered why it was still covered in the plastic they put on it in the factory. She had a lot of wondering to do. For the first time since she could remember, she was surrounded by people she looked like. She wasn't a chink or a nip or a wog. She could walk down the street and no-one'd take the slightest notice of her. But Dtui was right. She was a frigging imposter. There was an alien inside her that wouldn't never really understand what these people was thinking or feeling.

37

By the time they got to the Malaysia Hotel, Saifon knew that old taxi better'n her pink Chevy. She'd got to practice her Lao with Dtui, and it surprised her how it was all still in her head. It was like it was in storage in a little room up behind her ear some place. They got to know Dtui better'n some wives know their husbands. He give 'em the address of his relatives and said to be sure and look 'em up when they got up there.

The Malaysia was a happening hotel. They'd only chose it cause Waldo wasn't happy about lying to the immigration guy. Waldo probably never told a real honest-to-goodness lie in his life. This way he could say he was going to Malaysia and really mean it.

The reception area wasn't that big and it was crammed with all kinds of deadbeats, drunks and hookers. The deadbeats was mostly Thai men. And the drunks was all Western guys, even though a lot of 'em could of been fitted in the 'deadbeat' section too. It looked more like a whore house than a hotel. And it was only four in the evening.

A little bell-guy in uniform took 'em over to the elevator, and when the doors opened, there was two half-dressed women in there. It was kind'a their office. They must of rode up and down all day preying on tourists. When they saw Waldo with Saifon, they assumed what most people did, that he'd already gotten his gal.

The semi-naked broads was angry. This was their territory. They said something to Saifon in Thai. She answered 'em in English.

"I'm sorry. I don't understand." She smiled even though she knew what they'd said.

"You no Thai? You looks like Thai."

"Where you come from?"

"I'm American."

"Yankee? Right on."

They looked at the big fella.

"You wanna go three way?"

"Maybe four. Okay?"

"No. Thank you."

In the surprisingly nice room, the bell-guy showed 'em how to switch on the TV, and the air conditioner, and offered 'em things to smoke, swallow, inhale or inject. They politely refused.

It hadn't occurred to either of 'em to get two single rooms. The two beds was so small, when Waldo lay down on one, he looked like a hippo on a wafer biscuit.

"Maybe we should of gotten two doubles," Saifon shouted from the bathroom. She was bursting for a pee, but I guess you really didn't need to know that.

"No. It's okay. I'm so bushed I could sleep standing up. Hey, Saifon."

"Yeah?"

"What's a three way?"

She laughed.

"It's where you get to be the beef in a burger."

"Oh. I see." (He didn't.) "Ain't you tired?"

"Yeah. But I got a call to make first."

-o-

By the time she got around to it, there was more noise coming out of Waldo asleep than out of the pig waiting room at the meatworks. So she went down to reception and called from there. It weren't much quieter.

She made her appointment and was feeling pleased with herself until this scrawny little English guy from Yorkshire or some other darn place where people ain't learned how to speak right, come up to her. He was wearing a string singlet and soccer shorts. He'd been out in the sun for the first time in his life and was glowing like a stoplight. He breathed beer in her face.

"All right. Come on. You'll do."

"I'll do what."

"Blimey. One who speaks English at last. How much for sucky sucky?" He demonstrated with his thumb.

"Sucky sucky?"

"Aye. Hurry up. I'm already half mast." Before she could stop him, he grabbed her hand and put it on the flagpole. She pulled away and got that evil look in her eye that spelled trouble. She cleared her throat and straightened her spine.

"Well, hell. We'll sure have to do something about that, won't we." He had barely enough time to raise a smile before her knee solved his half-masting problem for the day, and probably many more days to come. He went down like a blown tire and his stoplight red turned to green.

She wasn't sure he could hear her but she told him anyway,

"There's whores, and there's ladies. Ninety-nine point nine percent of women in this part of the world are ladies. I'm a lady. You should'a asked."

38

Look, I'm gonna have to call me a time out here. It's crossed my mind that most of you out there got no idea where Laos is, or what the heck was going on there when Waldo and Saifon was in the region. There's probably some of you don't give a hoot.

But I believe, if you're planning to enjoy the rest of this book, you gotta really understand what the hell I'm yakking on about. I guess I could put in bits of knowledge here and there so you pick it up accidental like. But you probably spotted already that I ain't exactly Hemmingway, and I ain't much good at being subtle.

So, here's what I'm gonna do. I found this book, see. It's like a history book but it don't use no fancy words. So even you can probably understand it. I found a bit that talks about Laos in the sixties and seventies. Well, I copied it out and I'm gonna stick it in about here.

I know. I know what you're thinking. But it ain't exactly stealing you see. My dear departed English teacher taught us all how to do para-sailing or something-or other. All you gotta do is change words here and there and no one can tell.

You might notice a slight change of style round about here. Hope it don't spoil your reading.

By 1970, the population of Laos had declined (that means 'got smaller') by a third, to a little over two million. Those who hadn't died in the bombing had fled to neighboring Thailand. Although the news hadn't made it into the newspapers back home, America had been using Laos as a secret base to attack North Vietnamese positions since 1964. That was bad news for the Lao as the Vietnamese supply route, the Ho Chi Min Trail, ran plum through Laos.

During their secret war, the Americans dropped two million dollars worth of bombs on Laos every day for nine years. Shit. That worked out to half a ton of ordinance for every man, woman and child in the country. As the pilots were instructed not to bring back any B52s, those that weren't used on the enemy were dumped indiscriminately. The Air America pilots all based inside Laos wore no uniforms and didn't appear on US Government payrolls. Officially, they didn't exist.

The war was coordinated by the CIA from a headquarters near the Lao border in the Thai province of Udon Thani. In order to limit the influence of Laotian communists, the CIA had been shoring up a number of corrupt and inefficient Lao governments even long before the secret war began. The Royal Lao Army was funded almost entirely from Washington, and the capital, Vientiane, enjoyed an inflated war time economy that the rest of the country didn't get a share of. Vientiane in those days was a city of drugs and brothels and uncontrolled profiteering.

The Lao socialist movement, the Pathet Lao (PL), was largely a Vietnamese creation. It's senior members all had direct or familial connections to North Vietnam and were trained by the Viet Cong. But the Pathet Lao found sympathy and ready recruits to join its ranks among rural Lao families bombed for no damned reason by supposed allies.

Another reason for public interest was the royal presence of Prince Souphanouvong as a leading cadre of the Pathet Lao. The "Red Prince" had been converted to communism whilst working on the docks at Le Havre along with another convert, Ho Chi Mihn. While the Red Prince led communist troops in the North, his half brother, Prince Souvanahphouma (and you don't have to learn all these names) was heading various CIA puppet governments in Vientiane.

Because of a natural Lao reluctance to wage civil war against its brothers and sisters, the CIA was forced to recruit most of its ground troops from minority, Hmong villagers in the mountains. It was thanks to the Hmong the CIA was able to hold off the Vietnamese as long as they did.

There were still around 200,000 US troops in Vietnam as we entered 1971 (when Waldo and Saifon arrived in Bangkok). While Nixon refuted accusations that Laos and Cambodia had suffered incursions, there were constant US supported South Vietnam raids

across both borders to hunt out Viet Cong bases. In February, a
massive invasion of Laos was planned.

So you see when Waldo and Saifon arrived, they didn't
know nothing about what was happening in Laos cause it
was all a goddamn secret. (This is me speaking again by the
way) Now you gotta hand it to them CIA guys, hiding a
whole frigging war for nine years. It's hard enough hiding an
illicit moonshine still in the woods. You'd think someone
would of heard something wouldn't ya?

It sure didn't get to Waldo and Saifon's ears. They
thought they was perfectly safe. They thought there was two
fat ass countries between them and the war. But they was
heading right for it. Exciting or what?

-o-

Saifon thought she was getting everything sorted out. She
had this phone number you see. It'd been with her for
fifteen years. When she first got away from the traffickers
and she was being uncooperative with the social services,
this woman come to see her.

They was looking for a place for Saifon to live. Some
family dumb enough to take in a wildcat without no English.
You can imagine folks like that weren't queuingaround the
block.

So this Lao wife of someone important comes all the way
from DC just to see her. She couldn't understand why. And
this pretty old lady sits Saifon down and talks to her. She just
talks. Don't ask no questions or nothing.

There'd been this interpreter come to see her before. He
weren't that friendly and he asked all these direct questions
she didn't feel like answering at the time. She didn't know
where she was or why, so why should she answer questions?
But this old bird didn't ask her nothing. She talked on about

where they was, and what was happening there, and the price of milk, and all.

An hour she talked and no one's sure if it was because Saifon was afraid she wouldn't never stop talking, or if she just got ready, but she started talking back. Everyone was amazed. She didn't tell the pretty old lady what happened to her. No, she wasn't ready for that. But she talked a lot and it made her feel better. The woman never pushed. She told her if she was ready to talk about stuff she should give her a call. She wrote down her name and number in Washington. She wrote it in Lao and English and both of 'em was equally useless. Saifon couldn't read then.

-o-

Fourteen years passed before she was ready to talk. In them fourteen years she'd run away from a state home and three do-good church-going foster families, quit school, had a million jobs, and lived more on the street than under a roof.

She'd been raped, but she'd never whored. She had some damn fool notion inside herself that her body wasn't something for sale. Somewhere along the line she'd picked up dignity. It weren't the 'not living in cars or peeing in bushes' kind of dignity. It was the 'too proud to beg, too proud to sell your booty' kind.

God knows she could of bought herself out of her shitty life if her dignity hadn't stopped her. She saw other girls living okay by spreading their legs, but they looked kind'a naked to her, even when they was dressed in their expensive clothes. They didn't have no dignity and she did. If she lost that, she'd be frigging nothing.

So it was. After them tough fourteen years, once she'd decided to be Bat Woman and save the world, she phoned the number in Washington. It was the goddamned Lao Embassy compound. They told her the woman had left the States some ten years before. But after some very persuasive cussing, they hunted around and found a number for her. It was a number in Bangkok, which was odd, but better than nothing.

-o-

There in the reception of the Malaysia Hotel she'd phoned the number without a lot of hope in her heart. Old people got a nasty habit of dying. She was already old back then in New York. She would of been old plus by now.

But what do you know? This crunchy old voice answers the phone. The conversation went something like this:

"Hello?"

"Is that Mrs. Pornsawan?"

"Yes it is. Who's speaking please?" Saifon got kind'a choked up for a while. "Hello."

"Yeah. Well, you probably don't remember me, but my name's Saifon."

"Yes?"

"I met you fourteen years ago, in New York. I was about eight at the time and ... you come from Washington to talk to me. You give me your number. I guess you don't remember."

"On the contrary. I remember you very well. You were giving the social services people a hard time. I believe you bit a nurse who was trying to test your blood." Saifon laughed.

"Yeah. That must of been me."

"And are you ready to talk to me yet?"

"If you got time to listen."

39

Mrs. Pornsawan give her the address and they arranged to meet the next day. That's why Saifon and Waldo was on a dirty cream-coloured bus jerking its way through the crazy streets of Bangkok. The bus was crowded so there weren't nowhere to sit. Waldo took up so much space he stopped ten normal-sized Thais from getting on. He was still getting a kick out of all the sweating. The folks on the bus and in the street looked at him like he was Godzilla. It didn't worry him none. He just smiled at 'em and they smiled back and not one bird dropped out of the sky.

"Hi. How you doing?" he asked 'em, and they laughed and he felt happy. It didn't occur to him once that they might of been making fun of him.

Saifon wasn't embarrassed. She wasn't the embarrassing kind.

They arrived at Ngam Duphli Street a long time after they should of. The bus didn't move no faster than the houses in Mattfield traveling down to Roundly's. Plus when they got to where they thought they was going, they found out they'd given 'em the wrong information at the hotel. In fact the address they wanted was about four minutes' walk from the frigging hotel. Saifon was pissed. Waldo was happy as a drunk. This sure beat Indiana in his book.

They arrived at the big old brick house a couple of hours after the appointment. Saifon hated being late. But she got the idea it was expected in Bangkok. Mrs. Pornsawan opened the door herself. She was a lot skinnier than Saifon remembered her, real old in fact. Her skin was stuck to her bones like tissue paper. But them pretty almond eyes was still in their sockets smiling at her guests.

She welcomed Saifon in Lao, then for Waldo's benefit she switched to English.

"Welcome to my house. My goodness. You've grown into quite a beautiful young lady." Saifon blushed out loud. Waldo beamed and held out his hand.

"How are you ma'am? My name's Waldo. I'm Saifon's daddy." The old lady shook his big old hand and didn't look in the least surprised.

"I'm so pleased she found a daddy with such a nice smile." Waldo laughed. "Won't you both join me for a cool drink in the garden. Mr. Waldo, I can see you're finding our tropical heat a little moist."

"I'm sweating like a hog on a spit, ma'am." Saifon nudged him in where his rib could of been and he got the idea he'd spoke in bad taste again. But Mrs. Pornsawan seemed to enjoy a bit of bad taste. She chuckled all the way to the back of the house.

"The yard was like a little jungle with one of them white gazebo things in the middle of it. There was a big fan on the ceiling and the temperature out there was some ten degrees cooler than the street.

Once they'd got settled, there was Saifon and Waldo, Mrs. Pornsawan and a little quiet guy sitting round a white iron table on white iron chairs. She did introduce the quiet guy but it was one of them names with more letters than the entire alphabet, so Waldo decided to forget it before it over-taxed his mind.

The quiet guy was about the same age as the old lady with dyed black hair and a black pencil moustache. He must of been good looking in his day but he was squeezing the tube now.

Saifon blurted out the people-smuggling story as soon as she could. The others sipped on tall glasses of iced red stuff. A little square girl in a long skirt kept on running out of the house and topping them up.

When Saifon was through and any questions was answered, the old lady nodded her head.

"I thought something like this at the time. I wish you'd been able to talk about it then." She caught Saifon's frown. "Oh. Don't worry. I understand perfectly why you couldn't."

"Why'd you come and see me in New York?"

"You were the only live one we had." Waldo's straw had buckled and he was sucking like his life depended on it. He give up and looked over.

"You had dead ones?"

"Yes, Waldo. There were possibly two before Saifon. One was certainly Lao. She was able to say a few words before she died at the hospital. There was an expatriate Thai nurse on duty in emergency that night. If she hadn't been there, we would never have heard about it. The nurse recognized the language and went over to listen. She managed two sentences; 'They sold me,' and 'The Chinaman bought me.'

Then she gave in to her injuries. She had been repeatedly …abused over a long period. There were no missing children reports so the police came to see us at the embassy. My husband was the Lao ambassador at the time. He was busy with the matter of rescuing the country so he handed the matter to me."

Waldo felt sick about the story but real proud to be sitting next to an ambassador's wife. Given Waldo's normal social circle, this was almost as good as a queen, he reckoned. He got super respectful.

"That was a shocking story, your majesty, but …"

"Waldo, you may call me Porn."

He was honored, but he didn't think he could ever bring himself to call a high class lady something dirty like that. She went on.

"Following that first death, the police were looking for repeats. There was one other, a girl around the same age. They found her washed up in New York Harbour. She could have been Lao. She wore wrist strings typical from a Lao ceremony. But she was dead so we couldn't be sure.

You, Saifon, were the third. That's why I went to see you. The police and the embassy really needed some help to solve these murders." Saifon raised her eyebrows.

"Gee. I'm real sorry."

"As I said, it was no fault of yours. You were quite traumatized."

"Why do you suppose they'd go to the trouble of smuggling kids all that way, Mrs. …Porn?" Waldo asked.

"As they were all girls around the same age, I have to assume it was for sex." Waldo went through four shades of brown before landing on something purple.

"Sex? But … but these was little girls."

"Exactly."

"Waldo's got a real pretty view of the world, Mrs. Porn. He don't see people for what they really are," Saifon put in. "It's been fifteen years. You don't suppose them people are still selling kids do you?"

"It's unlikely. The embassy in Washington didn't hear of any more cases after yours. But, as I truly believe people will continue to do wrong for as long as they get away with it, it isn't completely out of the question. And with the ongoing war, there's more access to orphans and to transportation. There's plenty of money to be made in trafficking people."

Waldo couldn't believe what he was hearing. He wasn't saying the old lady was a liar or nothing like that, but it just didn't seem right was all.

He was developing a taste for the red stuff. It was tart but sweet at the same time. Mrs. Porn told him it was from some berry he'd never heard of. He'd drunk so much of it he was sweating red stuff. Mrs. Porn went on.

"And it's possible these smugglers learned from their mistakes and stopped making them. Saifon, what exactly is your intention for coming here?"

"I figured I'd go find the old bitch that sold me and …"

"You don't intend to go into Laos?"

"Sure. Why not?" Porn and the quiet guy looked at each other.

"Hmm. Your government appears to be better at hiding the truth than I gave them credit for."

"You mean we ain't at peace?" The old lady creaked to her feet. Waldo stood and give her a hand.

"Thank you, Waldo. Why don't I leave it to Soup to educate you as to what is really happening in our country? I have to go and find something for you. And perhaps we should think about some lunch."

Saifon and Waldo sat silently waiting for old Soup to get boiling. It was like she'd forgot to put him on the gas before she went. Waldo had checked on him a couple of times through the morning to see if he was still breathing. He sure didn't talk much. But once they'd give up on him, he started up.

"You'll have to excuse my English. It's rather poor." Waldo smiled.

"Heck, Mr. Soup. If we excused English like yours, there wouldn't never be no forgiving English like our'n." That got a smile out'a the old guy and set him bubbling. Waldo sure had a knack of bringing out the best in people.

Soup was spilling over by the time he got around to telling 'em exactly what Mr. Nixon was really doing to his country. But I guess I pushed them soup jokes as far as they're gonna go.

40

"Who you talking to, Waldo?"

"Aretha."

"Oh. OK. Sorry. G'night."

"Night."

Saifon was sleeping in the top bunk. Waldo was underneath her, if you know what I mean. They was on the train cluttering up country towards the Lao border.

When you're on a train in Thailand, you think every station you go through is alive. It don't cross your mind that it's only alive 'cause the train's there. At every stop, people ran up to Waldo's window and yelled at him like he was their last hope. He could only guess what they was saying.

"Eat my frigging quails eggs or I'll beat your head in."

"Buy my leaky plastic bag of sickly sweet cordial or my family'll starve to death."

Waldo being who he was found himself in possession of a lot of junk he didn't need as the train chugged its way to the northeast. Kids with nothing worth selling googled their eyes at him and coins somehow levitated out of his pocket and into their hands before he knew it. Orchids that was wrenched from trees an hour before was being waved at his face and he knew they was gonna be dead in another hour but he bought 'em anyway.

Train watchers sat at every station puffing on cheap cigarettes that stained their fingernails brown as the rest of 'em. Their job, that no-one ever asked them to do, was to glare at every passenger, every carriage, and every nut and bolt on the train before it pulled out.

Officials in brown uniforms and blue flip-flops stood at attention holding up their red flags even when their arms was tired and sweat dribbled down their cheeks. Miserable porters with empty push-carts and empty eyes left it to the very last second before they'd believe they didn't have no bags to carry. They watched the train slide out from the platform and wondered what they was gonna do for a drink that night.

But as soon as the train was gone, life on the station was gone too. The sellers went outside to their noodle stalls or their shops. The kids bought gum and candy. The guards put down their flags and wrote a report about how the train had come and went. The watchers got up from their benches and went off to boast to each other about how many nuts and bolts and smiling black faces they'd glared at that day.

Being in Thailand had turned Waldo into a watcher too. He noticed everything, everything that was different and everything that was the same. When the train stopped in Khorat for half an hour he almost didn't make it back on board. Saifon, who was still in her shitty mood shouted at him when she saw what he'd bought.

"What the *rather* d'you need with six packs of toothpaste, Waldo? We're supposed to be traveling light, remember?" She didn't fluster Waldo none. He held up one of the packs like he'd discovered something magic in the store. Under the brand name was a picture of the blackest minstrel you could ever see, wearing a tall top hat and a jaw-breaking smile.

"Look, Saifon honey. 'Darkie Toothpaste'. We even got our own brand out here." His smile was every bit as broad as the minstrel's and I guess that was the moment on the trip that got Saifon back on the positive side of the track.

"Waldo, you gotta be the ...." They laughed clean through to Burirum.

-o-

Now it was night. The ceiling fan flustered the sleeping car curtains as it circled from one side to the other. Waldo was mighty impressed at how a regular train carriage with seats could turn into a long bunk bed dormitory so easy.

116

"Sorry, Reet. Where was I? All right. So we have lunch with the old lady and the quiet guy. They sure give their kids weird names here, Reet. We wouldn't of called our kids Porn and Soup. I know that much.

When Mrs. Porn is sure we still planned to go to Laos in spite of it being a danged foolish and dangerous thing to be doing, she gives us some packages and a letter to deliver. The quiet guy, Soup, he turned out to be real knowledgeable. I got the feeling he would of preferred to be coming with us, but there was something stopping him. "Very soon," he told me. We got on real good in the end. You wouldn't believe how interested he was in pool balls. We yakked on all through lunch and most of the afternoon.

Reet, you'd of loved it here. The people are real friendly." He lowered his voice. "Saifon says you can't trust the Thais, but I think the type of life she's had made her suspicious of everyone. I'll love her out of that for you."

The guard had closed and shuttered all the windows before everyone got bedded down so kids at the stations couldn't reach in and grab your valuables. But Waldo bent the rules some and unshuttered and opened his. He was on his side watching the night go by. There wasn't a lot of lights, just the odd yella lamp glow here and there and the headlights of cars in the distance. But the sky. Man, the sky was something else. A billion one-eyed cats was looking down at him. It was so beautiful.

There was smells, too. Nothing smelt like Indiana here. The Thai countryside smelt of temple smoke and bicycle oil, and mouldy dogs and burnt chili. And all them flowers he didn't have names for that Aretha would of liked so much.

This was all a kick, man. It vexed him that he let so many years of his life go down a toilet hole like Mattfield. Why had he left it this late to start living?

"Night, Reet honey."

-o-

117

The sound of the wheels was New Orleans jazz.

Jelly Roll was keeping time. Waldo was twenty. Aretha was sixteen. They was wearing their matching T-shirts in the middle of winter. They'd took their coats off so Jelly Roll could see what big fans they was.

In the break, Jelly Roll come down and talked to 'em. Waldo said it was cause of the nice embroidering on the shirts, but Aretha had an inkling it was cause the weather had made her nipples big as plums . She was the prettiest thing there, and it's true, Jelly did have a problem keeping his eyes off her chest. By the end of the day the whole coloured orchestra had come to take a look at the stitching.

Waldo couldn't stop talking about how friendly them boys was. They even invited him and Reet back to their lodgings. Aretha didn't want to go for some reason. But all the attention sure had made her frisky. That explains what happened at the back of South Bend terminus.

That wasn't the Aretha he talked to every evening. He talked to the Aretha in her thirties, the one that was sensible and loving and rounder. The rounder she got, the less attention other guys paid her. She never cheated on him. Not ever. But her and Waldo got tired of the attention. That's why he fed her up so good. Getting her fat was what got him even fatter. He loved them evenings of listening to all their old music together, getting fat together.

They still talked a lot, him and Aretha. But they never did get around to the thorn in his side. They just talked about the good times. Any little thing could bring back them happy memories. So, the sound of the wheels was New Orleans jazz whether they planned it that way or not.

41

Ubon, at the end of the rail line was a town without no obvious organization. Buildings had been dropped here and there like empty crates out back of a supermarket. But Saifon and Waldo didn't have to stop there long enough to give it no heed. Within thirty minutes they was at the bus depot on a taxi truck waiting to take off to Mukdahan.

Waldo never did really get his tongue around all them long place names. It weren't just that you had to remember the name. You had to say it right too. If you raised a sound, like when you ask a question, you plum changed the name of the town. No one had any idea what you was talking about.

No, Waldo had to get by with his English, and with his hands. His hands could pretty much speak any darned language they wanted to. Oh, and he had Saifon. She was still fighting with the driver over how much he could charge Waldo for taking up three seats. The difference come to about two M&Ms, but like Saifon said, it was the principle of the thing.

Waldo watched the boys and the young men waving their arms and shouting at folks coming and going. They was touting for passengers for their own busses. It was like they believed if they flapped hard enough and busted their lungs yelling, someone might just change his mind and go north instead of south; buy a ticket to Bangkok instead of going home.

There was watchers at the bus station too, but they was covered in a layer of dust from all the arriving and departing. And there was this same depressed women in a long skirt with the color bleached out of it. He'd seen her with her tray of charred chicken wings in the capital, at every station they'd come through, and in front of every hotel. He wondered if it was one of them franchises.

The driver lost the battle and Saifon climbed up back. There was a crunch of gears and a stalling of engine, and that delayed their taking off. Restarting it involved some funny business under the hood that et up another three minutes. But that was good news for a guy that turned up late. He called something out to the driver.

To Waldo, he sounded like any other Thai. But when he climbed in and shimmied his backside onto a seat, Waldo was surprised to see a guy a few shades browner than himself, probably hazelnut or mocha coffee. He was a good-looking boy, somewhere between forty and fifty. He wore jeans and a white T-shirt, and had a canvas bag over his shoulder. When he saw Waldo he smiled and held out his hand.

"How do you do, sir." Waldo shook it. He was surprised to see an American way out there in nowhere country.

"You a air steward?" The man laughed.

"No, sir, I'm not. Do you ask that to everyone you meet?"

"Just not used to being a sir, that's all."

"Where you from?"

"Indiana, born and raised. Name's Waldo. Waldo Monk. This is my daughter, Saifon."

"Miss." He *wai*'d at her. She just nodded back. "You know, I could see the family resemblance right away."

"Tell the truth, me and my wife didn't actually, you know, produce her."

"Waldo, he knows that." Saifon looked away as the truck bounced its way out of all the bus ruts.

"Oh. Right. Right. What are you doing all the way out here, son?"

"I'm a spy."

"You don't say. I guess you ain't a very good one, if you go blurting it out to everyone." Saifon laughed. So did the guy.

"I could try to keep it a secret, I guess. But you and Saifon are probably the only two people on the border who don't know what I do. So it'd be a waste of time. I'm … well, I was the only ex-African in the region. Word of mouth gets around pretty damned fast out here. The name's Wilbur."

They shook hands again.

"Mighty pleased to know you, Wilbur."

"And what do you do, Waldo?"

"I'm, …I was quality control officer at a pool ball factory."

"I see. I won't pry any more. I guess you wouldn't tell me anyway."

"Tell you what, boy?"

"What you do."

"Heck, I told you didn't I?"

"Yes, sir." He gave one of them knowing winks. "And, Saifon. I guess you work in a pool ball factory too, right?"

"Not nearly as long as Waldo."

"Okay."

Wilbur had met all kinds of 'experts' in this or that in his time on the border. Their covers were usually better than this, but he knew when to stop pushing. So, as there weren't much point in asking them about their lives at the 'pool factory', he ended up telling them about his. That pretty much filled up the eight bone-crunching, muscle mauling, spine jarring hours it took for that old truck to get to Mukdahan.

-o-

The CIA had bullied him into accepting this second tour and had him based in Savannakheth, on the Lao side. That happened to be where Saifon and Waldo was headed so they was real interested to know how things was going there.

Man, that boy could talk. The CIA, he told 'em, was like a big old lobster pot. It wasn't that easy to find, neither. But once it was there in front of you, you had to be one hell of a dumb lobster to climb in. 'Cause if you had any brain at all, you'd know there weren't no way you was gonna get out of the thing. You know that but you crawl in anyways.

It seems the lobster people got in touch with Wilbur when he was serving in the military. He'd been one smart brother in school and went on to college and all. The army was pleased to have him but not too clear why he chose them over some of the fancy companies that was courting him.

Wilbur didn't fancy corporate life too much, or the people that lived it. And he was hankering after a family, and he felt the kind of girl he was after would go for an action man over a suite. He liked women with spunk. He figured in the army he'd meet the kind of gal you don't run into at a company cocktail party.

He went up through the ranks like some hot-assed rocket and he had enough glitter on his chest to dazzle any gal. Mary walked up to him at a Christmas ball. She was wearing a pink dress and he'd seen that dress and the pretty nut brown lady inside it a hundred times in his dreams. I guess she'd seen him too, 'cause she just said, "What kept you?"

He smiled and said, "Sorry. I wasn't sure where you were."

And that was that. Saifon kinda lost interest about this time and her mind wandered. But Waldo was a sucker for a love story whether it was bull or not. He noticed something about the way Wilbur talked about his wife, but he didn't see it as his place to mention it.

Wilbur and Mary got married a month later and before they knew it, they had themselves three children. That was kinda it. He had the family he'd dreamed of, was already a full major, and his army career was all up. He would of been the envy of any man. That's when he lost his mind.

It was one day after a racket ball tournament he'd just won. He was all sweaty and on his way to the shower when this old guy in a suit comes up to him and puts his hand on Wilbur's arm.

"Hi, Wilbur," he said. "you getting enough?"

"Enough what?" he asked, but he knew he was getting hit on. He didn't have nothing against fruits but he didn't like it when they tried to drag him into the basket with 'em.

"Out'a life."

Wilbur knew exactly what the guy meant and he was just gonna get rough with him when he pulls out this brochure. A friggin brochure. Can you believe it? He was recruiting for the CIA and he had this glossy colored leaflet that showed all these perfect people with their thirty-two teeth having fun as CIA operatives. There they was in tracksuits vaulting over eight-foot high walls. There they was in glasses in the classroom learning nuclear bomb defusing skills. There they was seeing the world; riding camels, boating down the Amazon, parachuting into pretty scenery without a trace of ack ack.

"You know why I agreed?" Wilbur asked Waldo. Saifon by this stage was already asleep against the shoulder of the fat lady beside her. Waldo didn't know. "I agreed because all but one of them perfect people was white, and that one black guy didn't look real. It was like they cut and pasted him in later. His head looked too small."

So that was why Wilbur joined the CIA, because some guy's head was too small. I guess there are worse reasons. And that's why Wilbur was here on the Thai/Lao border coordinating an unofficial war. Because America wasn't really at war in Laos, Wilbur wasn't really there. If he got in trouble, the Pentagon'd deny all knowledge of him. So he'd gone from being a decorated hero to being an invisible one. I guess that's why he did so much talking. Being invisible can make a guy lonely.

This laid-back spying attitude wasn't exactly what Waldo expected from the CIA. He thought those guys wouldn't give nothing away, not even if their toenails was pulled out one by one. It was night when the truck dragged itself into Mukdahan, and by then, Saifon and Waldo knew the entire blueprint for the secret war. Every last two million dollar bomb of it.

Wilbur went off to one of the CIA's secret locations in Mukdahan, but he give Waldo the address and phone number, just in case they got in trouble.

Mukdahan weren't much of a town if you compared it with some world famous city like South Bend. The two main streets that sat vertical to the river was pretty much it. There wasn't a hope in hell of finding anyone that spoke English. Most of the shop signs, them that could be bothered to put one up at all, was written in Thai.

Saifon had found a new love since they'd arrived in Asia. It was called 'sleeping' and when she weren't doing it, she was planning it. So once they'd booked their rooms at the Mittrapap Guest House, she couldn't be bothered to even go out for something to eat. She was too tired to look around and Waldo was too excited not to.

He walked around town some and give the locals something to point at. They'd seen plenty of Americans over the past few years but I guess you never get tired of laughing at an American: specially a big fat one. He didn't mind none. It was all done in good nature.

Just like that piper guy, Waldo reached the market with a tail of little kids dragging along behind him. He was freaked by all the unusual sights and smells. He needed someone to explain him through it all cause he didn't know what the hell he was seeing or sniffing. There was fruit like some alien experiment that went wrong, and bits of animals hanging down on wires, and big gunny sacks full of what might have been grass. And I don't mean the lawn variety. The market people shouted and flashed them famous Thai smiles and offered him tastes of stuff there weren't no way he would of put in his mouth back in Indiana.

He hung out there till the kids went home and the market started to wind down. Then, with one bag of little spring rolls, and another bag of milk that weren't exactly milk, he went down to the river and sat himself on the bank.

He'd heard about the Mekhong, followed it on Aretha's atlas from China, through Laos and Thailand, Cambodia and finally Vietnam and the South China Sea. But on the map, it sure weren't as grand as he was seeing it now. There was one full moon low in the sky and one more squeezed out across the water all the way from Laos on the far bank.

If he had a camera - well it probably wouldn't have come out, being night and all. Even if it was one of them Japanese cameras that do all the work for you. Because there weren't a camera in the world could do justice to what he was seeing. And if a camera can't describe it, I sure as hell can't.

"Aretha," he said out loud. "You seeing this, honey? I sure hope you are cause I'd hate for this to be just for me. Man, it's beautiful.

He munched on his spring rolls until this sorry excuse for a dog come and made him feel guilty. So, even though he hadn't eaten nothing substantial since the train, he give his dinner away. But the view filled him up. He slurped the sweet white stuff up through a straw and him and the dog just sat there appreciating the scenery for an hour. He got back to his room after midnight.

The Mittrapap guesthouse must of been hosting an interstate cockroach convention. Good old American roaches had the decency to be wary of people. But these little Thai suckers was curious. They crawled all over you, sightseeing, like you was the Himalayas or something. Saifon and Waldo spent the night wrapped in sheets, hotter'n hell. Didn't sleep a damned wink.

42

They was both zombies when they walked out of the guesthouse in the morning. It wasn't with what you'd call confidence that they got on the ferry to cross the river to Laos. Waldo didn't believe for a second the airplane from the States wouldn't fly, but he was convinced this lump of old tin wouldn't float. It was jam packed with vehicles and crates and almost the entire population of Southeast Asia. It was sitting so low on the water he got a sideways view of fish swimming past.

There was no sign of Wilbur and they kind of missed him. He'd said if you looked like you knew what you was doing on the Lao side, no one would stop you and ask to see your papers. As they didn't have none, that would of been a good thing. But talking about it and doing it, wasn't the same.

The ferry crashed into Laos like it wasn't expecting it to be there. Waldo sprawled on top of a herd of pigs. They was real pissed about it. Him and Saifon had split up. She blended in with the market traders and the day trippers.

He held himself up to his full height and marched past two ragged guys at the immigration post. He nodded at them and they nodded back. They didn't even ask to look at his passport. They was probably postmen or something.

When he found Saifon at the busy day market, she'd already gotten directions to the address Mrs. Porn had give her. It was an *auberge*, and that's French for a small hotel that's seen better days.

They thought they was gonna have to do a lot of explaining but it seems they was expected. The owner was all over their bags and showing 'em to their rooms and feeding 'em up before they got a chance to say nothing. They sure was honored guests. No doubt about that.

-o-

But that little French building was a creaker all right. When Waldo was upstairs walking around you could hear the rafters and boards groan clear to Vientiane. The owners obviously didn't have the money to fix the busted staircase, or re-hang the non-fitting doors, or do something about the window slats that didn't open or close.

Truth was, they hadn't seen more than a dozen paying customers there for the past year. The yanks had places of their own. The French was long gone. The Laos sure didn't have the money to stay in an *auberge*. But for some reason, they didn't seem to be trying too hard to attract custom. They just sat around.

When you go visit someone that ain't got much, and they give you half of what they ain't got much off, it makes you feel real special. But it can make you feel uncomfortable too. The larder out back of the kitchen wasn't no better stocked than a bus shelter. If you wanted food you had to tell the owner the day before and he'd go looking for it. As Waldo and Saifon was honored guests, they wasn't allowed to pay for nothing. The rooms was free and the food was, "taken care of".

The old couple that ran the place, Mr. Mrs. Wongdeuan, fought like billyo when the guests tried to force money on 'em. They would of starved to death sooner than accept a single *kip*, and a *kip* couldn't of bought you the leg of a snail in them days.

So it was, to try to keep the housekeeping bill down to a minimum, Saifon had to invent lunch and dinner engagements. Her and Waldo would waltz off like they had an appointment and sneak over to the ferry port where they'd eat at the bamboo stands that catered for the day-trippers. They put up with the flies and the smells to be kind. They thought they was being smart too, but in a little town like Savannakhet everyone knew what strangers was doing. There weren't a lot else to do there. The Wongdeuans assumed Waldo and Saifon didn't like the way they cooked.

-o-

Now, I gotta say, that little old *auberge* was a bit of a mystery. As far as Waldo could see, him and Saifon was the only two guests staying there. But on more than a few occasions he'd seen travelers arrive at the door and get turned away. There was always a whole lot of folks there in the daytime, whispering and looking jumpy. But at night it was quiet as a goldfish bowl.

Now it turned out that Mrs. Porn and the quiet guy had something or other to do with the Pathet Lao, the PL for short. This here *auberge* was one of their, what you call, candlestine bases. 'Cept there weren't much candlestine about it. Most people knew what was going on there. They could'a gotten bombed any time. But Saifon and Waldo didn't know nothing about that till later.

-o-

Waldo's enforced diet was important in a way I ain't mentioned yet. I guess it saw the start of a change in him. With the lack of food and all the sweating he was doing, Waldo noticed that his weight was falling off him like snow off a tree. It weren't a pretty sight but he'd took to standing in front of the big cracked mirror in the bathroom and looking at himself naked. It wasn't immediately obvious to no-one else, but Waldo could tell there was a lot less of him than what he'd brought over from the States the month before.

"What you doing in there, Waldo?"

"Doing?

"Yeah."

"Well, I'm looking at myself naked in the mirror."

"Oooh. That's disgusting. Why did I ask? I gotta teach you to lie, man. Listen. Wongdeuan got me a car with a driver. I'm going off to look for the old witch."

"Great. Hang on. I'll get dressed."

"Waldo, you ain't coming."

"Sure I am. I ain't letting my daughter go off alone into the jungle."

"No. I mean you can't come. The driver said we're heading off through territory where you're the enemy. And as I ain't yet thought of a disguise that'll stop you looking like you look, I sure ain't about to get myself shot just so's I can have me some company."

"Well "

"Nothing we can do about it, Waldo. So you just keep looking at whatever it is you're looking at, and I'll see you when I get back."

"Well …"

43

What you remember from when you're eight, ain't all that useful when you get to be twenty four. Saifon recalled trees and hills and huts, but that don't get you no place. 'Excuse me, I'm looking for this, like, big tree.' She knew her aunt's name, but being as there was under two hundred telephones in the whole country, there weren't no directory to look through. Besides, her aunt didn't have no running water, electricity, or walls, so she sure as hell didn't have no phone. So this search was gonna take some time.

The only thing she had to go on was something her aunt always said to her, "You carry on like this and I'll send you straight back to Ban". 'Ban' was a Thai word that meant 'town'. On the Thai side, every other village was Ban this or Ban that. But it weren't so common in Savannakheth. There was only three that she could find.

The PL driver had instructions from his boss to visit all of 'em. He'd also give her a letter saying she was representing the PL. If they got stopped by the Royal Lao Army, the RLA, she was supposed to eat it. It was writ on paper as thick as cowhide so she had a bottle of beer with her in the back seat to wash it down.

With this letter, she was sure to have the ear of village headmen. The locals could see that the commies was whipping yank backsides in Nam. It didn't take much sense to see that socialist forces in Laos would be running the show some day. Now was a good time to suck up. Without the letter she wouldn't get zilch. Her Lao was getting better, but she didn't talk, or move, or act like a Lao woman. They could all spot her as an outsider.

The first village, Ban Khong, was a sorry gathering of shacks that didn't have no feeling of homeliness about 'em. The stilts that was holding 'em up was all different lengths and breadths. You got the feeling they'd all been knocked down and put up again so many times the owners couldn't be of a mind to do a decent job no more.

A few sleepy old men crawled out from under their shacks and was almost on their knees, praying before Saifon got out the car. Now *wai*-ing like they do in Thailand ain't so popular in Laos so it was obvious these poor old guys was so brow-beaten they'd do anything just to get a bit of peace. A quick look of surprise did rustle through 'em for a second when they saw her, but they just went on praying and greeting and groveling, whoever she was.

They wanted real bad to be able to help, but they didn't know nothing. Saifon felt kinda sorry for 'em and asked if there was anything she could do to help them. It was obviously a question they never heard before. They looked sideways at one another from behind their praying hands. And even though they didn't have a dollar between 'em, and they hadn't et nothing but rice and stale vegetables for over a year, they couldn't think of nothing they wanted.

Saifon took a couple of twenty-dollar bills out of her purse, handed it to one of the guys and got back in the car. It was the same as if the fairy godmother'd come down in South Bend and handed a million bucks to a bunch of homeless guys. They was too stunned to say thank you.

The second Ban, Ban Se, was on a stream, and even though it could of been wishful thinking, she got vibrations from the place. The headman was a woman cause all the men was off firing bullets over the enemy's heads to earn a few cents a month from the RLA.

The year before, they'd fired over RLA heads when they fought for the PL. Laos was like that in them days. You'd be about to run your bayonet through some enemy soldier and realize he was your uncle.

The woman was tough and suspicious. She read the letter Saifon give her and said, "What do you want here?" The letter was upside down so she figured the woman didn't read no better than she did. She told her the story. She only had scraps of memories. Her ma's nickname. How her family got caught in crossfire and she was the only one survived. The aunt. She didn't say nothing about getting sold.

The headwoman spat betel nut on the dust at Saifon's feet. When she smiled it was like Muhammad Ali had smashed her in the teeth. Everything in there was rotten and stained red. She looked down at the outsider's clothes. They wasn't nothing fancy but they was clean and neat and western looking.

"I see you done good for yourself."

"I stayed alive, if that's what you mean."

"What I meant was money. You marry a Frenchman?"

"No. I live in America."

"America, eh?" She looked across at the driver and lowered her voice. "You got dollars?"

"I got dollars if you've got information."

"How much is information worth these days?"

"If it's good enough to find my aunt, twenty dollars."

The woman didn't know how to contain her excitement. The average yearly income, if you didn't count the criminals in Vientiane, was around fifty bucks. But she decided to push her luck anyway.

"I couldn't tell you for less than …forty." She unwrapped another betel nut from its leaf and popped it into her bloody mouth. Saifon sized her up.

"You know. If I had the choice between getting twenty bucks for doing nothing, and getting nothing for doing nothing, I know what I would of chose." She turned back to the car. The woman knew the girl was bluffing, but she needed the money too bad to play with her.

"Thirty."

"Twenty-five."

"Deal." Numbers ping pong was a national sport in Laos. The woman held out her claw and Saifon filled it with two tens and a five. You wouldn't credit how quick you can change a woman's mood just by giving her money. "I would of helped you anyway, honey. I don't recall the particular incident of your family getting wiped out. I married into this hellhole. Families get wiped out all the time in these parts.

But your aunt's name ain't that usual. (Souksaijai, Miss 'Happiness in the Heart', ironic weren't it.) I ain't seen her in a couple of years, but I guess the woman you're talking about lived out in the hills, about ten kilometers from here. She's about the right age, and she used to take in kids."

Saifon warned her that they'd be back if they found she was lying, although the woman's life was so miserable she doubted there was much she could threaten her with. That twenty-five dollars would probably make a difference to a lot of people. The woman seemed offended at such a possibility anyway but give the driver directions.

Saifon bounced around in the back seat and watched the jungle rise and fall on each side of the car. The driver had untold skill when it come to finding potholes. It was the longest ten kilometers she could remember. She still didn't feel it, that native instinct. She didn't feel like she was part of the country. She'd gotten too foreign. All her dreams of finding her roots was bounced out of her on the road from Ban Se. She wanted a hot shower and a hamburger and a couple of hours of mindless TV.

When the driver hit ten kilometers on his clock, he pulled over and asked some old guy dressed in a dirty cloth. He pointed to a patch of brown-green on the side of a hill, but something had already pinged in Saifon's memory. It hadn't changed none. This was where she'd toiled and suffered for the bitch for all them years. Her heart plopped down into her stomach like a turd into a toilet.

The driver stopped where one colour green ended and another one started. There wasn't no fences. She got out the car and looked over at a beaten up old bamboo shack on stilts. It had walls now, sort of, even though they was just straw sheets. Her legs weren't in no hurry to go to it.

Finally she got 'em moving and she walked up the little path. First thing she noticed was a beat up old motorcycle. And you'll never guess what thought come into her head when she saw it. She truly wondered if the money to buy the bike had come from her own sale. She wondered if the money had burned a hole in the old witch's pocket, and she'd bought the first lump of old shit fucking motorcycle she could find. Witch. She'd been robbed.

"Hello." There was a rustle from up in the hut, but no one answered. "Aunt Souksaijai, you up there?" Nothing again. She edged up the creaking steps till her head come level with the floor of the hut. And it was the weirdest thing, really. Inside was herself, looking at old magazines.

Of course, it wasn't really herself. That would of been just too weird even for a book like this. But there was a little girl in there, dressed and looking like Saifon must of when she was eight. She was dirty and there was a bad smell up there.

"Hello, little sister. I'm looking for Aunt Souksaijai. Does she still live here?" The girl didn't answer. She just kept thumbing through them old magazines the way her aunt always used to.

That was entertainment at auntie's. It was TV. It was cinema, play, education and the outside world. The pictures in her aunt's second-hand magazines was the only fun she had as a girl. Lord knows where she got 'em from. But if the woman ever caught Saifon looking at 'em, she beat the innards out of her. They was hers. So the only time she could sneak a look was when Souksaijai was off spooning with some guy, drunk.

She really knew how happy this young girl must be, looking at pictures and words she didn't understand.

"Sorry to disturb you. Do you know where Souksaijai is?"

The girl nodded. "Is she around here? I gotta see her." She nodded again. There was something missing in her eyes.

It was like they was just for seeing. Just for looking at the magazine pictures and nothing else.

"Do you think you could take me to her?"

The girl folded the magazines real neat and placed 'em exactly where she knew they ought'a be. She climbed out down the steps and walked barefoot along the rough grass between the rice paddies. Her aunt never had enough rice to sell, just to eat. That and some seasonal vegetables was breakfast, lunch and supper. When the drought come, or the rains was too severe, Saifon had to do without one or the other. There always seemed to be enough for her aunt though.

Saifon looked around her. That world looked a lot smaller than she remembered it. She tended the garden all by herself from when she wasn't yet four, while her nasty old aunt lay out there like an empress on her platform overseeing her empire, looking at her pictures.

She followed the girl off the land that was her aunt's and into the trees. Something stank back there. She could see her aunt laying in the shade of a tree. She still was a lazy bitch.

"Aunt Souksaijai, you asleep?"

She walked around the tree and got a clear view. She wasn't sleeping. There was flies where her face should of been. I think it's better if I don't describe the rest of her, just in case you're having lunch or something. Saifon staggered back. The girl stood there looking at the flies.

"Wh …what happened to her?"

"I killed her."

44

Mukdahan and Savannakhet sat opposite each other. There was only a river and a national border between them. But the feeling of them two little cities was as different as you can get. It was like some lab experiment where you got two bunnies in cages side by side. One bunny gets fresh fruit and vegetables and a little tender loving care. The other bunny has a permanent cigarette strapped to a hole in its neck, and no love.

I ain't saying the folks in Savannakhet smoke a lot. This is like an example. All I'm saying is the folks on the Lao side was different. They seemed, I don't know, sadder maybe. They didn't seem settled somehow. Savannakhet was poorer, even though people could cross back and forth as they liked, and there was a lot of the same stuff in the markets. The Lao just didn't have the money to pay for none of it.

There was a look in the eyes of the Lao like they just wanted to be settled and left to get on with their lives. They'd been at war with the French and with each other for over 200 years. All that war tends to make you a jumpy little bunny.

Waldo was real sensitive to the way people felt. They didn't have to speak his language. They didn't have to say nothing. He knew.

Wilbur invited Waldo for dinner at his place. They'd bumped into each other at the post office the day before. In a town the size of Savannakhet you have to try real hard not to bump into someone you know. It was a neat but naturally dirty place. There wasn't a clear gap between the dusts of the dry season and the muds of the rainy season. Most of the wooden houses wore a red dirt jacket outside. But the insides was spotless and cared for. You could hear the sound of sweeping way across the river.

Wilbur was just getting home from his tennis game when Waldo arrived on the doorstep with a bag of beers. Wilbur liked tennis so it was only natural he'd requisition some runway tar and gravel to build the town's only court.

"Good timing, Waldo. Come on in. How's your pool ball research coming along?" The guy had this weird habit of mentioning pool balls and then winking. It was beyond Waldo, so he didn't question it. You had to be a little crazy if you wanted to work for the CIA.

He walked into a home that was like one of them House and Garden magazine spreads. There was real classy pots, and expensive looking furniture, and at least a zillion dollars' worth of stereo equipment. He remembered his poor crippled record player at home and thought about how happy he'd be to have a quarter of the goodies spread out in front of him. Wilbur saw him drooling.

"You like music, Waldo?"

"Man, I love music."

"Go ahead and choose yourself some then. I've only got modern stuff, but you might find something there you like. Excuse me while I get cleaned up."

If you imagine how skinny one LP is, and you think of a rack eight feet long with three shelves full of albums, you'll know just how much music we're talking about here. Waldo was happy as a smiley T-shirt. He wasn't one of them cuss stubborn old folks that gets stuck in some music time-warp and thinks everything after that is crap. He was a with-it old timer.

He picked out the Chi-Lites' 'I like Your Loving' and put it real slow and easy on the beautiful turntable. It was just that he didn't have a university degree in electrical engineering so he couldn't fathom out how to play the darned thing. There was buttons everywhere. It was like when David took him up to the front of the airplane to meet the pilot.

"Hell, driver. How d'you remember what all them dials is for?" This was even more complicated. So he just pulled over a chair and sat back and looked at it till Wilbur come back.

"How you doing there?"

Wilbur walked out of the shower with a towel wrapped round his skinny waist. He had the type of muscly body Waldo was easing himself into. He come over and pressed a little button and the next thing you know they was surrounded by Chi-Lites. There was speakers all over the house.

"Good choice."

"Oh, brother. This is better than live."

"No, there's nothing better than live, Waldo."

"It seems like spying pays pretty good."

"Tell you the truth, this is just my hardship allowance. The salary goes straight to …my family."

"Hardship like this I can handle." Waldo didn't begrudge him a good salary. It wasn't like he worked in an office. In fact, Wilbur's life was most peculiar. He left home at seven in the morning and got in one of them Air America helicopters and they flew him to the front. And that's the war front I'm talking about, not the sea front.

There'd be bullets flying and mortars exploding and enemy attacking and soldiers dying all around him. And that was Wilbur's place of work. He'd spend the day there checking that his Hmong fighters was stocked up on ammo and spam, listen to complaints about conditions, dodge sniper fire. Then at five, he'd look at his watch, climb back in his helicopter and come on home. He'd play a few sets of tennis, have his dinner, and listen to music till the next day. And I swear I ain't making this up.

"Ain't you afraid they'll kill you, Wilbur?"

"My uncle George choked to death eating a pretzel. I guess that pretzel had his name on it. If it ain't a speeding car it's a rabid dog. Something's got your name on it. You can't be afraid of everything, Waldo, cause you just don't know what it is with your name on. And judging by the shooting practice I've seen, I'm more likely to get hit by one of our guys than one of theirs."

"Excuse me for saying this, Wilbur, but I get a feeling you ain't taking this war serious."

"Waldo, I hate this goddamned war. I don't know what the hell we're doing here. There's people freezing on the streets in New York, and we're spending money here like it's air. You wanna beer?"

Waldo didn't normally drink beer, but Biere Laos was kind of addictive. It weren't exactly slimming food, but for every pint he drank, he'd sweat ten. He wasn't built like a house no more. He was a cabin, heading for a hut.

"Sure."

They sat on the veranda overlooking the jasmine bushes. The maid had just watered 'em and it smelt like an aftershave factory out there.

"Stinks don't it."

"My wife would of been real happy here. She loved flowers."

"You know, out there where I go every day, there isn't so much as a leaf."

"You don't say."

"And you know why that is?"

"No."

"It's because we, that is, our government, dropped 200,000 gallons of herbicide along the Ho Chi Min trail so the Viet Cong wouldn't have nowhere to hide. I don't know if it'll ever grow back.

"200,000 gallons, Waldo. It stripped the leaves off the trees, the vegetation off the ground, and the skin off anyone foolish enough to be standing underneath those trees. And what are they guilty of? What was their crime? Being born, Waldo. They're guilty of being born where they were."

Waldo could see the guy was starting to get depressed. Beer and wars could do that to you. He went inside and changed the music to something happy. Ten minutes later they was out there doing a Supremes routine, singing into their bottles.

The maid and her boy come into the yard to watch the two crazy dancing guys, one burnt sienna, one mocha cream. If you gotta be bombed, be bombed by guys with rhythm.

-o-

Waldo got back to the guest house some time after midnight and something approaching drunk. He hadn't gotten in that state since Aretha passed away. He'd been afraid of getting to be a depressed drunk.

He'd refused a ride from his drunk friend and walked through the streets of Savannakhet singing out loud. He said 'sabaidee' (his Lao was almost as good as his Spanish) to anyone he met foolish enough to be walking through unlit streets that time in the morning. There was any number of reasons why he could of gotten himself killed just for being an American, but like he said to Wilbur;

"You never know what's got your name on it, so you can't be afraid of everything."

Wilbur agreed that those must of been the words of a very wise man, and he let him go. He didn't rightly know what 'sabaidee' meant, but Wilbur told him it was useful to know, and it did seem to get him home in one piece.

The light was on in Saifon's room and there was voices coming out. He knocked softly so as not to wake up the whole house.

"Who is it?"

"Diana Ross."

There was more whispers from inside before she unlocked the door and let him in.

"What time ...Wilbur, you been drinking."

140

"I know." He was surprised to see the little girl laid out on Saifon's bed, but not nearly as surprised as the girl was to see him. She pulled the sheet over her head. She hadn't seen nothing like him in her life, less you count buffalo. Saifon went over and talked to the shape under the sheet and she poked her eyes out from under it. Waldo give her one of his biggest smiles and waved.

"*Sabaidee*."

She went back under.

"I guess she ain't ready for you yet."

She scooted Waldo out of the room, followed him into the hall, and locked the door. His room was opposite, unlocked as always. They went in. He giggled when he saw he still had his shoes on.

"Naughty me."

"Waldo, this is serious. I need you to stop being drunk for a while."

"OK." He dropped back onto the bed but it found the will power not to collapse under him. She sat at his feet and helped untie his laces.

"Waldo, I found my aunt."

"Hey that's great."

"She was dead."

"OK. Then that ain't so great."

"She'd been dead a week, and …it weren't natural."

"Someone killed her?"

"That little girl you just met, her name's Nit. She clubbed the old lady to death with a hunk of wood."

"No." He tried to sit up. He failed.

"And you know why? Because she'd gotten sold, just like me. The old woman told her a week ago that someone'd be coming for her in the morning. She told her to wash her hair and put on a clean skirt. Nit remembered the same thing happening to her older sister. The woman took in the two of them. Their family got blown up. I guess Nit was too young

141

to sell straight off so she stayed with my aunt for two more years."

Waldo managed to get his legs on the floor and sit up. He was sobering up real fast.

"Man, fifteen years on and she's still pulling the same shit. That's incredible."

"Her sister was gone God knows where, and here she was about to follow her. She didn't want no part of it. She was scared, man. And she hated the old witch every bit as much as I did. But I don't know what it took to whack her to death. I couldn't of. She waited till the woman was out back taking a crap and she did it. She dragged her into the trees and waited.

When the truck come to get her the next day she hid in the rice and waited till it was gone."

"You think she'd recognize that truck again if she saw it?"

"I hope so. If she don't, that's the end of the trail. But she's pretty messed up right now. I gotta spend more time with her."

"You gonna tell the PL?"

"Not till I'm sure they ain't involved. I didn't say nothing to the driver."

"So, what do we do now?"

"Tomorrow we start our truck hunt."

"Right on."

-o-

Back in Saifon's room, Nit had climbed off the bed and was curled up asleep on the hard floor. But that was good. She'd been awake for a week.

45

"You know? I'm starting to believe you two really did work in a pool factory." There he went again. Wilbur's nervous wink was even worse when all three of 'em was together. Saifon and Waldo looked at each other and raised their foreheads. Neither of 'em could figure it out.

They was all on Wilbur's veranda. It was Sunday, the day of rest, so naturally Wilbur had a day away from the war. Nine to five warring had it's good sides. Saifon had decided to tell him about the kiddy smuggling minus her part in it. Waldo trusted him, but then again, Waldo would of trusted Hitler. They needed help finding the truck.

Nit was down in the yard watching the maid's boy, Pop, and his friends playing. She wasn't of a mind to play with 'em. She'd sat down with Saifon and drawn a picture of the truck. It looked like a closet. Drawing wasn't her strong point. But it did have some distinguishing points, no doors in the front, green paint, a Lao flag. Wilbur considered it.

"Looks like a Lao army truck to me." Saifon was relieved it looked like any kind of truck at all. "Only the Royal Lao Army would have a flag. You wanna drive over there and take a look?"

"You mean we can just go visit the RLA?"

"Sure. We pay their salaries so why not?"

So they did. They went in Wilbur's four-wheel-drive and the sentry just saluted and waved him through. They drove around the base. It was a big sprawling stretch of cleared land crawling with soldiers. There was nothing permanent about it. It was like they could just flee in terror at the drop of a hat.

They come to a motor pool where all the vehicles was covered in camouflage nets. Weren't a lot of point in that to tell the truth, seeing as the enemy didn't have no airplanes.

Three closets on wheels was parked at the rear. Nit pointed out one of 'em that had a Playboy centrefold taped behind the driver's seat. This poor deformed blond girl was finding it so hard to lift her own tits, she had 'em propped on the chair in front of her. Nit had seen that poor blonde girl before.

"Wilbur noted down the registration and walked into a large administration tent. He come back out with a piece of paper and a smile. They loaded themselves back in the four-wheeler and Wilbur headed off out of the camp.

"Where to next?" Saifon asked.

"That's it for the day."

"That's it?" She'd been hoping for something more confronting.

"Saifon, if you allow me, I'd like to follow up on this myself first. I can do it in a way that doesn't draw attention to us. If you guys did it, you'd be arriving back in Thailand in bin liners."

"We don't wanna put you to no trouble"

"You ain't, Waldo. Tell you the truth …" He looked at Nit in his driving mirror. She was staring blank as a snowdrift out the window. Saifon had her arm around her. " …I'd much sooner be doing work like this. There's nobody gives a damn about what happens to the kids. Schools are closed cause the teachers are all off fighting, and you'd never find a social worker all the way out here.

Whatever it is you two really do, I like it."

You probably worked out the, what do you call it? …the irony here already. Saifon and Waldo was getting cooperation from the CIA, who was supporting the RLA, who was fighting the commies. But Saifon and Waldo was also the honored guests of the PL, who was allies of the North Vietnamese who, if anyone's paying attention still, you'll know are the commies everyone else is fighting against.

While Wilbur was doing his ferreting around, Saifon and Waldo got 'emselves invited to the home of some real nice people that couldn't speak no English. It just happened that these was a senior PL couple just back from the caves in the north in Vieng Xai where the bulk of the socialist forces was getting trained up. Them caves up there was like something out'a Disney. They had hotel caves, and meeting caves, and office caves, and cinema caves. Hell, I wouldn't be surprised if they had a discotheque cave in them mountains too.

These old-timers was from an old Savannakheth family and it seemed everyone in town knew what they was up to but kept their mouths shut. Like I said, in them days you didn't wanna burn too many bridges. Who could tell who next week's Prime Minister was gonna be?

Saifon was the interpreter. Her vocabulary got way extended that night. When you don't use something for fifteen years it gets rusty. But it sure got a lot of oiling at this place cause they was more interested in talking to Waldo than to her. They didn't get much chance to chat with the enemy you see, not over dinner. They wanted him to understand where they was coming from. They was hoping he'd go back home and explain to the American people that all they wanted to do was stop the corruption and give the poor Laos a chance.

But this was Waldo they was talking to. The type of American people he knew, wasn't worth wasting your breath on. Of course, Saifon knew that, so there was times when she was getting a translation headache and she'd just say, 'Waldo, I don't know how to translate that. Just nod your head and look fascinated.'

'OK, Saifon.'

In the kitchen where they was getting stuck into sticky rice and Mekhong catfish, there was a parade of pictures lined up across one wall like post office wanted posters. The hosts told him these was all members of the Lao royal family, alive and otherwise. The photos was framed and glassed and seemed to've been dusted regular.

"Am I missing something here? Ain't the PL trying to get rid of the Royals, Saifon?"

"They say they ain't got nothing against 'em personally, and it's kind'a expected to have their pictures on your wall. No point in riling the neighbours, unnecessary."

There was one picture missing. The gap and the square of dark paint showed where it had hung.

"Looks like there's one they ain't so fond of."

"They say that's the only one they got any real respect for. That's the Red Prince, the royal that's fighting with the commies."

"So, they took it down?"

"They say they got it in a place of honor. You wanna see?"

The lady took Nit out to the yard to pluck some papaya from the tree. The man led Saifon and Waldo out to a back door that was locked. It was only a little box room with hardly enough space to kneel in front of the altar they'd built. There was tall skinny incense sticks smoking away on it and pretty Christmas tree lights, and scale model Buddhas, and toy animals and paper Lao flags on sticks poking out of jam jars. There was even a rice and banana snack on there in case them gods got hungry.

And looking down at the whole show from a nail on the wall, was the quiet guy, Soup.

46

Two days later, Waldo was still grinning from ear to ear. The old guy hadn't stopped grinning since he saw the Red Prince on that wall. Man that was a kick.

The house in Bangkok belonged to one of old Red's brothers, Prince Phetsarath, who was likely related to the pretty old lady, Porn. So that technically made her a princess. There'd he been, simple old common guy Waldo hand in hand with a princess, locked in serious conversation about the rules of pool with a live prince. His life had suddenly took on a whole new flavor.

And that old house in Bangkok was just as special as the people in it. It was there the Free Lao Movement was born and planned all its campaigns to kick out the French, then the Japs, then the French again. And it was there, when there weren't such a clear line between royalty and anarchy, that the PL took shape.

Old Red used to spend a lot of time at the house plotting and scheming while one of his other brothers, Souvana Phouma was playing at being prime minister. But he'd gotten frustrated by all the sitting around they was doing there and he rolled up his sleeves and got into the serious business of agitating. You wouldn't know it now, but he used to be a hell of a lot more agitated. Now he just went to the house from time to time to shake off the dust and relax when he got tired of the caves.

Them brothers was friends one minute, enemies the next. This, what they call, sibling rivalry ain't so hard to understand when you consider their daddy, the viceroy, had eleven wives and twenty three kids. Anyone who's had teenagers of their own knows one or two of 'em can tend to get rebellious. One out of twenty three ain't so bad, I guess.

47

When Mr. Kamphone come out of his house one Sunday morning, he found the rubber groundsheet was off his car and this big old black guy was standing staring at the yella Citroen like he hadn't never seen one before. Khampone stood staring at Waldo. Waldo stood staring at the car.

It was uncanny. The only car him and Aretha'd ever owned was a yella Citroen. It was a hunk of shit but it was the only car they could afford. It took 'em three years to drive it to its grave but they did get a hell of a lot of good times out of it in them three years.

It being the size it was, and them being the sizes they was, they couldn't never sit together in the front seat. So Waldo sat in the front and Aretha sat in the back with her arms around his neck. Off they'd go in that little yella box of French rust, never knowing how far they was gonna get before the thing overheated. It always overheated.

That's why they called their Sunday car rides their 'adventure trips'. Wherever it was the car started to give off smoke signals, that's where they'd stop and have their picnic. It sounds kinda crazy but with the car playing such a big part in their adventures, it was like it was helping plan the trips. It was like it enjoyed 'em as much as they did.

Aretha stayed up most of Saturday nights putting the hamper together. Of course they didn't always end up in some scenic spot. There was times they'd wind up having a picnic under a billboard on the highway, or in the parking lot of a diner. But that was the fun of it. They never knew.

They called the car Old Lemon, seeing as Citroen was almost French for lemon and that's what it was. And here it was. Not the same Old Lemon of course, but a passing copy. Waldo had saw it peeking out from under the rubber sheet and he couldn't resist having a look. All them happy days come flooding over him and he couldn't tear himself away.

Mr. Kamphone didn't know why this big guy was crying at the sight of his car and he couldn't ask him. For all their years of colonizing the country, the French didn't actually leave much of a legacy. They weren't much for roads and water systems and schools, and stuff like that. They left a lot of buildings that didn't match the local style at all, and wouldn't last long, and they taught a few maids how to cook frogs. But they sure left a lot of rusty old car bodies. Laos was a cemetery of dead French cars and them queer little mopeds.

Kamphone inherited this heap from his old boss. The man had fled the country when there was a chance he might get shot by the communists for making money from the down-trodden Lao peasants. He took with him the company parole and Kamphone's first wife. It was a fair swap in Kamphone's book and he looked after the car better than he ever looked after his wife. He couldn't afford to put gas in it no more so he kept it oiled and polished and free from dust under a rubber groundsheet.

It impressed him that this foreigner was so moved by his car. As he couldn't find out why, he went inside and come out with the key, and handed it over to Waldo. Waldo come over all mushy, and said a bunch of stuff. Then he hugged the poor little guy. That was more thanks than he needed and he started to wonder whether he'd just given his car away.

But Waldo pointed to his watch, hugged Kamphone again, and opened the car door real delicate-like. Kamphone hadn't never seen a man so happy to be having so much trouble getting in a car. When he was all in, he filled up the whole driver's side and half the passenger seat. The steering wheel was someplace under his left arm. It was like he was wearing the car.

But he sure knew where everything was and started it first time. Citroens sound like something cruel's going on under the hood even when they're new. But the screech was like music to Waldo. Him and Aretha used to cheer whenever Old Lemon was kind enough to start. So he cheered and found a suitable gear and edged gently out of Kamphone's yard. The Lao fella signaled to the gas tank and Waldo put up his thumb and away he went.

Kamphone wasn't too sure what he'd just done, or why. But the big guy sure did seem happy, and there wasn't that many happy looking people around in Laos in them days.

-o-

Nit and Pop was sitting out front of the *auberge* when this little yella car pulled up beside 'em and a sweating Waldo winded down the window. He smiled at 'em and said something in that language o' his and clicked open the back door. Every day with Waldo was a mystery. He called 'em in and in they got.

The kids was mighty impressed with the way old Waldo slid his way through the gears and glided smooth as syrup down the main street of Savannakhet. They didn't know where they was going and they didn't care much. If there'd been someone around who spoke English, and if he'd bothered to ask, that someone probably would of advised against his taking the road up to the north east of town. They probably would of told him there was a lot of trouble with PL up there and that it was the last place they'd send an American in a French car.

But there weren't no one around to give that advice, so Waldo drove north east. He spent most of the trip looking down the holes that appeared in front of them and trying to get around 'em. But when he did have a couple of yards of flat road, he took in the sights and the sounds and the smells.

I guess Waldo was expecting the car to overheat, cause he just kept on going. With the state of the road they hadn't gone more than ten miles in the first hour. But that was far enough to get 'em to the new administration zone that was controlled by the PL; the same PL that was shooting down American planes and sabotaging American concerns around the country.

Waldo was singing; 'Row, Row Row your Boat,' and the kids'd heard it so many times, they was singing it too. But they couldn't understand why he kept stopping and starting again in the wrong places. So they kept stopping and starting too. Waldo seemed to think this was real hilarious so they kept doing it. They loved to watch him laugh. It was the first time Nit really come out of her shell. They was all in a great mood when they reached the road block and the AK47's come poking in through the windows.

Waldo wasn't too worried about the war. He figured as he was living with PL and he was a close friend of the CIA, he had both sides covered. But them young soldiers in their new uniforms, they didn't know nothing about Waldo's contacts. They was fresh off the propaganda farm. They'd spent the last six months with a wise Vietnamese corporal who taught 'em just how cruel, sneaky and two-faced the American imperialists was.

They'd seen actual photographs of what the American imperialist lackeys was capable of doing. They'd seen entire red Indian tribes wiped out and scalped. They'd seen poor people froze to death on the streets of New York, and slaves hung by the neck from trees like apples in an orchard. They'd seen television pornography that even young children could watch while they was having dinner. They'd seen this guy John Wayne butcher a whole regiment of Asians while people in the cinema cheered and whistled.

And here at their barricade, terror had stepped out of the classroom and confronted them on their first day of active duty. *Not one thing the American imperialist lackey said could be believed. Nothing he appeared to be could be trusted.*

What evil trick was them Americans playing here?

They couldn't work out why he was being so cool about having a machine gun in his nose. The kids in the back seat figured Waldo knew something they didn't, so they relaxed too.

The young guards was wired but they still played it by the book. *No. 1. Get the enemy out of his vehicle. No. 2. Disarm and incapacitate the enemy.* Now in the book that was OK. But in real life Waldo had swelled up some since they took off from Savannaket. There didn't seem no way they was gonna get him out. They got them other two imperial lackey collaborators out and was searching them. But they didn't seem too concerned about things, neither.

The guards decided if they couldn't get the big guy out, they'd just have to go in and search him where he sat. But there was one last trick in his box of mind warfare. They didn't know it, but Waldo had been ticklish since he was a littlun. He couldn't stand no one touching him. So when the young PL guys started prodding and poking him, he pee'd himself laughing. That got the kids in a giggle-fit no one could stop.

The guards kinda stood back and watched. They was scratching their brains and looking at each other blank as suet. This weren't what they imagined conflict to be like. This was much worse.

They huddled together.

"What do we do?"

"They're technically prisoners of war. We should take 'em to the commander."

"Right."

"You think he …?"

"What?"

"You think he might be pissed that we didn't follow instructions?"

The kids was back in the Citroen having a fit. The car was vibrating like a spin drier.

"*You mean …?*"

"*I mean, No. 2. Disarm and incapacitate the enemy. No. 3. Extract*

basic information. No. 4. Shoot if they resist.

"*You think we should?*"

"*Should?*"

"*Shoot 'em.*"

"*Look, I …*"

"*Go on. Say it.*"

"*Nothing they taught us at orientation covered this. I think we have*

to use our initiative."

"*I don't know. That doesn't sound very …*"

"*Very what?*"

"*Very communistic.*"

"*Right. You're right. What would Ho Chi Min do?*"

"*Good point. What would Brother Ho do?*"

"*In this situation?*"

"*Yeah.*"

"*No fucking idea.*"

"*Me neither.*"

The old yella car was rocking and rolling around like some ride at a fun fair. All three of the invading army inside was laughing so bad it really hurt. Nit thought she was gonna burst open.

"*Or we could …*"

"*Let 'em go.*"

"*Pretend we never saw 'em.*"

"*It'd make our lives easier.*"

"*I ain't too sure I'm cut out for this work.*"

-o-

Three hours later, Nit Pop, Waldo and the funny wagon arrived back in Savannakhet. They'd stopped at some scenic spots, caught toads, and fixed a flat tire. The kids was sure they'd never have so much fun again in their lives.

Waldo filled up the tank with premium, and got the tire fixed before he took the car back to Mr. Kamphone. He seemed surprised to see it. Waldo give him $20 rental. Kamphone give it back. He figured he'd made up enough good karma that day already he didn't want to get greedy. He had a feeling it was his day. On an urge, he took the last ferry across the river, met a woman, and, as far as we know, lived a happy life. Weird how life works out, ain't it?

48

Wilbur looked shell-shocked when he turned up at the *auberge* and that was cause he was shell-shocked. He'd been exploded next to.

"You have a bad day at the war, honey?" Saifon asked him. He could see her lips move but he was still deaf as a plank from the blast. He yelled back at her.

"Sorry. Can't hear you, or myself. Mortar. I guess I bruised my eardrums. They hurt like hell. Am I shouting?" They could of heard him in Manchester, England. Saifon got a pad and a pencil and started writing down her questions.

"Will your hearing come back?"

"Oh, yeah." He yelled. "It only happened a couple of hours ago. But I wanted to come over straight away. I've got some top secret information for you."

It didn't seem right to be shouting top secret information on a balcony overlooking the street so they took him to Waldo's room and locked the door. Wilbur couldn't settle on nothing between a yell and a whisper, so he decided to write everything down too.

"I checked out the background of the truck driver. He used to be a heavy for the local mayor. The latter was involved in a lot of illegal stuff while the French were still here. His trucking company was doing very nicely out of Hmong opium harvests. The French weren't doing too badly out of it either.

When the RLA grew in influence, they took over a lot of the trafficking trade. The mayor started losing business to them, so he did what any good businessman would do. He bought himself a commission in the RLA. Once we started pumping money in, he found he could steal it a lot easier by being in uniform. He's a captain now, in charge of quartermaster's stores. He's exactly the type of person your PL friends want to get rid of."

Saifon and Waldo looked at each other like they'd been caught with their hands in the cookie jar. How the heck did he know about their PL friends? Maybe he was a better spy than he made out. They started to protest but he couldn't hear 'em. He just kept on writing.

"His dad was mayor fifteen years ago so it's quite possible he was involved in your abduction, Saifon.

Our people in Mukdahan monitor the traffic across the Mekhong. Your truck crosses over once a month. Technically it goes over empty and comes back with supplies. It went over a week ago so it's possible there were some kids on board. No one checks. But there's one that wasn't aboard."

He looked at Nit doing her Lao homework. Her and Saifon was learning to write together. They got some books from the market. Nit was doing better at it.

"I've got a list of places the truck picks up from. We're checking on them. I have to go throw up."

They was amused he'd bothered to write that last part cause he barely made it to the bathroom. While he was chucking, Saifon and Waldo thought things through. They come to the conclusion they'd have to wait three weeks for the next delivery, else they wouldn't have no evidence. When Wilbur come back he wasn't buzzing so bad and he agreed. But he told 'em they'd have to do the job right. They'd have to track the kids all the way. Maybe even to the States if they wanted to catch the masterminds behind it all.

That's when Saifon and Waldo realized how far out of their league they was. Saifon hadn't thought that much beyond doing what Nit had done. But Wilbur was right. The guys running this business wasn't gonna sit back and let it be shut down without a fight. He said he'd call on some Thai favors and see what he could fix up at home. When he'd gone, Saifon and Waldo sat either side of Nit. They didn't have to say nothing. They was both scared out'a their wits.

-o-

But they dug in. The RLA officers used to hang out at a café down by the river. By day it looked like the kind of place baby Jesus might of gotten borne in. Waldo called it 'the manger'. But by night with its pretty lights and painted serving girls, it was Time Square.

With so many uniforms and so much booze, there was fights guaranteed every night. At least one killing a month. The police, what there was of 'em, didn't have no control over the army, so the army did what it wanted. What they wanted could pretty much be found at the manger café.

You can imagine, Waldo wasn't delighted when Saifon announced she'd gotten herself a job singing there. It weren't just cause he didn't think much of her singing. Even if she had a decent voice it was still a dangerous place for a girl to be at night. He wouldn't be able to chaperone, neither. He'd stand out there like an iceberg in a corn patch, and there ain't nothing like beer for reminding a guy how grieved he is about his politics.

But Waldo had more chance getting a job in the national ballet than he did talking that girl out'a something she set her mind to. She told him there was the chance of getting to know this captain mayor and gather some evidence before the next shipment. The girls there knew him and said he was there often.

He hoped they'd listen to her singing the first night and fire her ass. She didn't know no Lao songs, and what she knew in English, she knew in keys the writers never imagined them getting sung in. But when she didn't come back early that first night, he knew she'd managed to bluff her way in.

-o-

So, sooner than worry, he put all his energy into babysitting Nit. Boy, that girl had problems. She'd wake up screaming in the middle of the night. She'd steal stuff and hide it under the mat. She'd get mad for no reason. But even when you're mentally screwed up like that, it's real hard not to like Waldo.

He fooled around all the time and got plenty of laughs out of her. She had a pretty laugh even though her teeth was all messed up. It was Waldo first got to coax a comb through the hair knots she had. It was Waldo got her to wear the nice dress they bought her and showed her the first photos of herself she'd ever seen.

She stuck them photos inside the magazines like they belonged there and Waldo always play-acted that he was seeing a magazine model right there in front of him. Him and Saifon had talked about not getting too close to her else she'd be messed up again when they left. But they come to the conclusion it was better she felt a little bit of love from someone sooner than none at all.

And, boy she loved old Waldo. She followed him round like her nose was welded to his backside. When Waldo helped old man Wongdeuan around the inn with fixing and moving stuff, she helped too. She was a fine sweeper. When Waldo went for his run around the yard, she ran round with him. He talked at her in English and she talked back in Lao and by some freak of language they managed to understand each other.

49

On Saifon's first night at the manger, she finished her first set of songs and was real surprised when they clapped her. She didn't have her skirt up round her ass or foam rubber down her brazier, so they must of been clapping her voice.

They weren't just being polite neither. There was eight singers altogether. Two of 'em knew Vietnamese songs. But none of 'em could sing in English and American music was big even then.

The system at the manger was exactly the same as the Inn Diana Butterfly. You get up on the stage, sing, show your stuff, and go down and sit a spell with the boys. You let 'em fondle some and lead 'em to believe they're your one and only. You help 'em drink, persuade 'em to buy something more expensive and something for you. Then when they think it's their lucky day, you gently break it to 'em that you can't go out back with 'em this time, but you surely will if they come back again. Men are vain enough to believe that shit.

If you get it right you can work up to eight tables a night, and have a dozen guys coming back just to see you. And the good thing is, you don't actually have to give out to none of 'em.

But, there at the manger, there was a couple of small differences to the system that messed her up. First, the girls all went out back with the guys cause they needed every cent they could get and tips wasn't enough. Second, in Indiana, the lady drinks they brought you wasn't the lady drinks the guys ordered for you. For example, rum and coke's all coke. But the barman bites a slice of lemon to the top of the glass that's been soaked overnight in rum. See? If the disbelieving guy smells it, he smells rum.

But here in Laos, the girls was expected to match the customers drink for drink, from bottles on the table. So you gotta be one tough mamma to get through the night. Some of the sixteen-year-old hostesses looked forty. Saifon spent a lot of her nights in the bathroom with a finger down her throat.

But in spite of her toilet habit, she sure was popular. The foreign ways she had about her, and the sense of humor she put on, and the fact she weren't easy, made her number one for tips. She didn't have no problem with the other girls cause she shared them tips around. She didn't need the money. In Indiana she was broke, in Laos she was a millionaire.

She was getting a kick out of the singing, but that wasn't why she was there. Four days had gone by and she still hadn't seen old captain mayor. No one knew where he was at. But then, on Friday night, there he was. He turned up late with a pack of soldiers decked out in stripes and colored bars and shiny buttons like they was going to a fancy dress party. He was short and lumpy and nut brown and old. He was a dog turd in a uniform.

The bouncers cleared a table near the stage of its bottles and its customers. They was half way torn between fighting and saluting. The brass sat down. When it was Saifon's turn to sing, she hitched up her skirt a couple of notches, put on enough lipstick to stop a fire truck and did the moves.

Next thing you know she's sitting at the front table as a guest of the jerks. She used up every round of ammunition she had. She played all her drinking games, told dirty jokes, and flirted like a whore. By the end of the night, captain mayor had her sitting on his lap and was making improper suggestions into her ear. She'd been stroking on his ego so she knew he was interested.

There was three places he could of took her. His wife and eight kids lived at one so that probably weren't the best idea. One was his barracks and he was afraid the long drive would of killed off his rising passion. So, he had the driver drop 'em at number three. That was a room in back of his old office down town.

Saifon didn't have no degree in it or nothing, but she'd studied drunks all her life. She knew how far she could push her luck with 'em. This lumpy little shit was safe. Getting her to come back with him had impressed the young officers, but he'd used up all his energy getting to this stage, and drunk ten times more than he'd intended. Weren't nothing left. The only thing between him and unconscious was gravity.

Soon as she had him laying down he was snoring like a baby. She took his keys and found the one he'd used to get 'em inside. On the wall in the office there was a dozen nails with bunches of keys hanging off 'em. They was probably spares for the staff or something. She found a match for his key, tested it on the door and put his back. Then she looked around the office in the light of a candle.

It was all so darned frustrating. There was cabinets full of documents and she couldn't read one of the frigging things. But she was sure there was something in that office that would get captain mayor in trouble. Someone else would have to do the reading.

Before she let herself out she undid the mayor guy's zipper and left his little old dick poking out. That way, when he come to, he'd assume …well, you know what he'd assume. That might be useful if she had to see him again. She walked a block from the office and caught a bicycle samlor back to the *auberge*.

50

Next time they saw Wilbur his ears was pretty much back to normal. They went to his place on the Sunday. The three of 'em, Saifon and Waldo and Nit walked there through the hot dusty streets of Savannakheth.

I guess the only way to describe what Savannakheth was like in them days would be to imagine a little village in Europe someplace during World War Two. Imagine you're strolling down the main street and there's German and British soldiers and French resistance walking around doing their weekend shopping, chatting with each other about how things are going at the front. And General Montgomery's at the grocery store buying corned beef and Mousellini's in front of the post office fixing the puncture in his bicycle tire.

That kind'a sums up what Savannakheth was like.

"How's your ears?" Waldo asked.

" How's your ears?" Nit parroted. She'd taken to repeating everything he said. It was real amusing for the first two seconds or so, but she did it all day. Course, she didn't know what she was saying but she did say it with a good old Indiana drawl.

She went off to find the maid's boy. She was taking a shine to him. He was about the same age as her missing sister.

Nit weren't in no trouble, with the law I mean. Even if they'd found Aunt Souksaijai's body (whoever 'they' was) they wouldn't of done nothing about it. These was war times and there was any one of a thousand reasons she could of been clubbed to death. Fact is, if you planned to club someone to death, this was the perfect time to do it.

"Getting better."

"What?"

"My ears, you asked about my ears."

They sat together on the porch. Saifon handed Wilbur the key and a map showing where the mayor's office was. After she'd explained, Wilbur smiled.

"You wanna come work for us?"

"Be a spy? Help you blow my country to f … (Waldo gave her the eye)…to Finland? Sure. How many helpless villagers do I get to bomb?"

"I guess that's a 'no'."

The chilled Biere Lao arrived like the Seventh Cavalry, just in the nick of time. Waldo took a long sip.

"Oh, man. How am I ever gonna live without this stuff? How we doing for news from Mukdawachamacall?"

"You take it easy grandpa. Sit back and sip your beer. It'll be the last one you get for a while. I've got some big news for you. You're both leaving for Mukdahan tomorrow."

"We are?"

"Why's that?"

"Well, let's just say there's a big party planned for the day after tomorrow that I'm not allowed to tell you about. It's gonna be loud and lively. But there's a number of folks around here that haven't been invited to it. When they find out the party's on, they're gonna be mighty displeased. It would be much better if you weren't around."

"I take it the people running the party didn't ask permission," Saifon asked.

"Right you are."

Waldo thought they was talking about a party and people not getting invited.

"Seems a pity to leave just cause of a party." Saifon and Wilbur looked at him the way you look at an ox pulling a plough. All that untapped power and potential.

"I'm sending the maid and her boy south for a few weeks till the government forgives us. If you want Nit to go along I'm sure she'll be happy to take her. Just till you get back."

-o-

A couple of hours later, Saifon was out in the yard with the kids. Nit didn't seem to mind going down country with the maid, as long as Pop was there, too. She did make her and Waldo promise they'd come back.

Waldo and Wilbur was sitting in the living room surrounded by Percy Sledge. They'd had too much beer: much too much. They was singing along;

"WHENA MAN LOVES A WOMAN, CAN'T KEEP HIS MIND ON NOTHING ELSE …"

That was the point in the song where they went off in opposite directions with the wrong words. Either that or Percy got it wrong again. For guys of a certain brown, you'd think they could of carried a tune between 'em. But if Percy could of gotten off that turn table and told 'em to shut the hell up, I know he would of.

"You miss your wife, Wilbur?"

"I try not to think about it."

"I hear you." He looked at his friend and wondered if this was the time to say what needed to be said.

"She ain't alive, is she."

Wilbur's mouth dropped open. "Why the hell you say a thing like that?"

"I'm sorry."

"No, man. I don't want a sorry. I want to know why you'd say something like that."

"There's two ways to miss a woman. You can miss her 'cause you ain't in the same place, but you wanna be. And you can miss her 'cause you know wherever you go, you ain't never gonna see her again. They's different. They look and feel different. That second one is you, Wilbur. You don't ever talk about seeing her."

"How d'you know she didn't walk out on me."

He said it like a joke but he wasn't laughing inside.

"I know what it feels like to be in love with someone who loved you back right up to the last second. I know that love didn't die in you two."

"God damn you, Waldo."

Wilbur took a deeper chug of his beer than he needed.

"Sorry, Wilbur. I didn't mean …"

"It's OK." He was upset; real upset. Waldo felt the mood in the room get heavy and drop. "You really are a piece of work, Waldo. I don't know how you do it. You get inside people, man. It's scary." There was a long silence. The first track stopped.

"She died in a car accident when I was here on my first tour. There was a lot of stuff I didn't have a chance to say to her. And that's the last thing I'm gonna tell you about her. You hear me?"

Waldo took a breath before his next line.

"Ain't nothing to stop you talking to her now."

"You what?"

"Just cause her body's gone don't mean she can't hear you no more."

Wilbur laughed kinda rude, like. "You crazy old coot. You should get together with some of my Hmong fighters up in the hills. They talk to their dead. There are ghosts all over the frigging place. Don't seem to stop 'em getting killed though. You're as crazy as them."

Waldo went quiet for a while and they both pretended they was listening to the next song.

"They ain't crazy, Wilbur. They let it out. Crazy people are the ones that keep it ins…"

"OK. That's enough before I hose you down. Don't talk like that in my home."

"Sorry, Wilbur."

"And stop saying you're damn sorry when you ain't."

"Sorry."

"I don't wanna hear no more."

"OK. …Just try it though."

"What?"

"Telling Mary how you feel."

"I'm gonna hurt you, man. I swear I am."

"OK. OK."

There was a real angry silence in the room when Saifon come in. She bumped into it.

"You two girls had a fight?"

"Hell, no."

"Course not."

She could see they had.

"Well, I'm on my way to the fridge for a couple of cold ones. I don't suppose I could interest you?"

"Yeah, I'll have one."

"Me too."

They sat sulking while she was outside opening the bottles. When she come in she decided to sit with 'em. It didn't help the atmosphere none, not until Waldo looked up at her and Wilbur and said; "You know this party? The one we have to leave for?"

"Yes, Waldo."

"Well, do you suppose they'll be having a barbecue?"

Wilbur snorted beer through his nose and nearly choked. Saifon went and thumped his back.

"Waldo," he said once he got his breath, "you're good. You really are good. When we meet up in the states when this is all over, I want to find out exactly who you are and who you work for. I can't wait for that story." He smashed his bottle against theirs.

"Cheers."

Waldo and Saifon cheered too but they looked at each other as if there weren't no hope for the party. As it turned out, they was right.

51

That little party upset a whole lot of people. If their entire economy hadn't been kept alive by the CIA, Laos would certainly of broken relations with Washington over it. The South Vietnamese army invaded Laos from the east. They bought along some ten thousand U.S advisors, which is a hell of a lot of advice you'll have to agree. Sadly, the advice wasn't that good.

If you're gonna invade a friendly country, the least you can do is win. But some fool in Washington couldn't read maps, and the nice spot he decided on for the battle, turned out to be a mountain range. They found themselves doing more rock climbing than invading. The North Vietnamese camped out in Laos just whipped their tired asses and sent the survivors scurrying back to the south with their tails between their legs.

You can probably find better descriptions of the battle of Xepon, but I don't believe in spoiling a good story with a lot of interesting information. All you need to know is, they came, they saw, they got beat. But they pissed off all the wrong people doing it.

So it was just as well Saifon and Waldo was in Thailand while all that was going on. They was staying in a secret CIA apartment they didn't have to pay for and waiting for news from Wilbur. You can imagine he had bigger things on his mind than them. They wasn't even sure the trucks would be able to cross over while the fighting was going on. So they didn't have a lot to do but wait. In fact there wouldn't of been much to write about if Waldo hadn't got himself shot.

Him and Saifon was going stir crazy in the apartment so they decided to go for a little trip. It was Waldo's brilliant idea that they jump on a bus and go visit Dtui's family. Dtui, you probably forgot, was the taxi driver that drove 'em from the airport in Bangkok. He'd told 'em he had a large family but he'd forgot to mention how most of 'em was gangsters.

They was real friendly gangsters, but in the twenty miles or so around where they lived, they was responsible for every illegal activity there was; pignapping, rice trafficking, moonshining, chicken gambling, fish poaching, you name it. And now, with a war just across the river, they had more illegal weapons than the entire police force. They was the Koknoy village mafia.

The next year, Coppola based the Marlon Brando role in the Godfather on Dtui's ma. Everything was there, the puffy cheeks, the thinning hair. There's no doubt about it.

When Saifon and Waldo arrived at the house that was surrounded by tall brick walls, they was met by two bare-chested skinny guys with tattoos and taken for an audience with Ma Marlon. She talked through one of the skinny guys like he was a telephone.

"What are they doing here?"

"What are you doing here?"

They told her.

"Dtui sent 'em."

"Dtui? We know a Dtui?"

"Sure, Ma. He's your son. He's driving cabs in Bangkok."

"Oh, Dtui. They friends of my Dtui?"

"That's what they say, Ma."

"Then you better feed 'em. Be nice to 'em. Any friend of Dtui's is one of the family. Show 'em some fun."

"Right, ma."

She waved her hand and the audience was over. They split Saifon and Waldo up then. Saifon they whisked out to the kitchen cause that was where women had fun in them parts. They let her join in the fish scaling.

Waldo would of been more hard to please if it hadn't been for Uncle Loo. He spoke about eleven words of English so they took him along to translate. They didn't get many Americans around there, so they drove him into town in the truck. For a special treat, they decided to take him to the most happening place in town, Crazy Moo's.

From outside it looked like another shophouse, but you should of seen the smiles on their faces when they led the big guy inside. He was surprised to see a pool table all the way out there. The balls wasn't standard size but they had a surprisingly good sheen and the balance was okay. The table warped a little to the northeast. He took all that in, in his first glance.

Crazy Moo suited his name. His sienna was a little more burnt than Waldo's and he had just the one long eyebrow. He'd brought the table all the way from Ubon and he made his living by charging eight cents a game. He was the district pool champion cause no one was brave enough to try to beat him. He played in just a pair of short pants with a pistol tucked in the belt.

Uncle Loo thought he'd explained to Waldo that he should probably lose to the guy. The words that left his brain said, ' Don't win this game or he'll kill you." But it come out like this: "No win. You die."

That, of course, Waldo took to mean, 'If you don't win, we're gonna kill you.' That could of been a joke of course, but looking at the faces of Crazy Moo and his own hosts, he could see these guys was all a few bottles short of a crate.

Now, I ain't mentioned it yet, but as QCO at Roundly's, Waldo had to check the balls for faults. Naturally, to see whether they recoil okay, you need a cue and a pool table. They had one set up out back. After thirty-eight years of hitting balls around, he'd gotten pretty good at it. He didn't play the game for pleasure. Why would you go play pool after work when you had to play with balls all day? But he was something of a genius at getting them balls into them pockets.

Of course Crazy Moo didn't know that when he called in all his neighbours to watch him whoop Waldo. There weren't much excitement cause they'd all gotten used to seeing him win. Most of 'em come just to get a first close up look at a big black guy.

But when he started playing, and was sending down balls from every frigging angle, they started to root for the wrong guy. They was playing best of three. Crazy Moo joked through the first game like he was getting thrashed deliberate, like, just to keep things interesting. But Waldo didn't seem to notice him stroking his pistol between shots. Dtui's relatives did.

"No win, die."

"No win, die."

"OK guys, I'm doing my best." But he still thought it was a joke. He was laughing along with the crowd, fooling around, doing trick shots behind his back. Crazy Moo's reputation was shrinking and wilting and sagging in front of everyone's eyes.

That's why, half way through the second game, with Waldo way in the lead, Crazy Moo shot him.

One of the skinny mafia guys shot Crazy Moo back. One of the neighbours shot the skinny guy. Uncle Loo shot the neighbor, and that sort of evened things up right. The other neighbors filed away saying what a good game it was and how they should'a had bets on it.

Dtui's relatives, the ones that survived the shooting, they was in a difficult situation. Their instinct was to run, but they'd promised Ma they'd look after the guest. And there he was bleeding on the concrete floor.

Them gangsters was stronger than they looked cause they managed to drag Waldo out of Crazy Moo's and into the truck. But he was lighter then cause of losing all that blood. The bullet had gone in an inch to the left of his belly button so it looked like he had a spare one.

They was nowhere near a hospital so they took him and the skinny guy to the meatworks. That was under Ma Marlon's sphere of influence, if you know what I mean. The head butcher'd done a lot of cutting for the family and he was pretty damned good with a knife.

They debated whether Waldo's bullet might of gone right on through to his stomach sack. If it did, it might just pass through his system of its own accord, natural like. But, as Waldo was passed out by this time, the butcher decided it'd be better to dig in there and have a look round.

As it was, it hadn't gone in too deep at all. They should make bulletproof vests out of fat guys. They dug it out, cleaned him up with spirits, and the butcher's wife sewed him up with turkey string. Waldo wasn't in no state to remember details.

52

Waldo come back to life. "I do something wrong?"

"You won a game of pool."

"I thought that was the idea. Where am I?"

He was back in the secret CIA apartment with Saifon leaning over him. He'd been out of it for three days. He lost about eighty gallons of blood at the pool game. It tends to tucker a guy out. For the first forty-eight hours he had a fever and a temperature of 120.

Pleased as she was that the butcher had kept him alive, Saifon called for a second opinion soon as they got him back to Mukdahan. She got in a real doctor. She had to convince him this yank with a bullet hole didn't have nothing to do with the war. He didn't want 'em ferrying in wounded in helicopters to his surgery.

But he did a good job on Waldo. He was cute too. Saifon couldn't recall the last time she'd dated a sober guy. She wondered if she'd ever have a man who loved her for her mind, for her heart. She had both. Just kept 'em out of the public eye in case they got damaged. It meant if some guy wanted to love her, he'd have to get to know her pretty good before he'd find any positive points. That was one of them catch twenty-two problems. But she knew one thing. She wasn't gonna give it away no more less the guy could convince her he wanted something deeper.

But it sure wasn't gonna be the doc. He assumed she was the big guy's fancy piece like they all did. He smiled polite like, refused a cup of coffee, and said he'd be back the day after. Shame of it was, he kinda liked her.

She was new at this nursing game. She guessed Waldo needed some sorta medicine now he was awake.

"You wanna beer?"

"You been looking after me?"

"Yup."
"I mean, like everything. Even the ..."
"Yup."
"Oh, shit."
"Yup."

-o-

Two days later, Waldo was already moving around pretty good. They hadn't heard nothing from Wilbur, but the fighting was still going on and they'd called a state of emergency in Laos. They reshuffled the government again. They did that so often there couldn't of been many Lao folks in the country hadn't been minister of something or other.

There was still RLA trucks coming over the river, but they wasn't sure Wilbur'd be able to get himself enough time away from the invasion to tell 'em when their truck was due over. So Saifon started hanging out in one of the cafés down by the ferry. It was lucky she did.

There was at least two army trucks on every ferry. It wasn't yet a month since the last shipment but she recognized the big naked blonde behind the driver soon as she cleared the customs shed. Saifon had the secret CIA motorcycle at her disposal. It had a CIA decal. When the beaten up old truck went past her, she followed it at a discrete distance.

Common sense told her the driver wouldn't be loading up on supplies till he'd dropped off the kids, if he had any. She tailed him out of town and along the north road. She wondered what the hell she'd do if he didn't have no kids this trip. They'd have to wait another goddam month.

About six miles along, the truck pulled into a garage. It was the greasiest yard she'd ever seen. All the parts, the old motors, and a couple of dogs was caked in oil. She rode past and stopped by the fence. She could see over it.

The driver got down and opened the back doors of the truck. Shoot. From where she was she could see inside. It was frigging empty. Two greasy guys lifted a slimy black engine into the truck and shut the doors. The driver and the dogs followed 'em inside the garage.

Saifon jumped over the fence and ran to the truck. She kept it between her and the office. She opened one of the doors and looked inside. One motor. No kids.

Now it wasn't like she was gonna scratch through the dust and find no nine-year-old girls in there, so it ain't clear why she decided to climb on in that old truck. Desperation probably. It was dark in there. It stank of grease and stale food, and sweat …and pee. It all triggered this ugly memory of fifteen years before. Her belly started wobbling.

She opened the truck door as wide as she dared and the light caught it. A little puddle deep in the corner. In that heat, any liquid would of evaporated in an hour at the least. She went over to the puddle, dipped her finger in and sniffed at it. Frigging pee.

Now that was weird, man. She'd followed the truck from the ferry. It didn't stop nowhere else. And trucks sure as shoot don't pee themselves. She supposed the driver could of done it on the ferry on the way over but most guys just relieved 'emselves in the Mekhong. And if he'd been bursting that bad, there sure would of been more than this little puddle. Probably hadn't been that much thinking gone into a puddle of pee since Sherlock Holmes. She just knew there'd been girls in that truck not that long before.

She turned round and there was these four mad eyes glaring at her through grease.

"Hi, dogs. How you doing?"They started snarling, so that told her they wasn't doing too good. But she didn't have time for being terrorized. She climbed down from the truck and ignored their growling and drooling and walked back to the fence like she was meant to be there. It confused the mutts long enough to see her over that there fence and on her bike. Them dogs was there thinking, 'dang, we shoulda bit that girl', when she rode back down the road.

She had to do some serious thinking before she got back into town. She wished she'd stayed on at school and gotten hold of some of that logic they was giving out, cause she was feeling pretty dumb now. She'd seen that truck drive away from the customs office beside the ferry. If she was right, the kids would of been handed over before then. That meant the ferry.

But that didn't make no sense. If you're going to the trouble of smuggling kids out'a Laos, there didn't seem much point in doing the handover on a crowded boat. You might as well hand them over before you leave. So that only left one possibility.

She parked opposite the customs shed. I say 'shed', but it was more like a hot dog stand with a room stuck on the back. All the business, the paperwork and the taxes was done up front at the stand. There was a crush of people there like drinkers at a crowded bar. Only officers got into the back room.

She walked along the side of the building like she was lost. There was a window with bars and no glass halfway back. For such a little room, she was surprised at how many people they could squeeze in there. There was plenty of uniforms but no kids. A big guy in the prettiest uniform saw her gawking and waved for her to get the hell away. And when he moved to do that, she saw 'em behind him.

There was two frightened little girls sitting on chairs against the far wall. They was about eight or nine. Saifon's knees went weak. She could of been one of them little girls. Not knowing what was happening. Not knowing where they was going. Now what the heck was she gonna do?

She only had Wilbur's number on the Lao side. But it was mid-day and he'd be off fighting his war. The maid was away with her family someplace. There wasn't no phone where her and Waldo was staying and she didn't want to risk going back there in case they shifted the girls. So she stayed put.

She found herself a view of the back door to the customs shed and got comfortable with some sodas and a bag of noodles. She could see everyone come and go so, unless they threw the kids outa the window, she'd know when they left. But they didn't leave for a hell of a long time.

At around five they shut the customs hut and pulled down the shutters. A lot of the uniform guys got on their motorcycles and went off home. With all the soda inside her, she was so bursting to relieve herself, she had to stay away from sharp objects. The nearest place to maintain her dignity was way on the other side of the market on a disused building site.

She was as quick as she could be under the circumstances, but when she got back there was a little brown van parked beside the building. It had driven over the grass and stopped up flush with the door like it was picking something up. But whatever that was, she'd missed it cause it was just pulling away. That had to be it.

So, she got on her motorcycle and give chase. Mukdahan wasn't New York. The suburbs didn't last long. Soon she was in countryside where the trees outnumbered the buildings and the evening shadows sliced across the road. She kept a good distance between herself and the van but she doubted the driver would of taken much notice of her.

It wasn't the busiest road in the country but there was a steady stream of traffic leaving the town and heading home. She was too focussed on the van to take much notice of anything else. That's why she was surprised when she felt a hand on her ass. She almost rode herself into a ditch.

Two young greaseballs had pulled their motorbike alongside .

"Hello, beautiful. Where you going?"

They was about sixteen and so cool they could of kept fish fresh. They was smoking and the ash was blowing back in their eyes. But they was too cool to take the cigarettes out. You know the type.

She couldn't believe her luck. On TV, when the good guy's following the bad guy, there ain't no road accidents, no breakdowns, and sure as hell no goddam pick ups. This was real annoying.

"Boys, go back to school. I hear you teacher calling."

The cool guy on the back with the hair was the spokesman.

"You crazy? We don't go to school." The driver grinned.

"We ain't never been to school." He said it real proud.

"That must be why you're both so dumb."

Big mistake. You should never tell dumb people they're dumb. It's too much information to be getting all at once.

"Yeah?"

"Yeah?"

"Yeah."

"Well, if we're so dumb, you ...whore, then how come we got this?" Yeah. Like having a gun disqualified him from dumb club. Saifon was starting to wonder if she was the only person in the province that wasn't packing a piece. Didn't seem right.

"OK, guys," She looked up and she was losing the van. "I'm in a hurry so I can't play with you today. Leave me alone, okay?"

The cool guy with the hair pointed the gun at her.

"Pull over into them trees or I'll kill you."

So this was their dating MO. The lengths some guys would go to get a little action. They was the same all over the world. She didn't appreciate having a gun poked at her.

"Oh, please don't kill me," she said like she was scared or something. "Here, take my money." The guys grinned at each other.

"It ain't your money we're here for, babe."

She fumbled in the cloth roll in front of the seat and come out with a half inch wrench. She leaned forward like

Annie Oakley and jammed it between the spokes of the guys' front wheel before they could do nothing about it. She barely got her hand away in time.

Man, it was better'n the circus. Them guys and that bike must of done three frigging somersaults before they landed. The gravel on the road peeled a foot of skin off the pair of 'em, and the gun flew up ahead about twenty feet. When she stopped to pick it up, she looked in her mirror to be sure them cool guys wasn't dead. She was impressed. In spite of all the flying they'd been doing, them cigarettes was still alight in their mouths.

OK. She got back in sight of the van and went another mile before she ran out of gas. Frustrating reading ain't it. Like I say, this wasn't a movie. (Less you're some fancy Hollywood producer and you wanna make a movie out of it. I'll give you my number at the end.) In a movie she could of waved down a passing car and said, 'Follow that car.' But she waved her arms round like a hen that didn't know it couldn't fly, and not one car stopped for her. The van was out of sight and she was real mad. So she took out her gun and pointed it at the rider of the next motor bike that come past.

She did a deal with the owner. He could have her nice new CIA machine and she'd take his piece of shit on wheels. He probably would of agreed to that even without the gun.

Even full throttle, she couldn't get that old lawn mower to go better'n forty miles an hour. It didn't like that neither. It was bucking like a mule. She was sure she wouldn't never see that brown van again. But in spite of the way it was looking, this must of been her lucky day. The van was up ahead, turned into a short drive, waiting for someone to open up two big green metal gates.

She rode slowly past, just as them gates was wide enough open for the van to pull inside. There weren't much to see in there, a big yard, a couple of houses, and a big tin barn. The gorilla that opened the gates looked straight at her riding past. He did a gesture that involved his mouth and his fist that she recognized as a moron version of oral sex. Disgusting!

The gate closed and she rode over to a spot on the far side of the road where she could take everything in. Less you was one of them Olympic pole jumpers, you couldn't of gotten over the wall around that house. The green gate was the only way in. She was in the middle of frigging nowhere and they hadn't even invented goddam mobile telephones yet. And if that weren't serious enough, the sky was turning mauve and she was gonna be stuck out there in the dark.

She really didn't have no choice if you think about it. She pushed her old bike over to the gate and hammered on it with her fist. The gate gorilla opened it wide enough for her to see the gap in his teeth and the glint in his watery yellow eye.

"Yeah? Hey, honey."

"You got any gas in there? I can pay for it." He opened up some more so she could see the belly he had hanging over his belt.

"The pretty lady ran out of gas did she? Now ain't that a shame." He knew she must of come back cause she liked the look of him. He looked her up and down, mostly down. She was wearing flared pants and a t-shirt like them frisky city women wore. He looked like he wanted to suck her in like a vacuum cleaner.

"Well, do you or don't you?"

"Oh, I got some gas, but it's gonna cost you, and I don't mean money."

"I guessed that. Where'd you keep your gas can?"

You'd have to figure, opportunities like this didn't come along every day to a middle-aged gate keeper with a face like a rat. He had to grab it when it did. He had instructions that nobody from outside was to get through them gates. But this was an emergency.

"You gotta keep quiet. Don't let the boss see you." She was in. He led her around the back of the guard post to a hut. It looked like he'd put it together himself …with his feet. "This is my place."

"You surprise me."

"Go in." Yeah, really. Like she was gonna just crawl on into a box with a gorilla without no romancing or nothing.

"Gas first. Then we can…you know."

Oh boy did he know. The gas was in back of the guard post in big metal drums. He held an empty beer bottle under the spout and danced on the foot pump till gas come out. Pumping was plain uncomfortable given how excited he was. He took the bottle over to his hut and crawled inside.

"I got your gas, honey. Honey." No honey. Now where the hell had that girl run off to? He'd lose his job if they found her hanging around the houses. Even he wasn't allowed in there. He couldn't go no more than ten yards from his hut. So, he couldn't even go looking for her. Damn women. No wonder he'd strangled his mother.

Now what was he gonna do with the ox boner she'd left him with? He paced up and down to take his mind off it, waiting for unemployment. She'd be back.

But she wasn't back for another twenty minutes. He was in his guard post keeping his boner entertained. She snuck up on him.

"Am I disturbing you?"

He fell off his chair.

"Where you frigging been? You ain't allowed in there. I told you that."

"Yeah. But your boss called me over. Didn't you see?"

"The boss?"

"That's right."

"You sure it was the boss?"

"Chinese looking. Short grey hair. Gold tooth. Name of …"

" …Koonnay Yort. Right. That's him. What did he say?"

"He said it was kind of you to help me with the gas. He asked me on a date. I guess he liked me. He wants me to go home and get dressed up and come back later. So, if you'd give me the gas. He said there's no charge for it."

"Oh, all right." He went over and got the bottle.

"You gonna let me out?"

He unlocked the gate.

"What about his wife? Didn't she say nothing?"

"His wife? No, she seemed to like me too."

The gorilla slammed the gate harder than it needed. How come the rich, smart guys always got the cute girls, and the dumb, ugly, poor guys with bad breath ended up jerking off?

53

She was on her way back to Mukdahan. Of course she hadn't met the boss. He was busy in the barn with half a dozen other shady looking guys. But she did talk to the kids. They was in a barred room at the back of the house. There was four of 'em including the two latest. All girls. All scared out of their minds. She talked to them through the bars and found out where three of 'em come from. The other one was too freaked out to speak. One of 'em heard the guard say they'd be taking 'em to Bangkok on Friday. This was Wednesday. She had a day to do something, whatever that was. She wondered if Wilbur had lost interest now his war was going bad. She wondered what she'd do if one of them mortars landed on him.

There wasn't nothing familiar about the house. This wasn't where they'd brought her to when she was smuggled. And she didn't recognize the boss. By the look of his place and the cars in the yard, smuggling kids was a boom industry. He must of took it over.

She almost missed her CIA bike in the shadows. It looked like the guy she'd done the deal with didn't have no gas neither. She switched back and the borrowed gas was just enough to get her to a little gas station. They had a phone there. She rang Wilbur's number so long it croaked. You'd think a spy would have a goddam answer machine wouldn't you.

But she had more luck calling Mrs. Porn. She ate up everything Saifon had to say. She took down details of the place, the names and the connection from Savannakheth, and told her to call back the next day to see what they got.

Saifon was excited and anxious at the same time. The acids was flowing in her veins. This was all stimulating stuff. She couldn't wait to tell Waldo all about her day. But it looked like she'd have to. When she got back to the apartment, the door was open and he was gone.

She went down to ask the old landlady if she'd seen him. In his state, he shouldn't of been out. The old lady had gotten into a rogue batch of betel nut and been high as a crow all day. Her eyes was still going round. She couldn't remember nothing.

So Saifon sat upstairs and waited. It was weird. There weren't that much you could do in Mukdahan. Half an hour and you would of seen everything there was to see. But she sat for an hour and there was still no sign of him. And why did he leave the frigging door open? That wasn't like him. And how come the refrigerator and the cupboards was bare?

She went down and tried Wilbur again. There was still no answer. Then she wondered if the cops had heard about the shooting at Ma Marlon's and dragged Waldo in to help them with their inquiries. So she went to the police station, and the hospital, and the doctor's surgery, but no one had seen him.

The mystery was solved when she got home. There was a note pinned to the door. It was in Thai. She couldn't read it. She thought the landlady had left it so she went back down. The woman was o-d'ing. She had so many betel nuts crammed in her mouth she couldn't talk. She was belly up on the floor choking and giggling. A betel nut o-d would be a horrible way to go. Saifon had never seen nothing like it.

"Where did you get the nuts, mother?"

"Gurgle. Gurgle."

Saifon helped get the nuts out of her mouth so she could speak and flushed her out with tea before she could get any sense out of her. If she didn't know any better, she'd say them nuts was spiked.

"I just found 'em on the doorstep this morning. Don't know where they come from. Delicious but."

"Can you read this for me?"

It took her some time to focus cause the letters was running around the paper. But when they settled down they give up a terrible secret.

"We've got the American. Give us one million dollars and stop bombing Laos or we'll kill him."

Saifon was shocked. How the hell do you kidnap a 300 pound guy?

54

Waldo was in the kitchen of the kidnapper's place eating cake. It didn't fit in his diet but extreme times call for extreme measures. The kidnappers was all nice guys, polite and all, and they all spoke English pretty good. But they was torn. Three of 'em thought they should truss him up and bruise him some. The others wanted him dead. It weren't nothing personal. They wasn't killers. They just needed to make a political point now they'd screwed up the mission. Being 50-50 they decided to let Waldo have the casting vote.

-o-

They knew they'd blown the job as soon as they saw the big guy propped up on the bed. It was either a great disguise or this wasn't no CIA operative.

"Hi, guys. What can I do for you?"

Most people would of been disturbed to see a bunch of masked men carrying semi-automatic weapons come bursting in through the door. But Waldo saw the funny side of it. Weren't very much that could shock him no more. And besides, he was already on life overtime he didn't have no right to be claiming. If it hadn't been for Saifon, he'd already be up listening to Jelly Roll and all them other dead guys, live.

"What do we do?"

"Hell if I know."

They switched to English.

"You stand up."

"Sure thing, young fella. I guess I stopped bleeding enough." He pulled back the covers and they could all see the bloody dressing round his gut. It just made matters worse.

"*He's injured.*"

"*What do we do with him?*"

"*Let's just leave.*"

"*We can't go without him.*"

"*Why not? He's not who we came for.*"

"*How do you know that?*"

"*Look at him. Does he look like CIA to you?*"

"*Well he must be. They wouldn't let him stay in the secret CIA apartment if he wasn't.*"

"*Perhaps he's a general.*"

"*Even the Americans wouldn't have generals this size.*"

"You guys mind if I sit back down for a spell while you sort this stuff out?"

"What? Okay. Sit."

"Much obliged."

"*We can't leave empty handed after all the planning.*"

"*I reckon we can still get a ransom for him.*"

"*And what do we do? Carry him out in a blanket?*"

"*I'm not carrying him.*"

"*Me neither. I got a bad back.*"

"*Maybe he's scared enough to come without a fight.*"

"*He doesn't look scared to me.*"

"*I'll ask him.*"

"Mister."

"Uh hu?"

"Are you afraid of us?"

"I don't reckon I am. No offence intended."

"Is OK. Would you mind coming with us?"

"Where we going?"

"I can't tell you."

"Is this like one of them kidnappings?"

"Kidnap? Yes. That's the word." Waldo laughed.

"Now who do you think would be interested enough in me to give a shit?"

"The CIA?" He really laughed at that.

"Hell, boy. They wouldn't give you a slab of bubble gum for me."

"I told you."

Even through the masks Waldo could see this look of disappointment come over all their faces. He felt like he'd let 'em down. He didn't like letting folks down, old Waldo. So he thought about the situation for a while.

"I guess the US embassy in Bangkok might be concerned about one of its citizens, specially with all the secrets they're trying to keep and all."

"You really think so?"

"It's worth a try. You'd need some publicity mind. Maybe some photos. You private or affiliated?"

"I'm sorry?"

"You members of a group?"

"Yeah. Communist Party of Thailand. This is a stand against what your government is doing in Laos."

"And Vietnam."

"And Cambodia."

"OK. Well, I can see a point in that."

"You can?"

"Sure I can."

"So, you'll come with us?"

"I reckon I could. Hand me that pen and paper over there. I just need to leave a note to a friend of mine. Don't want her worrying none."

"He can't leave a note."

"Why not?"

"Are you kidding? A kidnapping's supposed to be scary. The people who find him missing are supposed to panic. That's the point."

"You're right. We'll let him write it then come back for it."

"OK. I guess that's about it. I don't suppose you guys wanna give me an address or a telephone number I could … No. I guess you wouldn't." He put the note on the pillow. "We'd better be off. One of you guys wanna grab that tray of medicines and dressings over there? And you can get me some fresh underwear and clothes from the closet. You got anything to eat at your place?"

"Not much."

"Well, we better stock up. Bring anything you can find out there in the kitchen. There's some juice and stuff in the refrigerator. Help yourselves."

It turned out Waldo was every bit as good at organizing a kidnapping as he was at quality controlling at Roundly's. They helped him to the door and down the stairs. The landlady was high on the opium-laced betel they'd left her so there wasn't no witnesses.

-o-

He'd been in on the discussions from the start. They needed to send some photos to the US Embassy to show they wasn't messing about. They all agreed on something of him looking tortured and holding the daily newspaper. It was the killing they couldn't agree on. They had this camera, see, belonging to the brother of one of the guys, and he wanted it back that night. So they decided to shoot his gory murder as well as the newspaper pictures, just in case the embassy didn't come up with the million.

They spent most of the evening on it. Waldo had 'em in stitches. Then they started passing round the rice wine. They had a hell of a good time. The boys was all ex-university students from Bangkok. They wasn't expecting to be rebels and terrorists. They just wanted to be Communists. But with all that was going on in the countries around 'em, Communist was a dirty word in Thailand.

55

It was naughty of 'em to take Waldo's note from the pillow, but they was confused, so you could forgive 'em, right? But it left Saifon with two mysteries on her hands, and she was starting to feel like she was doing it all on her own. It wasn't till she lost Waldo she knew how important his being there was to her. She had a rough night with all them thoughts and problems going around in her head. Didn't sleep for a second.

So, by six she was already on the phone to Laos. Wilbur's number rang a thousand times before he answered the darned thing. He was drowsy. Sounded like he'd been up for a week.

"What?"

She was so relieved to hear his voice she blurted out both stories in Technicolor and didn't give him no time to answer. When she was done she felt kind'a faint. It crossed her mind she hadn't done enough breathing. Wilbur didn't answer right away. He was likely considering about everything, or maybe he went back to sleep. Then he said,

"Wow, Saifon. You make my war pale into insignificance." But that was probably sarcasm.

"Yeah. I'm sorry, Wilbur. I know you got problems of your own."

"No, girl. A promise is a promise. I'm sorry I let you down with the truck." He was starting to wake up. "Look, I'll level with you. I haven't got anyone in Mukdahan free to stake out the smugglers' place on short notice. You know anyone that could tail the truck as far as Bangkok?"

"I might have. I gotta make a call after this. Can you do something from Bangkok onwards?"

"That I can promise. And I'll show you how you can get through to my field telephone. Now, as for Waldo. Anyone chooses a 300lb guy with a bullet wound in him as a kidnap victim has to be lacking in some of the finer skills of hostage taking. So I wouldn't worry too much about getting him back. I want you to call the embassy in Bangkok. Talk to a lady there name of Demetria. She's a very cool person and she can solve that problem for you I'm certain. Tell her you talked to me and explain what happened. Use the word 'communist' a couple of times."

"You think the commies are behind this?"

"Who knows? Just say the word. If you can find a fax machine anywhere, send her the note you got. OK?"

"OK. Thanks."

-o-

At the USIS offices inside the grounds of the US embassy in Bangkok the phones did so much ringing the staff only looked up when they was quiet. It was like everyone wanted to know what America was lying about, 24 hours a day. The information service took on four extra staff to read out press releases and make intelligent guesses as to what Mr. Nixon might want 'em to say to the international reporters camped out on Wireless Rd. It seemed like there was always two more phones than there was people to answer 'em.

Now, phones just ring, right? They don't ring different for different callers. You can't tell from the ring if it's your aunt Ada or the Queen of Scotland at the other end. Well, embassy people got a knack. They know when there's trouble coming over the phone. Demetria Johnstone knew. She got a tingle just before she picked up her phone that told her she'd be better off ignoring it. But she didn't.

"Hello?"

"Can I speak to Demetria?"

"Yes, speaking.'

"I was given your phone number by Wilbur Groves.

"Oh, oh."

"I just sent a fax to your office. It's a copy of a ransom note."

"Ransom? Whose?"

"His name's Waldo Monk. He's an American citizen. I sent a copy of his passport too."

Still holding on to the phone, Demetria tried to get across to the fax but the cord was too short.

"Hold on." She put down the handset and retrieved the two sheets at the top of the tray. She was reading the note as she picked up the phone. "Oh, my."

"Can you read it?"

"Yeah. They teach us tricks like that."

"Well you know what?"

"What?"

"The kidnappers. They're communists."

Wilbur knew in that embassy full of paranoid people, Demetria was the paranoidest. Just the sound of the word set her teeth chattering.

"Communists?"

"Sure as I'm standing here holding the phone." She was sitting down.

"An American citizen in the hands of desperate communists. Heaven preserve us."

"Amen, sister. Amen."

"Listen, dear. Word can't get out about this. It would cause a great deal of panic in the expatriate community. Where are you?"

"Mukdahan."

"OK. Just sit tight. I'll be there as soon as I can. I have a liaison officer at the Thai Ministry of Interior. I think we'll need him there too. Don't forget. We keep this just between us. Don't do anything silly."

"No, ma'am."

Saifon put down the phone in the post office, walked over to the fax and arranged for the press release to go out to all the wire services.

56

Things started to move fast after that and it wasn't just cause I suddenly noticed I ain't even close to finishing this here story.Demetria and some Thai secret service guy flew to Udon Thani that same day and drove all the way across to Mukdahan in a rental car.

Saifon met 'em in the evening. Demetria was a big, happy saddle-brown woman who'd spent most of her sixty-two years in government service, following her husband around the world. He went and got himself killed early on in the Vietnam conflict by looking the wrong way. He was a general, the type that couldn't ever find a desk to suit him. Demetria and him could of retired long before Vietnam but they wasn't the retiring type, I guess. After walking away from a thousand battles without a scratch, he walked himself under the front wheels of a number twenty-one Saigon municipal bus. He must of forgot they drove on the right over there.

The secret service guy, Sisamone, he was just too good looking to be real. He was the type they cast in movies to play the hero. You know them guys you never see in real life? Saifon never did trust guys that looked too damn good. She was always looking for reasons to hate 'em. Most made that easy.

Once they was checked into the old Hotel Muk, they listened to Saifon's story about how they'd come to the region to trace a dear aunt in Laos who had sadly passed away before she could talk to her, and how she'd misplaced Waldo. (Wilbur told her not to say about the kid smuggling if there was a Thai service guy there. He was probably the most trustworthy man you could meet, but better safe than sorry.)

Sisamone was eager to show the women how valuable he could be. He had a brainwave right there in front of 'em. He reckoned they should let the local radio station know where they was staying. That way the kidnappers would know they was in town and how to find 'em. That was a real smart move.

57

"Hi."

"How you doing?"

"You must be Waldo."

"Well, that's right. How in tarnation you know that?"

"I came to Mukdahan to rescue you."

"Is that right? That was very nice of you. Thank you. What's your name?"

"Demetria." Waldo thought about it for a bit.

"That's a real pretty name."

"Thank you."

"You're welcome. Would you like some cake?"

Waldo and Demetria got on real good at the kidnappers' place. She got over the shock of herself getting kidnapped real soon, with Waldo soothing her nerves. It had shook her up some to see five guys in masks at the end of her hotel bed at five in the morning.

Her and the general had been in some tough spots in her life. But she never had to look down the barrel of a gun before. Not even in New York where she was born, and that's gotta be some kind of a record.

I guess Waldo didn't have no choice but to be nice to her, seeing as he was responsible for her being there. When the boys heard on the radio there was someone from the United States Embassy in town, he dropped in the suggestion that they might as well kidnap her too. So they did. He figured two hostages was better than one, and someone from the embassy had to be worth more than him. Couple of the guys started calling him, 'boss' already.

58

If Laurel and Hardy would of been Laos, they would of been Suk and Sivilai. You ain't never seen two funnier looking Asians in your life. Suk had a waist that was somewhere down around his knees. He had so many chins, one of 'em was his belly. The only meat on Sivilai was his tongue. You see them two together and you think some guy's been separated from his skeleton and he's walking around with it figuring how to get it back in.

But, man, them two was dedicated to the Pathet Lao. They sure was. There wasn't a thing they wouldn't of done for Porn and Souk. It's just that the PL couldn't use 'em much on account of the way they looked. Secret agents gotta be invisible. It don't help if they give the impression they're gonna launch into a comedy routine. It was heartbreaking for the two guys stuck in an office doing paperwork.

So you can imagine how delighted they was when they got their first mission. They was Thai-based PL with legal, well, almost legal, Thai papers, so they was perfect for the job Porn give 'em. After the briefing, they went up to Mukdahan and met up with the Lao/American girl and she give 'em the background.

Both of 'em fell head over heels in love with Saifon, but thanks to their loyalty to each other neither of 'em confessed their feelings. Suk knew Saifon would of chose him and it would of crushed his friend. Sivilai knew the same thing only in reverse.

They was camped out in their van down from the compound on the Ubon road when the truck come out. There was two guys to do the driving and it stopped at the first gas station and filled up. You never filled up in the northeast less you was planning a real long trip. It was a box truck but Suk climbed up on the roof of their van and could see that there was vents open on the top. That had to be the dispatch they was watching for.

Suk and Sivilai shared the driving and kept their distance just like they'd seen at the movies. Next morning they found they was coming into the outskirts of Bangkok. A couple of times they almost lost the truck in crazy traffic. The deeper they got into the city, the crazier it got.

At nine in the morning that old truck stopped in front of a pair of fancy iron gates at a big, dumb-looking mansion near the docks. It pulled inside, the gates shut, and the boys knew they'd just done a real good job of spying. For sure, they was going on to bigger and better things.

59

Things started to get serous when the pictures the commie boys took arrived at the embassy a day later. In fact you could probably say the situation got a little out of hand. The guy that did the developing sent off the whole frigging lot of 'em, alive and dead. He didn't really get the part about saving the post-mortem Waldo till later. But the effect was real effective.

It soon become clear to everyone at the embassy that them kidnappers wasn't kidding. Look what they'd done to the poor old guy. He was laying there dead in a pool of blood like a french fry in tomato ketchup. (The tomato ketchup part was right.) Them pictures was shown to the cops and the secret service. To the military, they was a prayer come true.

You see, if you wanna keep control on people, you gotta give 'em something to be afraid of. In Thailand's case it was 'communism'. Commies was the boogy men that ate your kids, and did unmentionables to your grandmother. It wasn't unknown for 'em to creep in your bedroom at night and bite your head off.

Course they never did none of that stuff, but the army wanted everyone to think they did. And this set of pictures was living color proof that them commies was cold-blooded murderers. Somehow, them pictures accidentally got leaked to every newspaper in the country.

And that's how Saifon found out Waldo was a goner. She was on the train to Bangkok and a lady come through the carriage selling newspapers. Waldo's bugging-out eyes and flapping-out tongue was right there on Waldo's head that was lying in a pool of blood. Even the black and white newspaper picture was gory as hell.

Saifon probably wouldn't confess to how she really felt when she saw that picture. She didn't do emotions too good. She never let herself get too close to no one so her feelings didn't get a lot of exercise. She thought she'd run out of tears long before she hit sixteen.

But Waldo was different. She'd let him in all right, the big gumball. She done everything she could to keep him outside in the snow but that fool shoveled his way through it. Once he was in, she didn't have no choice but to love him.

"You okay, miss?"

The two ticket collectors was looking at her like she was a leak in the washroom.

"Course I ain't *rather* okay. You goons think I'd be sitting here bawling my *rather* eyes out if I was *rather* okay? You *rather* fucking idiots." But she said all that in English so they didn't have a frigging clue what she was talking about. They snipped the corner off her damp ticket and left her to her ranting. It took her all the way to Bangkok. She was full of that lump you get that ain't explainable in no medical way. She cried till there weren't nothing left. Every hill the train went past reminded her of him. Her landscape was flat without him. I thought of that. Pretty ain't it.

-o-

She got to the capital determined that Waldo's death wasn't gonna be in vain. Bangkok had even more surprises waiting for her. Mrs. Porn's driver was there to meet her at the station and take her back to the house on Ngam Duphli Street. By the time she got there, she'd already decided not to tell no one about Waldo. She really hated people feeling sorry for her.

"Great news." The old lady met her at the door and kissed both her cheeks like the French people do. You always worry if you cleaned your face properly in the morning, when that happens. Mrs. Porn couldn't wait to tell

Saifon her news so she put her arm round her waist and dragged her through the house to the garden. She couldn't see the misery behind Saifon's sunglasses. She didn't know then that Saifon's horizon didn't have no hills on it. "Our men kept track of the van all the way to Bangkok. It dropped the girls off at a house near Klong Toey, at the docks."

They sat in the gazebo and the same maid bought the same drinks out that Waldo liked so much. Saifon hadn't slept all night but she was pushing herself to keep a focus on the lady's story.

"Do we know who lives there?"

"The owner of the house works for a shipping company. By rights, if we look at his position, he shouldn't have a big house and a nice car but he has both. He also has a bar and one or two minor wives. So he obviously isn't living off his salary alone."

"You found all that out in twenty-four hours?"

"Oh, my dear, it's so nice to be presented a problem that's small enough to take control of." Funny. Saifon didn't see the problem being small at all. "There are two ships attached to that particular line leaving tomorrow, a tanker and a freighter. We'll be watching the house very closely. I imagine they'll take the children on board early, before the dock workers get on duty."

Saifon thought about the girls and recalled something one of her street sisters told her once. She was teaching Saifon how to cheat at cards and there was this one tactic where you lose a couple of hands even if you got good cards. This makes the mug you're playing think you're crap and bet heavier. She said,

"Sometimes you gotta sacrifice a few soldiers to win the war." She thought that was good advice, less you happened to be one of the soldiers. The four kids they was sacrificing on the boat was all gonna end up a mess like she did. They'd be on the tanker, tired, stinking and confused. None of 'em knew where they was going. They wouldn't understand why everyone knew they was there but didn't do nothing to help 'em. Winning the war didn't mean a frigging thing to them.

"I'll need the address," she told Porn. "For when I call the CIA guy." That's what she said, but she needed it for another reason too. She wanted to let the girls know they was gonna be alright.

During the afternoon, she had a long talk with an old guy in a suit that Mrs. Pornsawan dragged in from some Ministry. The old lady must still of been somebody. She told him everything about the trafficking and what she knew from Mukdahan. She didn't say nothing about Waldo. He seemed real interested and wrote stuff down and promised he'd get the guys that was running the business.

She wondered why this important-looking guy would come himself and not send some secretary. Porn put her straight once he'd left. The Thais was keeping an eye on things in Laos and it still wasn't clear what side they should be on. So they played on both of 'em.

After the calls was all made and the plan was all set, she had a nap and a think. At six, she lifted some unfashionable clothes from a closet and went for a taxi ride.

-o-

Knock. Knock.

"Hello?"

"I'm here to see Mr. Jaroon."

The maid didn't bother asking what she wanted. She was a maid, not a doorman. She unlocked the gate and stepped back to let this over-powdered young woman in dark glasses into the yard. The dogs sniffed at her like she was dinner.

She got took into this grand new house that had more concrete than the Lincoln Memorial. Concrete was all the rage then for folks rich enough to build with it. Mrs. Porn was right. You didn't get a house like this on seventy three dollars a month.

The maid left Saifon in a kind of expensive holding pen and went off to find the boss. The room was a mess of styles that didn't match. Money can buy you stuff, but it can't buy you taste. There was an ugly mirror by the door so guests could look at themselves and decide if they was good enough to be there.

She looked in it. She was sure Mrs. Porn's men wouldn't recognize her in her glasses and hat. She'd worked out a cover story that wouldn't blow the whole operation and she'd run enough scams in her life not to be nervous. In fact there was only one thing that could of happened to screw everything up.

When Jaroon the shipping company guy come in she felt like she'd been hit over the head with a baseball bat. He come out of her memory like an old sink unit being ripped out of a wall. He'd been in there hiding for fifteen frigging years and she didn't know it. He wasn't changed at all from the little guy that ran his smelly hand over her chest when she was eight. His hair was sitting further back on his head and his belly was rounder, but there wasn't no doubt.

"Can I help you?" She couldn't bring herself to say nothing. "Miss?" Them few stalled seconds dragged out for what felt like a goddamned hour before she could make her voice work.He was getting restless.

"Ah, yeah. I'm with … I'm with the Jehova's Witnesses."

"The what?"

"We're an international religious organization that spread …"

"How did you get in here?"

"Your maid let me in." She'd lost the desire to playact. She just wanted to get out. All them years and he was still there. She imagined how many petrified little girls he'd manhandled. How much money he'd made from the flesh of children. She wanted to kill him right there.

"She shouldn't have done. I've got better things to do. I don't have time for rubbish like this. She'll show you out." He turned his back on her rudely and walked out. Her legs was wobbly. She heard him bark and growl at the maid before the girl come running back in with tears in her eyes.

"The boss says you gotta go. Now." She led her back to the gate, unlocked it, and almost pushed Saifon out into the street. She knew the watchers was around somewhere so she walked a block and turned a corner before she stopped to catch her breath. She'd never felt nothing like it, but she knew already that what she'd been pretending was a load of bunk. She wasn't doing all this just to help them kids. She had her own angry inside her that needed clearing out too.

60

Demetria and Waldo was getting on okay. I don't mean nothing romantic mind. They was both in love with dead people. But they'd been sharing a room for forty-eight hours and you get to know someone pretty good when you're stuck in a little space together. There certainly was some electricity.

"Waldo. Do you think we should consider escaping?"

Well, of course he didn't think that. He was in cahoots with the kidnappers. The last thing he wanted was for the hostage to get away. He tried to convince her they wouldn't be in no danger as long as they didn't do nothing stupid. But she was a feisty broad who'd married into the army. She'd watched a lot of training movies.

"Demetria. Just relax, girl. Think of this as a couple of days paid vacation."

"Right. I always put myself through stress if I need to relax. I always take my vacations in rooms without windows in the middle of God knows where."

"So I guess you're used to it then, Demetria?"

See? That was another reason there hadn't been no romance. Demetria was as deep as Lake Michigan. Waldo … well, Waldo wasn't.

-o-

Sisamon, the secret service guy was going nuts. It was his first big assignment. They'd sent him to the northeast to rescue a kidnap victim. That victim was horribly murdered. His only ever idea led to him also losing a high ranking US embassy official. She would likely get chopped up like the first guy.

203

The story was all over the local papers. Thai journalists was crawling all over the place. And foreign war correspondents sick of being fed bullshit in Bangkok, had come up for this juicy little piece too. It was a sneaky way to write about the secret war without writing about the secret war, if you know what I mean. 'US Embassy Official Kidnapped by Thai Communists.' What could they possibly be protesting against?

Sisamon's career was on the line. He had to find Waldo's remains and Demetria before the press did. He started hanging out with 'em in the hotel bar at night, scrounging for tid bits. He got the lead he wanted from a very well known reporter whose grasp on secrets got looser the more drinks he had inside him.

"Have another bottle, Athit."

"Well, just the one more I suppose. Got to hang on to the little money they give me in Bangkok. Now, if I had a *Washington Post* budget, I'd have kidnapper's banging on my hotel door at three AM too."

"The *Post* talked to the kidnappers?"

"They sure did. But this is just between you and me young …what's your name again?"

"Kwun."

"Right. They got a world exclusive for a mere four thousand bucks. Can you believe it?"

"I didn't see that in the *Post*."

"Ah. They're hanging on to it. The reporter wants to skip town before it's published. He doesn't wanna be tortured by them Thai secret service pigs. You wouldn't believe what those animals do to you to get information."

"You'll have to tell me sometime - when we're alone. What makes this reporter think the kidnapper's genuine?"

"He had a note signed by the first victim, and the embassy broad's ID."

"So, what's stopping the reporter from leaving? He's got his story."

"Not all of it. He sent a bunch of questions back to the gang. He'll meet his contact for the answers tomorrow."

"Is that so?"

-o-

He went to see the *Post* guy for a friendly chat at 3AM. They'd have to fix the lock later. He took his press liaison officer, Mr. Kritijak with him. His job was to hold the knife at the Post guy's throat while they discussed sources. Press freedom didn't ever make it to Mukdahan.

So when one of the student kidnap guys went to meet the Post guy for a follow up, he got jumped by half a dozen military guys.

61

"Mr. Waldo, can you come with us please."

"Oh no. What are you going to do with him? Leave him alone. Hasn't he suffered enough?"

"Now, Demetria. Settle down. I'll be fine. They just want a little chat, I guess. Isn't that right boys?"

They took him out to the kitchen and sat him down.

"We've got a problem, Waldo."

"A big one."

"What's up?"

"They grabbed one of our men, the Thai army."

"Now that's too bad. What do you think they'll do to him?"

"They'll torture him. Make him tell 'em where we are."

"You think he'll talk?"

The boys thought about it.

"I would."

"Me too."

"And me."

"Then we need to rethink. You guys been getting much publicity?"

"It's all over the news. Radio. TV. Here and overseas. It's been huge ever since you died."

"OK. Then if the Thai soldiers rescue us, you'll be the bad guys. What say you let us go? Before they mess your boy up too bad."

"But, what about the money?"

"You could pretend the money wasn't never what you was doing this for. You'd score more points. Make a lot of friends. And you already got money for the interview, right?"

They yakked about it in Thai. Waldo helped himself to a cup of tea.

"What happens to our friend after you get back?"

"Leave it to me. I got an idea."

See what I mean? Waldo was at his best when he was lining up plans like he was racking up balls. He was a natural organizer. The commy boys let him and Demetria go just as soon as he'd finished his tea. They put 'em in the truck and drove 'em back into town.

-o-

"You're a very brave man, Waldo." Waldo blushed. Even in the dark shadows at the back of the car, he could tell his cheeks was purple.

"No, I ain't."

"Yes, you are. I understand exactly what you've been doing here."

"You do?"

"Course I do."

"Shoot."

"I know you must be every bit as concerned as me, but you've been putting on this brave face to protect me. To stop me worrying. I think that's so noble, Waldo."

They was sitting side by side and he could feel her warm hip against his. She leaned in towards him. "You know what these bastard commies are capable of just as well as I do. We've all heard of the atrocities. And you know that you and I are being driven into the valley of death this very minute."

"Demetria. We ain't …"

She put a finger up to his big lips.

"No. Enough. Waldo, I love what you've done. I admire you. I know my dear husband would've done the same."

"I "

"I'm going to kiss you, Waldo."

"That ain't necessary, De …"

"Don't say any more. I know." She sobbed a pair of well-spaced sobs. "I know this is the end. I want the last memory

I have to be the taste, the warmth, the strength of a man I respect."

Now, Waldo knew this was kind of the over-sixties version of the, 'What would you do if you knew the end of the world was coming in half an hour?' scenario. He should of told her the truth right then, but for some reason, he kept his trap shut. Well, no that ain't exactly true.

She threw her mouth at his. It weren't one of them platonic, cheek kisses neither. It was a tonguie. Waldo hadn't had no one else's tongue in his mouth for fifteen years. It felt kinda crowded in there. Thing was, he didn't exactly fight her off. Thing was, he kinda liked it.

The guys in the front seats witnessed what was going on in the back. It turned their stomachs some. In their culture, old folks didn't do that kinda thing in public. Hell, in their culture even young folks didn't.

They was rescued from further embarrassment 'cause the dim lights of Mukdahan city limits appeared up ahead and they both shouted,

"Look at the dim lights of Mukdahan." But whatever was going on in the back seat didn't stop right away.

-o-

Demetria believed she was on her way to purgatory right up to the moment they dropped her and Waldo out back of the hotel. The first thing she saw when they took off her blindfold, was a stack of beer crates and she knew they sure as hell wouldn't be serving no beer in purgatory.

"Oh, Lord. We're safe." She sank to her knees and thanked each and every department in heaven.

Waldo said goodbye to the boys and they told him they'd miss him. They give him a souvenir frog on a stick. The stick went up through the frog's rear end and out its mouth. If you spinned it round the frog made croaking noises. Course it was wood, not a real frog. That would'a been cruel.

-o-

For a day, Waldo and Demetria was bigger than Nixon and Kissenger. They got interviewed a billion times. There wasn't no explaining how Waldo managed to claw his way back into the world of the living after his gory and well publicized death. A lot of folks kind of admired the kidnappers for being able to fake it without him knowing.

Waldo come out of it all looking pretty damned good in the world press and the commies didn't do too bad either. It was only in Thailand they suffered. One paper even said Waldo was interfered with, but I bet that would'a pushed the reader's imagination just too far.

-o-

Waldo still had one lose end to tie up. Sisamon called him in to identify the captured commie. He was already pretty beat up. Demetria only ever saw the kidnappers in masks so Waldo was the only eyewitness.

Agent Sisamon made the mistake of inviting a gallery of press to come and view the identification. He had one of them photo opportunities in mind where Waldo's standing pointing at the bad guy and Sisamon looks all modest and handsome in the background. That's what he had in mind.

But naturally, Waldo said he hadn't never seen the kid before. Sisamon's insides dropped.

"But you can't be sure."

"Yeah, I'm sure."

"Take another look."

"Son, I could look at him till my eyes drop out but it still wouldn't turn him into a kidnapper."

"Maybe you didn't see all of them."

"Oh, I saw 'em all right. I et with 'em. I played cards with 'em. I sang patriotic songs with 'em. Just to save my life, mind. Less he went out and got a new face, this ain't one of the guys that kidnapped me. I may be dumb but I ain't blind."

Now you probably realize, that was a hell of a big deal for Waldo. He hadn't never lied before. Not deliberate. He shifted across to his left cause he figured if the Lord was gonna strike him down, he didn't wanna give Him a sitting target. But there weren't no bolt from the blue and to tell the truth, he kinda liked the feeling that come with a bare-faced lie. He figured he might even try it again sometime.

All the press guys in the room suddenly had another story for tomorrow's front page. They took pictures of the bruises all over the guy and made sure they got Sisamon's name right. They even got close-ups of him with what looked like tears in his eyes. It was touching really.

The cops didn't have no choice but to let the non-kidnapper go. He kindly refused to make a complaint against 'em. In fact he just wanted to get his ass out of there. There was a look between him and Waldo when he walked out the door of the police station. No one else saw it, but Waldo knew he'd just saved a life. He wondered, up in the Lord's account book, if it made up for the life he'd took. Soul math.

And you're probably wondering about what happened in the hotel that night between Waldo and Demetria. And I guess you're gonna have to keep on wondering, cause I sure ain't gonna write about that kinda thing.

62

Wilbur hadn't slept in a bed for a week. He was aching real bad, but he had a lot of fence-mending to do. His Hmong fighters was mighty disappointed. They'd been expecting a big push from the south for quite some time.

There was this movie you might of seen. It was about what was left of a British army unit in Africa. They knew one more Zulu attack and they was buzzard food. Just then they hear the sound of reinforcements coming round the mountain. The bugle's sounding the charge. They're so relieved they eat up the last of their rations, and they're so happy they fire the last of their ammunition up in the air. And round the corner comes the bugler - only the bugler.

That's how the Hmong felt when their reinforcements give up and went on home. It was Wilbur's job to convince 'em it weren't the end of the world, even though, deep down, he believed it was. He could see the edge.

So when he got back to Savannakhet, he felt lower than he'd been since he started his second tour. There weren't no other yanks around cause the Air America guys was told to lay low for a while. Local people looked at him different around town. He thought they was maybe seeing him human for the first time.

Even the RLA that was living off the food he put on their plates seemed to be wondering whether they was on the right side. He didn't know what to say to the RLA command 'cause he didn't yet know what excuse his fart-ass government was going to make for screwing up an unlawful invasion. He had to wait for an announcement.

So, as he couldn't do nothing about the big picture, he decided he should work on a little one; something he could do right. With his two best Hmong pals and a bottle of Bourbon, he drove on down to the boarded-up office of the ex-mayor. They blasted open all the cabinets with a quiet jelly and loaded the files into the 4WD. They replaced 'em with PL propaganda leaflets just for effect, and stood back till the flames took hold. Unseen, they rung the town bell to warn people there was a fire, and when they was sure all the neighbors was out of bed and safe, they left.

By the time they'd put out the fire, the old wood office was a heap of ash and the fire had been so hot, even the metal cabinets was molten.

That night, the old couple in the *auberge* was woke up by the rattling of the gate and the griping of the dogs. They come out to find out what all the fuss was about, and on the front stoop they found three piles of official and unofficial Savannakhet documents.

They didn't read 'em all that night, but they saw enough to know what they had their hands on. It suddenly weren't no surprise they'd shut down the provincial prison. All the criminals was running the town.

Over the next month, the files went by truck to the Ho Chi Mihn Trail, and from there by donkey and bicycle to the north. When they arrived at Vien Xai, a team of PL clerical ladies went through 'em and started the paperwork for criminal proceedings against most of the Savannakhet administration for when they took over.

But Wilbur weren't of a mind to wait that long. And he weren't convinced the ex-mayor was gonna sit around and wait for the PL to come gunnin' for him. So he planned a little ceremony in advance. He had three kids of his own. Two of 'em was girls. Every time he thought about the trading going on through Savannakhet, he recalled his girls at the same age and his blood boiled.

Captain mayor was alone in the mess tent slurping on a bowl of beans. The chubby little fella looked up and saw Wilbur come in through the mesh door. He slowly pushed his plate away from him, stood without no, what you'd call 'enthusiasm', and give a sloppy salute. Them was the rules.

"Sit down, captain." The captain sat. "Now, let's see that again."

"See what?" He didn't bother with a 'sir'.

"Let's see you stand to attention and salute, politely." The captain laughed and took up his spoon again. These American 'advisors' got a bit too big for their boots sometimes. He might of been a soldier somewhere back along the trail, but here he weren't diddly-squat. Now he even wished he hadn't saluted the first time.

When the beans was just about to leave the spoon and slide down his gullet, he heard a click. He turned his head to see Wilbur with his service revolver in his hand with the barrel pointed directly at his beans. He was about to laugh again till Wilbur shot that goddamned bean bowl and made a hell of a mess of the captain's uniform.

Being as he was from 'stores' and hadn't been shot at before, the captain thought the bean sauce was blood. It was as close to death as he'd ever gotten and he fell into some kinda shock.

"Now, I said I'd like you to stand at attention and salute, politely."

When the MPs and a couple of cooks come running in, they found the captain bolt upright saluting stiff as a train signal. Wilbur had his gun back in it's holster and he was just standing there. One of the guards asked him what happened.

"Must of been the beans," Wilbur told 'em. "The plate was mined. It just exploded. Ain't that right, captain?"

Captain mayor nodded and when Wilbur beckoned him to follow, he went along like a baby duck. "You, men. I want all the other plates checked. This shouldn't have happened. You understand me?"

"Yes, sir."

Him and the captain walked out to Wilbur's 4WD, and drove off. The soldiers started going through the stack of tin plates real careful. They hadn't never seen mined bean plates before. Them communists. They was as sneaky as you could get.

The 4WD drove out the gate without stopping, and off down the lane. Wilbur noticed there was tears in the captains eyes.

"Now, quit that. It riles me to see a man in uniform cry."

"You ... you aren't going to kill me?

"Oh, I'm gonna do much worse than that."

Old captain mayor balled his eyes out at that. He really was a damn wimp when you got down to it. He was begging and pleading and sobbing so bad, Wilbur had to take his gun out again. He fired out the window but the captain could feel the bullet whoosh past his nose. That sure as hell shut him up.

Once Wilbur'd got his attention, he started to tell him all about the rednecks back home and all the stuff they did to old guys that messed around with little girls. He made it real graphic; didn't leave nothing out. And unfortunately for the captain, his English was so good he understood every darn word.

When he couldn't take no more, he stuck his head out the window and threw up. Most of it decorated the side of Wilbur's car and that really got him pissed. When you're trying to stop a guy from castrating you, the last thing you wanna do is throw up over his 4WD. Wilbur slammed on the brakes and got him to clean it up - with his uniform - then put it back on.

They drove northeast on an unpaved road they wasn't supposed to be on. After about ten miles, they come to a clearing. Wilbur stopped. Way up ahead there was a bridge. After the crossing the road got narrow and there was tight brush crowding in on it from both sides. The track seemed to veer round to the right then disappear behind the vegetation. This was the spot Waldo had told him about.

"Stay there." The captain sat quaking and stinking. Keeping the bullet-proof truck between himself and the far side of the clearing, Wilbur went to the rear of the car and took out a sniper rifle he used for hunting. He come alongside captain mayor's door and opened it.

"You see this? I got four gold medals for shooting one of these. You know what that means? That means I could shoot a bean off a button from four hundred yards."

The captain trembled and looked down at his tunic. Wilbur went on, "I'm gonna give you a chance you don't deserve. It's kind of like sport, you see? You ever run before in your life?"

"Y ..yes." But it was clear from the shape of him, that must of been a hell of a long time ago.

"OK. You're gonna run. You're gonna run along this road. Acr…" The reflection of a rifle sight glinted for a second from across the clearing so Wilbur knew they was being watched. "Across that little bridge and along the track. I don't think it would be a good idea to run off the road and into the bushes because this is one of the heaviest mined roads in the province.

You're gonna run, and your goal is to get to that bend in the road up ahead before I shoot you. If you run straight I've got a better chance. So you have to zig and zag all the way so it ain't easy for me. You know what I'm saying?"

The captain mayor was sweating like a dog and smelling even worse. "All right. Get going. I won't shoot till you're over that bridge. You can't say I'm not a fair man, now can you?"

The captain got out of the car and jogged towards the bridge slower than most people walk. Halfway across, he stopped to look back and saw Wilbur with the rifle to his shoulder ready to shoot. So he kept on jogging like some wingless old chicken in boots. And he zigged and he zagged and the first bullet whistled just over his head, and his speed somehow doubled till he was kicking up clouds of dust from the clay road. And he didn't dare look back once a second shot clipped his ear.

The bend in the road was up ahead and he tensed waiting for a third shot. He knew once he was around that there bend, and if his heart didn't give out, he was gonna make it. That third shot didn't never come. He stuck close to the inside of the bend and ran and ran till he was sure he was outa sight.

And there was hope. Up ahead round that bend, there was a barricade, and through the salty sweat that was stinging his eyes, he could see that there was men in uniform.

But them men in uniform was just boys fresh from PL orientation. They hadn't seen a lot of action. The only enemy they'd encountered in their week at the barricade was an American in a yella Citroen. They'd thought about that a lot since they let him go. They decided they should of arrested the guy and let the commander sort it out. They sure would next time it happened.

Captain mayor could see the soldiers up ahead but they was blurry seeing as he was just about to pass out. They was pointing their guns at him, so he waved his arms over his head and shouted that he was unarmed, and a captain in the Royal Lao Army. He knew he was saved, but he fainted anyway.

63

"You didn't tell me your father was kidnapped."

Saifon got a sick feeling in her chest. She'd been crying like a baby all frigging night again. Her pillow was so wet she nearly drowned. She couldn't stop thinking about the kindness the old guy had showed her. All the love. She remembered his simple common sense and his smile that made her feel warm and safe. She remembered his joy at every day things that made her notice stuff, too. It didn't seem fair that he was dead.

"I couldn't."

"Why on earth not? I could have helped."

"Helped what, Mrs. Porn? Raise the dead?"

"Don't be so morbid."

"It ain't called 'morbid' if it's real death."

"Real death? Are you mad?"

"He's dead. Waldo's dead, Mrs. Porn."

"Don't be ridiculous."

Saifon was getting irritated with the old girl.

"I seen the body, ain't I?"

"Really?" She laughed and it made Saifon mad as hell.

"Yeah. Really. In the goddam newspaper."

"I must admit I don't believe I saw that particular newspaper. We don't get them delivered every day. But I did see today's. And I assume you didn't." She called the maid and told her to bring the paper. She come running in with it like it was alive.

Glaring out of the front page was this big picture of old Waldo's smiley face with teeth all over the frigging place and some brown woman holding onto his arm like they was married or something.

"What the f …? What's it say?"

"It says they were rescued."

Saifon sort of collapsed on the couch like all her joints come unglued at the same time.

"But …but I saw the frigging body. There was blood all over the place." She didn't know whether to cry or dance.

"It says they faked the death pictures."

"They faked ..? The sons of bitches. They kept me awake for three frigging nights."

"Ah. Now I understand why you've been such a pain in the bottom since you got here. You thought Waldo was dead."

"I tell you. He really will be when I get my hands on that big burnt sienna son of a …" Tears was streaming down her face like Niagara Falls. "He won't have to fake nothing when I'm done with him." Mrs. P hugged her.

"You should have told us, dear. You should have shared your grief."

"I ain't that good at sharing." She was pretty damned good at shaking though.

64

It took the freighter three weeks to get to the US. It didn't go to New York like they did fifteen years before. It went straight to Norfolk so it could start loading up with supplies for Nam. The Customs was never too fussy about searching an empty American ship when they had so many full foreign ones to keep 'em occupied. So, as usual, the crew just marched the kids down the gangway to a waiting station wagon. The driver took 'em overland to a place just outside Washington where they got fed a real meal and cleaned up. The next morning they was dressed up real pretty and dragged on over to the Lido.

The Lido was a private cinema, the type of place you could rent for functions or dirty film showings. The owners just took your money and left you alone. This morning in question there wasn't no film showing. There was a meat market. There was an auction of little girls. Since the early days of mistakes in New York, the smugglers had streamlined the business. They only dealt with Asian or Asian-American brokers. They was all regulars and they knew when the next shipment of girl meat was coming in. The goods was inspected, the dealing was done fast, and the satisfied customers would leave with their property in under two hours.

The security was strict, but for once the FBI operation didn't get screwed up. They rounded up eighteen guys in suits and rescued nine girls. At the same time there was a series of arrests at the docks in Norfolk. Then there was CIA monitored arrests at the docks in Bangkok, raids at the houses of all the company officials, and a commando-style raid on the compound in Mukdahan.

The arrests in Washington pushed over a whole goddamned domino trail of contacts and suspects and villains all the way up through to New York. They all sung like canaries, cause basically, guys that do this kind of thing are all chicken-shit cowards. Let's face it, if a guy's gotta use a nine-year-old girl to get his rocks off, he sure ain't a man. Know what I mean?

65

Saifon forgive Waldo for being dead when he got to Bangkok, but she sure made him suffer first. The case of the kidnapping and trafficking of little Lao girls saw so much attention in the papers and on TV in Bangkok, Jaroon the shipping clerk was already tried and convicted by the population. But, back then, it didn't matter a queer coyote what the population thought. All that mattered was how much he was prepared to pay to blindfold old lady justice. If they didn't lynch him on the way to court, he had a fifty-fifty chance of getting let off.

So on the second day of the trial, after folks'd read in shock about what went on the day before, even more of 'em turned out to show their support. They was everywhere, up trees, balancing on fences, trying to catch sight of the witnesses and the accused. There was press and cameramen and ladies in bleached out skirts selling charred chicken wings.

It weren't like in the US where they have ushers to keep out the rabble. If you was rabble and you could squeeze in, you squeezed. There was a hundred or so people crammed in the twenty-foot square room. They'd been smart enough to get there early. There was one ceiling fan doing its dangdest to stir up the stale breaths that filled the court already. But it was hotter'n hell in there.

Waldo sat beside Saifon on the front bench. It was supposed to be for witnesses but there was rabble there too. Cameras was flashing at 'em, and questions was flying at 'em, and by nine of the morning when it was all supposed to start, there was a circus feeling in that little room.

The two prosecutors sat up front on their perch on the left, and the two lawyers was on the right. One of the lawyers sat behind a red nose that generated as much heat as the sun was doing. He reminded Waldo of Divine and wondered if he got his from gin, too. They was all flapping official documents in front of their faces to try to cool things down. But them long black capes they was all wearing didn't help none, less they was packed in ice underneath.

The four little girls, just arrived back from the States, had faced their interrogation on day one. Saifon wasn't allowed to be in there with 'em 'cause she was a witness herself. That rosy nosey lawyer bamboozled them poor little girls with big language. He called 'em liars and had 'em all crying and tripping over each other's stories.

By the end of the day, they was so confused not one of 'em could positively identify Jaroon the clerk, even though they all knew it was him. Don't forget these was Lao girls. Thai and Lao languages got a lot in common, but they didn't understand most of what they was being asked. In them days, nothing in the law said the lawyers and the judges had to make things simple for 'em. So they was answering yes when they meant no, and no when they meant yes.

-o-

It was nine thirty on day two by the time the accused turned up in the room. There was booing and hissing from outside before he appeared through the back door. It was probably wise they didn't bring him through the front. He was chained by the ankles and had to hold it up so he didn't stumble. He was wearing dark blue pajamas and a nasty smirk. He didn't look too concerned about his situation, if you know what I mean. He looked at Saifon but he didn't recognize her from her visit to his house.

A minute later, three old guys in black robes come in through that same back door which set a lot of people wondering. They climbed up on the highest perch right at the front of the room and set the ball rolling. The audience shut up at last, 'cept for the babies.

The judges spent a while summing up what happened the day before. Waldo didn't understand nothing and Saifon wasn't of a mind to interpret all the legal stuff she was struggling with herself. While they was waiting for the trial, Mrs. Porn had give her lessons in law jargon and how to stay polite, even when you're fuming inside.

The time come for Saifon to go sit on the witness chair, and if she'd heard right, things was looking good for Jaroon the clerk. She was the only other eye-witness and what she'd seen was sixteen some years before. There was a lot of space for error there.

When they called her name she stood and walked forward to the witness seat. She was looking real elegant and poised in a nice dark silk suit Porn leant her. She sat down real calm and crossed her ankles so them horny judges couldn't see up her skirt. She smiled at the lawyers and waited.

She got through the basics without no mistakes; name, age, nationality, and all that. But then rosy nosey started to get frigging personal.

"What do you do for a living, Miss Saifon?"

She waited for the prosecutors to object but they just sat there.

"I'm a professional singer."

"And what kind of establishments do you sing in?"

"What type? I sing in music restaurants."

"Music restaurants? I've never heard them called that before." He laughed. The prosecutors didn't object to that, neither. "Isn't it true that you were working in a brothel in Savannakhet for the past month?"

She didn't even flinch.

"No."

"No, what? No it isn't a brothel or no you weren't working there?"

She looked up at the judges.

"Sirs? I thought I was here as a witness in the trial of that scumbox over there. I didn't realize I was on trial myself."

Rosy nosey got in before they could answer.

"Judge, I need to establish the moral background and therefor the reliability of the state's prime witness."

"Why, hell," she smiled. "Why don't you just ask me if I'm a whore?"

The lawyer's nose kinda spread to the rest of his face and the audience chuckled.

"Very well. Are you, or have you ever been a prostitute?"

"No."

She was doing a real good job of not thumping that tomato of a nose.

"I remind you, you have sworn to tell the truth."

"Well, that's an interesting mess you gotten yourself into, ain't it? Here you are checking on my morals to see if I can be trusted to give evidence against your client. But now your telling me I swore to tell the truth so I can't be doing no lying. That means you ain't gonna believe me one way or the other.

But let's suppose I am a prostitute. You know it don't make a shit of difference as to how honest I am. There's honest whores and there's lying whores. Just like there's honest lawyers, and lying ones. 'Cept you don't get to see too many honest ones."

The audience let out a little whoop and she swore she saw two of them judges smile. The prosecutors just sat there like they was poached. It was getting obvious where Jaroon the clerk had his money invested. The lawyers gathered 'emselves for a counterattack.

"Miss Saifon, when do you claim you saw the defendant, Mr. Jaroon?"

"I *claim* I saw the defendant in June, 1955."

"You must have a remarkable memory. Can you give us the exact date, please."

"Well, I'm sorry. I can't "

"You can't give us a date? Then how can we establish where the defendant was on the day in question?"

"Well, that's easy. I can tell you. He was beside me on a cot with his hand up my skirt." The audience kinda booed when they heard that, and the middle judge told 'em to shut up again. Then he told Saifon to just answer the questions that was asked. She thought she had. Rosy weren't finished.

"If it was such a big day in your life, pray tell us why you can't remember the date."

"I was an eight-year-old girl straight out of Laos. We didn't have no electricity, no newspapers …"

"No education."

"No education don't make you stupid. A lot of stupid people graduate from universities."

"Of course we aren't suggesting you're stupid. Your imaginative use of our Thai language tells us how brilliant you are." He laughed at his joke and waited for the audience to join in. They didn't. "So, let me see …"

-0-

The way we heard it later, them lawyers went through every little detail of Saifon's twenty-four hours in Bangkok. She had to admit it was a crazy twenty-four hours. So many things was confused. She spent most of her time locked inside things without no windows; the truck, a room, the hold of the ship. She didn't see a lot of daylight. She sure as hell didn't see the Grand Palace or the Emerald Buddha. Sightseeing weren't included on that tour. She'd heard stuff, folks talking, traffic, the radio, enough to convince herself where she was, but not enough to convince a court.

By the time they'd pulled them twenty-four hours to pieces, the lawyers had convinced the judges that she probably hadn't been in Bangkok at all. She could of gotten on a tanker anyplace, if indeed she did get on a tanker. If indeed she *was* trafficked.

Clutching for straws she said,

"I recall one of the sailors saying how many hours, how many days we was out of Klong Thoey docks."

"Oh, thank God. So all you need to do is produce this time-keeping sailor and all your problems are over. You have kept in touch, I hope."

Rosy nosey was looking real smug and cocky. Jaroon the clerk leaned back in his seat and looked across at Saifon with that same smug expression. She knew if they didn't convict him after all this effort, she'd have to kill him right there in the courtroom. She wasn't gonna let him walk out of that place a free man. Rosy was still showing the audience how clever he was.

"So your presence in Bangkok, the validity of your abduction, and the guilt of our client, all comes down to whether you can prove you met him in 1955. Tell us, how did he look then, when you saw him as he slept ' beside you on a cot'. That seems very close."

He was getting to her. She might as well kill him too.

"He ain't changed much. He's got the face of an old pig now and he had the face of a young pig then. A pig's a pig." The audience snickered.

"Really? So in 1955 he looked very much the same as he looks today?"

He reached back to his satchel and pulled out a large black and white photo. It was of Jaroon with a full head of long hair, glasses, and a lot less meat. It was taken at a party while he was fooling around, pulling some stupid frigging face. Of course it didn't look like him then or now. "This is a photo of Mr. Jaroon in the year 1954. He certainly doesn't look the same to me."

He handed the photo to the court cop who stood there looking at it. The other lawyer poked him and told him to take it to the judges. They passed it around. Saifon looked at the two silent prosecutors. They was obviously only there for balance. She was on her own.

She cleared her throat and straightened her spine. Waldo had seen her rear for an attack enough times to know something serious was about to happen. When she spoke, it was in a new voice that hushed all the mumblers behind her.

"We didn't sleep." The lawyers looked up, smiling.

"I beg your pardon?"

"I said we didn't sleep. He wasn't on the cot long enough to sleep."

"I don't think we need any more …"

"You asked me what he looked like then."

"Yes. Well …"

"Yes, well he didn't look like that jolly guy in the photograph. I'll tell you how he looked. He looked naked. That's how he looked. And to a little girl, a naked pervert is the biggest and scariest thing there is."

The accused spoke up.

"I never …" The lawyers shut him up in a hurry. Rosy come to his rescue.

"I think we've already shown the witness didn't know the accused in 1955. She's obviously never met him. There's no …"

Saifon looked into the creep's eyes.

"His hair was greased back then and he stank. He stank of aftershave lotion. I'll never forget that smell." One of the judges opened his mouth to speak, but she give him one of her stares and he backed off. "You think I'dforget a thing like that? You think his face would ever go away? You think I wouldn't see it in every nightmare for the rest of my life? You think I could be mistaken about the most frightening moment I ever knew?

"Prove it? You want me to prove it, Mr. Tomato nose? All right. I can prove it."

The room was so quiet you could hear the fly ramming the screen on the window. She looked over at the prosecutors. "One of you stuffed owls care to give me a pencil? A sharp one."

There was something about the way she said that, give Waldo the heebie-jeebies. One of the prosecutors bought her a pencil and a bit of paper and she burned a hole in his double-crossing head with her eyes before snatching 'em from him. She put the pencil in her right hand and smiled at Jaroon the clerk. One of the wheels seemed to fall off his wagon, there.

She looked at the empty paper for a second then leaned over it and started to draw. The fly at the window stopped ramming so's he could listen to the scratching of the pencil. Even the babies was mute. All them necks was straining trying to get a peak over her shoulder.

When she leaned back so did everyone else in the damn room. She called over the cop and folded the paper in half before she give it to him.

"Take 'em this."

He give it to the middle judge who opened it slow and studied it. His eyebrows took off like dragonflies. The other two judges couldn't stand it so they stood up and come over to sneak a look too. They was just as shocked. The middle judge fixed his old eyes on Saifon.

"Could you explain what this is all about."

"Well I ain't no artist, judge, but surely you can see what it is."

"It looks like …"

"It's his dick."

For a few seconds there weren't no air in the room 'cause everyone sucked in at the same time.

"I don't …"

"Them circles on the side. They're moles. I got a real close look at 'em in 55. I can't never forget 'em. Show me two men with a little dick like that and two big moles on one side and I'll surely believe in miracles."

There was a whole mess of confusion in that room for a while. Rosy went to consult with a seriously sweating Jaroon. The other lawyer went to look at the picture along with the two crooked prosecutors. The judges got into a huddle, and the audience was excited as hell. That excitement got out of the room and into the street and the crowd outside suddenly filled up with hope.

Saifon turned around and give Waldo a little smile. He just couldn't wait to find out what the hell was going on. The judges climbed down from their perch and two of 'em went out through the back door. The other one called over to rosy.

"We'd like to see your client in the back room for a few seconds." Jaroon weren't too pleased about that prospect.

"I ain't going." He weren't looking quite so smug now. In fact he was looking real pale. It was like someone had found his tap and drained all the blood outa the guy.

He was still screaming and objecting when the two cops hauled him kicking out to the back room accompanied by the cheers of the audience.

"I ain't showing you nothing. She never saw that. I never …"

And the door at the back slammed shut and the yelling got muffled and the audience buzzed.

-o-

About two minutes later, three smiling judges come back to their perch. But interesting enough, Jaroon didn't come back out. Neither did the lawyers. Jesus knows what they did with 'em. But the middle judge cleared his throat and announced in language that weren't exactly legal jargon; "He's got a little dick with two moles on it."

There was a cheer you could of heard in Indiana.

-o-

229

That was the turning point of the trial, sure enough. The newspapers started to call it the 'moley dick' evidence and it stuck. It set a precedent that found a meaningful place in Thai legal history. Thammasat University wrote a unit around it for their law degree called the 'moley dick riposte' and I heard they're still teaching it today.

But more important, once Jaroon and his lawyers knew they was screwed, they started to implicate every man and his dog that had anything to do with the racket. And as it was too big and loud to just vanish at the wave of a magic billfold, all the Thais that was involved ended up rotting in jail. Even the goddamned rich ones. That was probably the last time justice was seen to be done in Thailand.

66

On their last day at Mrs. Porn's, before they was due to fly back to the States, Saifon and Waldo was making the most of their last evening. Waldo and Soup was having a last series of pool. Waldo spent an hour teaching him how to screw (that's a pool term) and he was getting pretty good at it.

Saifon and Porn was out in the gazebo thing getting pickled on real French wine. Mrs. Porn put on her glasses and read the label of the bottle they was presently guzzling from.

"You know, dear, exactly what it is we're consuming here?"

"Wine?"

"Well done. But it isn't *just* wine. It's very *old* wine."

"Don't worry. It still tastes OK."

Porn laughed

"It doesn't go off, Saifon. It gets better the older it is."

"Yeah? Sounds like Waldo."

"I think it's time to wean you off beer and onto the finer things in life. This particular wine, for example is from Bordeaux and if you were to buy it in New York, it would cost you approximately $2,000."

Saifon choked on it.

"Shit."

"We'll also need to work on your vocabulary when describing fine wine."

"$2,000 for grape juice? You gotta be kidding me. How did you get hold of it?"

"We stole it from the French. We've got a cellar full of the stuff."

"Good for you. Here's to stealing from the French. Cheers."

"Salut." They chinked glasses and chugged. "I feel we've had quite a lot." She refilled four glasses but there was only two there. "Oops."

They was lying back in them wooden recliner chairs looking up at where the moon would of been if this wasn't Bangkok. Porn thought about Saifon leaving the next morning and come over all emotional.

"Saifon."

"Yeah?"

"I'm sorry."

"What have you done?"

"No. I'm sorry about what happened to you when you were little. When that beast …"

"Ahh. It weren't so bad."

"Wasn't so bad? But he …"

"No he didn't."

"What?"

"He just fiddled around a bit. I screamed and kicked so much he give up."

"But he was naked. You saw his …His …"

"No."

"No what?"

"No he wasn't, and no I didn't."

"But you said …"She shook her head and gulped at her wine.

"Yeah. I know. But that greasy, strawberry-nosed lawyer was wiping the floor with me."

"You lied?"

"There weren't no bible or nothing."

"But how did you know?"

"About his …?

"Yes."

"I asked around. I found out where he liked to go drinking. When I was there having a few beers who should I meet but the young gal that collected the glasses. And you'll never guess what he got her to do on more than one occasion. She was thirteen. I give her a few dollars for her trouble and she give me some details."

"You little minx."

"Do you hate me?"

"Saifon. I couldn't love you any more if you were my own despicable daughter. You are really something special." She leaned over and give her one of them French kisses. Not the … well, you know what I mean.

"What's a minx, then?"

From inside the house they heard Soup cheering and screaming. He'd beaten Waldo again. Probably won another dollar. It was odd how bad Waldo had got at the game since he found out Soup was a prince.

67

So, even though Saifon and Waldo was heroes in Thailand, there probably weren't a soul knew nothing about it stateside. They was in the departure lounge at Don Muang International airport. The news on the TV showed American and South Vietnamese troops invading Cambodia. The botched invasion of Laos hadn't taught 'em much. They was screwing this one up too. Most folks stateside wouldn't be hearing about that neither.

There was body bags lying all around and choppers ferrying wounded. (On the TV. Not at the airport.) Waldo must of been moved by all them bagged dead guys cause he decided that was the time to tell Saifon something he hadn't never told no one else in his life. Not even Aretha. The place was crowded and noisy and sticky but sometimes the moment chooses itself. You got no say in it.

"I took a life once, Saifon."

"Yeah. Right." She didn't believe him but he looked so repentant she couldn't really ignore what he'd said. "Who was it?" He let his eyes swerve off across the terminal.

"Ralph."

"I don't believe you. When?"

"June 3rd. 1955. It was a month after Reet Passed away. You know. I took her death real bad. But Ralph, he couldn't live without her. He didn't eat, couldn't sleep, just let himself fret on after her."

Saifon couldn't understand how she could of known Waldo all this time without this Ralph character coming up in conversation. Something just didn't hang right.

"You never told me about Ralph."

"I never told no one. Shooting Ralph ain't something I'm proud of."

"You shot him?"

"In the head."

"Jees, Waldo. How old was he?"

"Dunno. Must of been about twenty I guess."

"Jees."

"He'd been with us most of his life."

"Living with you and Reet?"

"Yeah. He was unbreakable, you know? He fell out of windows, got run over by cars. He even had his foot sliced off by a goods train."

"I see. Now, Waldo, this ain't a person we're talking about here is it?"

"Of course not. Hell. What do you think I am? Ralph was Reet's cat."

"You shot a frigging cat?" She laughed.

"He weren't just a cat, Saifon. Aretha used to say he was an angel been sent down from heaven to watch over us. And I reckon that was true, cause when Reet took off, Ralph's soul left on the same flight. There was just his body left on the sofa.

"I watched it get skinnier and skinnier and it just killed me. I took my old revolver out the closet. I carried what was left of Ralph up to the quarry and I blew his little brains out."

"Then I don't see a problem. You were being kind, that's all."

Waldo had come over pale. He was drained as a goat in a meat shop.

"No. There's a problem. Oh boy there is. I ain't never been able to tell Aretha what I did to her cat."

"Waldo. She'd understand."

"I don't think so. You see? It's worse than just the …the killing."

"What can be worse than killing it?"

Waldo looked around at all the folks desperate to get out of Bangkok. He lowered his voice.

"Saifon. I hated that goddamned cat. I hated it from the first day she bought the scrawny runt home and started feeding it up."

"Why didn't you tell her?"

"I couldn't. She loved the son of a bitch. I knew it was like a child to her. I tried to like it. Really I did. But it knew I didn't like it. It knew, and it didn't like me back. When Reet was around it'd be all sweet and loving and stuff. Then, soon as she went out, the little vermin would hiss and spit at me and pee all over the place. Every time it left I wished a pack of rabid dogs would get it.

"So, you see? I wished it dead for most of it s life. Then as soon as Reet wasn't around no more, I made it dead."

"Waldo. You killed it cause it was fretting."

"On the outside, yeah. That's what I thought I was doing. I thought I was putting him out of his misery. But deep down, I was putting him out of my misery. I read all about it. It's called 'psychological'. That means your body does something your head tells you to, and you ain't got no say in it. Now, how in tarnation can I tell Reet that?"

"You old assassin, you."

"It ain't a joke, girl. I was so filled with remorse and prodded by the firey finger of the Lord, I didn't know what to do. His lifeless body looked like one of them fur collars. I took the bus up to Lake Michigan late at night and threw the goddamned gun in the lake.

It was after that I went in search of the Lord to beg for redemption."

"Over a frigging cat?"

"I told you, Saifon. In Reet's eyes it was like our fluffy, four-legged baby.It was like I'd blown our baby's brains out. Aretha was already suffering from being dead. I didn't want to make it worse for her."

"Being?"

"Dead AND mourning."

"So you been doing the mourning for her. All this churchgoing and talking to the Lord."

"I guess."

"You gotta tell Aretha."

"No. I can't."

"You told me didn't you?"

"That's different. You're my girl."

"That's just it. How long I been your girl and how long's Aretha been your wife? You owe her."

"You reckon?"

"Damned right I do."

"Jee."

Waldo sat and considered it for a long while. Saifon didn't want to interrupt his considering so they just sat quiet till the woman announced their flight was ready to board. Everyone stood up and got in a long queue 'cept for Saifon and Waldo. Even when the queue was down to a little waggly tail they was still stayed sitting. Waldo looked at the people with one eye and the TV screen with the other eye. At last he asked,

"Saifon."

"Yeah, I know." She reached for her bag.

"Why we going back?"

"What?"

"Why we going back to the States?"

"Why?"

"Yeah. What do we have to go back there for?" She thought some.

"I don't know."

"Me neither."

"You wanna go back to Laos?"

"Do you?"

"I guess I could."

"Me too."

68

And that was how them two ended up staying. Just like that. And I mean staying. Neither of 'em went back to the States. Not for thirty odd years. Not till till two months ago.

Saifon and Waldo had made a lot of friends of one type or another up on the Lao border. With the war still going on, visas and working permits wasn't easy to get a hold of so they figured it'd be better if Waldo didn't spend all his time on the Lao side. Wilbur fixed him up with a job on base at the US commissary in Udon Thani. He was working in the store there for a while, selling stuff to spies and pilots. He was great with figures. At weekends and on his days off, he took the bus over to Mukdahan and visited with Saifon and the skinny mafia guys and the commy students.

Things was going real good till Wilbur turned up in Udon. Waldo had missed him, but he didn't want to see him like he was by then.

-o-

Wilbur'd hardly knew a day's sickness in his life. Health was something he never thought about. He didn't take no precautions against tropical diseases, not cause he was ornery, but because guys that don't never get sick, don't know what it feels like.

It started with a kind of lethargy. He didn't feel like leaping out of bed. He walked when he would normally of jogged to the chopper. He felt it most in sport. He normally got through three sets of tennis without breathing heavy. But these days he was tuckered out after just the two. Then he could barely get through one.

He decided he needed a tonic. The guy they all lovingly called the witchdoctor at the RLA clinic give him some stuff that looked like shampoo and tasted like vomit. He asked Wilbur if he'd happened to see a captain they'd been missing for a couple of months. Wilbur didn't know nothing about it.

In Savannakhet after a series of defeats, Wilbur didn't get a lot of sympathy from the Lao army for the way he was feeling. There was troops dropping like flies from dysentery and malaria. He understood only too well how they felt about his being poorly. In fact, for a long time he kept it to himself. But now it was gone too far.

"Man, you look like hell, Will."

The helicopter pilot was an old crop duster from Kansas. Him and Wilbur'd been close for years. Wilbur saw his own reflection in the guy's shades. If there was worse than hell, he looked it.

"Where you going, Hank?"

"Udon. Wanna come? I think you should."

"Yeah. I guess I'd better."

Hank dropped him on the lawn out front of the clinic at the RTAF compound. He only had to walk twenty yards to the door but he barely made that. He should of been there two weeks earlier to give himself a real chance. The hepatitis already had a hold, and he weren't going no place but in the ground.

Oh, he fought. Man, he fought it. He hung on there for a month when most other guys would of pulled the pin. A lot of friends that knew him and respected him come to visit between missions. But there was one guy camped out in his room for the whole time.

"Sir, you understand it's contagious?"

"I know it."

"Wouldn't you like another room?"

"No ma'am. Thank you."

Waldo weren't going no place. They had a lot of meaningful talks in the time he was there. There was three that Waldo remembers real well. The first one went something like this: "I been talking to her, Waldo."

"Who's that, Wilbur?" He'd said, 'who's that, Wilbur?' but he knew already. They was up on the roof of the clinic and there was more stars up there than you could count in a lifetime.

"To Mary."

"I'm glad."

"It really helped. It made me feel …calmer. You always right, man?"

"No. I made a mistake once. It was 1937."

"Really? I would like to have been there for that."

"It won't happen again. What you telling her?"

"Mary? I tell her I love her. Tell her I've never loved anyone else. Tell her all the stupid things I've done. Tell her I was too bloody-minded to take all the inoculations they recommended."

"Do you tell her how many people come by and visit? How many people love you?"

"You think they do?"

"I know they do. And Mary oughta hear it too."

The second big talk come about a week before the end. Wilbur was looking kinda orange by then. They'd been joshing about it. Waldo complained Wilbur was sliding through the Dulux paint chart so quick he didn't have time to get down to the store and see what color he was.

When he'd stopped laughing about it, Wilbur remembered something.

"You recall what you gave me when we first met, Waldo?"

"Don't reckon I do."

"You gave me two packs of Darkie toothpaste." Waldo giggled.

"That's right, I did."

"And you were so pleased they were making toothpaste just for us dark folk. You didn't see nothing wrong with it, at all."

"There's something wrong?"

"Right. You know, Waldo. I'd always gotten mad when I saw that Darkie toothpaste. I always took it personal. I guess I'd gotten so paranoid about being the only black, sorry, the only mocha cream guy around, that I was waiting for insults. I was expecting people to be looking down at me like they did at home.

That toothpaste was an attack on my blackness. So I thought. Then you come along and you think it's the greatest joke on the planet. And I go on home and I think about it. The people that made the toothpaste didn't have a thing against me any more than the Pillsbury Dough people had against big round white folks. Whatever bad feeling I got from it came from me, not it.

And after that I looked at the way things were around me here. People didn't judge me for what colour I was. They judged me for what I did with 'em, and for 'em. Most of 'em hadn't ever seen a person of colour before so it occurred to me I was a clean slate."

"Maybe a blackboard."

"Yeah. Maybe a blackboard. But you did that, Waldo. You wiped my blackboard clean. I don't know how you do what you do, but you sure do it."

Waldo had that combination feeling of embarrassment and ignorance he was getting a lot lately. A lot of folks was seeing stuff in him that weren't really there, and he didn't know how to go about putting 'em right.

The last big talk was the night he went. Waldo knew his buddy was going. If the truth was to be told, by that stage they was both looking forward to it. If it had to happen, Wilbur wanted to still have the strength to think right to the end.

They was lying side by side on the single cot. The Wilbur of a year before wouldn't of fit on there by himself.

"You promised, Waldo."

"What's that, man?"

"To tell me what you do."

"Oh, Wilbur."

"Come on, bro. I'm outa here. I ain't gonna tell nobody in this life. There ain't a secret so deep you can't tell a dying man."

Waldo didn't know what to say. He was hurting for a sign from The Lord; some way he could make Wilbur believe. He didn't want his friend to go to his grave thinking he'd lied.

And suddenly it come. It come plain as the nose on his face, and through it. It come floating up from the bed pan beneath the bed. At the same time as the stink come to his nostrils, the name of B.O. Bulokavic come into his mind.

With tears of laughter streaming down his cheeks, Wilbur listened to the story of B.O. and how he married the girl without no nose, and the poem he read at the wedding. Then there was the night at the Inn Diana and the boys that found true romance with the Hollywood showgirls. And he heard how Saifon disguised herself as a Japanese and bought Mattfield from old Roundly's daughter.

Wilbur didn't laugh so much that it hurt 'cause by then there weren't nothing hurting no more. Hepatitis ain't the most painful disease, but it drains every ounce of strength you ever had. It don't really give you nothing but, man it's a thief.

So even though he didn't laugh till it hurt, Wilbur laughed till there weren't no more water in the reservoir to make tears no more. There weren't no doubt in his mind after that. No cover in the world could come up with stories like that. Sure as eggs is eggs, Waldo was a QCO in a pool ball factory, and that just made him even more remarkable in Wilbur's mind. The guy had to be an angel.

Wilbur was tuckered out from all the mirth he didn't deserve, so, with his weak hand clasping Waldo's, he said goodnight and went to sleep. And that was the end of Wilbur.

-o-

"Aretha, honey. There's someone coming up there I'd like you to take care of for me. He might need some help finding his wife. You was always good at finding stuff.
And Reet, I love you. Don't you forget that."

69

Saifon pretended she wasn't too concerned about Wilbur, but she was. Waldo didn't see her cry about it, but she did. She stayed busy to keep her mind off it.

When she'd got back over to Savannakheth, she stumbled on a deal. Like I said, everyone knew it wouldn't be long before the commies took control. In the early seventies, a lot of folks with reasons to be afraid sold up and got out.

The owner of the bar I been calling the 'manger', he had every right to be scared, what with all the sinful earnings he'd been living off all his life. He bought himself a visa to Australia and almost give the place away. Saifon still had some of her savings left over so she bought herself the bar and all the paperwork she needed to own it. Them was good days for picking up bargains from folks that was planning on a trip. That included stuff like passports. Before the end of 1972, Saifon was Lao again.

She learnt herself Lao reading and writing so's people couldn't cheat her. She put walls on that bar and turned it into a Bar and Grill, something like Moose's place but without the class.

Now I ain't told you yet what she was doing with all this money while it was still rolling in. She didn't forget them little girls. No sir. Some that was rescued in the States, they let stay there if they wanted to. Most of 'em did cause they didn't have nothing to come back to. Don't forget they was pretty screwed up already. But there was some that wanted to come back to Laos. It did worry 'em some that they'd been sold, but what happened in the States was so frigging horrible they just wanted out of there.

That's where Saifon come in. First off, she took in the four girls they'd just put on the boat. But one by one, the social services people in Washington sent back others. Saifon bought a big house on the river for about twenty cents and moved in there with the girls. She hired a private teacher to help 'em get through schooling and tried to give 'em the love they was all missing. It weren't easy. She worked hard to make that house a home.

One evening, Saifon was up on this bamboo ladder. It swayed from side to side like the bamboo wasn't dead yet. She had a pot of off-white paint and a brush made out of donkey mane. The insects was just lining up waiting to jump, splat into the fresh paint. The front of the house was starting to look like a slab of chocolate-chip ice-cream.

A voice come up from below.

"If you painted in the morning you wouldn't have so many insects, you know?"

"Well, believe it or not, I did start painting this big heap of shit in the morning, but I've only got one brush and one me, so I'm still up here."

She looked down to see who she was talking to, and nearly fell off the damn ladder. Standing there looking all ruddy and well fed and happy, was Nit.

Saifon come sliding down the bamboo like a monkey with a paint tin over one arm. The brush was still up top stuck to the wall with the critters. She weren't too sure if she should grab hold of the girl 'cause the Nit she remembered weren't a great one for physical contact. But she got her answer when Nit threw her arms around Saifon's neck. They didn't give a damn about the paint that was splashing over the pair of 'em. Nit was crying like a baby.

Saifon looked up over her shoulder and there was Pop and his ma, Souk looking back at her. She shook off Nit and went over and give 'em both a hug.

"You all just get back? I guess you been at Wilbur's place, already?" Souk answered.

"Yes."

"Then you know."

"He left some money for us with the neighbors."

Her and Pop both hung their heads like they'd lost something important. There was these maid-master relationships all over Asia where the maid was real polite and the master went round telling all his friends the servants loved him. That was bullshit. You might suppose that was a fact in about one percent of cases. But in the case of Wilbur it was true as day.

"So I guess you ain't got nowhere to go."

"There's another American in his house now. He's got a Thai wife and she already took a maid."

Pop cut in.

"And besides, the Americans ain't gonna be around for much longer." Souk slapped the back of his head, but not hard enough to convince anyone she meant it. Saifon handed Pop the paint and dragged Souk towards the house. She swept up Nit on the way.

"OK. The good news is I'm looking for a housekeeper myself, and a little guy to fight off the insects while I paint this crumbly old house."

Nit looked up at her with her big eyes.

"What about me?"

"You? Hell, you don't have to do a damn thing. You just sit back and eat. You're family."

And that family kept on growing.

-o-

By 1975, the restaurant and the house was both booming. But that's when the shit hit the fan. In the December of that year, Laos become the Peoples' Democratic Republic. The Pathet Lao Socialist forces marched peacefully into Vientiane, calm as you like, without firing a shot.

If the truth was to be told, there probably wasn't that many people left in town to shoot at. Most of the upper classes and the intelligent folks and them that had made enough money, had all fled across the Mekhong river in bathtubs, and closets, and anything else that would damn well float. They took their valuables with 'em. So there wasn't that much left for the PL to start a new republic with. But them old commies did the best they could with the nothing they had.

Saifon's restaurant suddenly took a nose dive cause the royal military wasn't getting paid no more and them that didn't flee the country, burnt their uniforms and registered with the communist party. Like I said, Laos was a very forgiving country.

The new socialist government announced there was gonna be cutbacks for a while, just till the republic got on its feet. Now, for country folks that had nothing already, cutting back didn't make no difference. Half of nothing's pretty much the same as nothing.

But the commie way of cutting back wasn't so bad. After a while, the poor people was getting rice and basics in a national share out. They was doing better than ever. So for a while, if you was used to starving, communism was a real good thing. The new government took over businesses and salvaged what was left after the rats had all deserted the ship.

Politics ain't my strong point, just as a lot of other things ain't. I imagine, like most good ideas, communism worked pretty good in the early days. But as time went on and with people being the shits they are, there was those that tried to make a few bucks on the side. It's one of them things that if everyone ain't rowing together, the boat stops moving. You know what I mean? If pure communism didn't work in a country like Laos, it ain't gonna work no place.

See what happens? You write a book and it makes you smart.

By the time Laos become a republic, Saifon had thirteen girls at her place from thirteen to eighteen years of age. Eight was from the smuggling. Five come in off the street.

They loved that old place. They called it the Raindrop house for obvious reasons.

But without no income from the restaurant, Saifon really didn't know how she was gonna make ends meet. Waldo started bringing over supplies on his boat. He was like a one-man import business, with oars.

Then there was one day when he was sitting in the living room looking fitter than Jessie Owens from all the rowing, and handsomer than Sydney Poitier from the dieting. He was down below two-hundred pounds for the first time since he was about twelve. Him and Saifon and the girls was singing songs and playing games and having a gay old time when Souk the maid comes running in like there's a catfish up her ass.

"The Pppppp ….The Pppppp"

They looked at her. She was shaking like a jelly. Saifon asked the girls,

"Can anyone tell me what the hell she's saying?"

"The Ppppp ….The Pppppp," the girls all said.

"That much I got myself. Souk, you wanna take a deep breath and try that again?"

The maid sat down and fanned herself with a magazine.

"The …the …the President's outside."

"The President of what?"

"Laos." The girls didn't know whether to hide or go put on make-up.

"Come on."

"Really. He's in a big black car. He wants to know if he can come in." One of the girls collapsed like a sandcastle when the tide washes through it. They give her snuff to bring her round.

"You didn't just leave him out on the doorstep? Jee. What does he want with us? We ain't done nothing."

Waldo was standing to attention, adjusting his T-shirt. He was just about to be exposed as an illegal alien in front of the President of Laos.

"What if they want to close this place and take the girls away?"

"Over my dead frigging body. He'll have to fight me personally if he wants to touch my girls."

"Wrestling or Judo?"

The voice come from the doorway. There, dressed in a white suite with a white tie like the doorman at the Inn Diana whorehouse stood the quiet guy, Soup. Waldo smiled like a sunrise.

"Soup? Hell, it's good to see you. You ain't the President."

"I am too."

"He certainly is. Did well for himself, didn't he?" Mrs. Pornsawan come out from behind him dressed in a pretty Lao skirt and blouse. There was a little posse of armed guys buzzing around, checking the girls for weapons and the cushions for bombs.

"Well, I'll be a sheep's you-know-what." They almost shot Waldo when he went over to President Souphanouvong to give him a hug. He slowed down some when he saw the guns pointed at him.

"Waldo. Long time no see."

"President. Well, gosh darn. Ain't that something? I ain't never shook hands with a president before."

"Then you'd better do it." He waved away the guards, and him and Waldo greeted each other like old bowling buddies. Mrs. Porn give Saifon a hug.

"We lost track of you," the old lady said. "We only found out you were here two days ago. Communication with the south isn't so good. And these, I take it, are your girls." The girls was all sprawled out on the floor *nopp*'ing the visitors. That's as polite as you can get in Laos short of digging a hole and climbing in it. They was all shitting 'emselves at being in the same room as a Prince who was doubling as a president. Saifon and Waldo scored a few brownie points with the girls that day.

After the shock, they all sat down for tea. The girls was on their best behavior. Didn't spill nothing. Didn't say nothing embarrassing, well, almost nothing. Porn and Soup was real proud of what Saifon had done for 'em. They didn't want to take the girls away. Hell, no. They wanted to give 'em more.

While Waldo and Soup and the bodyguards was off playing pool on the table Waldo had made by hand, and the girls was doing their chores, Mrs. Porn had took Saifon off to one side.

"Saifon, dear. You know we have a lot of girls who lost families in the bombing. Most of them were forced into prostitution to stay alive. We need somewhere to keep the younger ones."

"Well, I tell you, Mrs. P. If you don't mind 'em eating dirt and drinking river, they're all real welcome here." Saifon was so proud to be asked to do it she almost had a chest there for a second.

"I know times are hard but I think we can help. We can provide basic rice and canned food and seeds and cuttings for fruit and vegetables. And I can get you staff. We can probably do something about that restaurant of yours as well. Perhaps make it an official socialist party venue for regional meetings and functions. You interested?"

"Is the Prince communist?"

"I take that as a 'yes' then. We have a deal?"

"You bet." She hugged Mrs. Porn then ran over to the pool table to hug her dad. It really messed up his shot. While she was explaining her new deal, Mrs. Porn come over to the table and sank three straight spots. She was either born lucky or born with a pool table in the loft. Soup patted Saifon on the back.

"And I believe you've become Lao again. That qualifies you for a medal."

"A medal?" She blushed like the back end of a baboon. "I don't want no frigging medal …sir."

"Too bad. It's a government decree. You have no choice."

Waldo was smiling outside but unhappy inside. That was another one of them psychology moments he'd read about. He was feeling left out of things. Oh. He was happy for Saifon. Course he was. But this was looking like one of them 'don't call us, Waldo, we'll call you' moments. Here he was playing pool with the president and he didn't even have a visa. He was an illegal alien and the guilt was too much for him to bear.

"Soup, I got a confession to make."

"Ah, yes. Waldo." Mrs. Porn give him his cue back. "I hear you've been in Thailand for the past four years."

"Yes, ma'am. On and off."

"So I assume your Thai is quite impressive."

"It could probably impress anyone that don't speak it."

"Now, don't be modest. As Thai and Lao are quite similar, I don't imagine it would take you long to master Lao, given the chance. I'm thinking, with all these young girls alone in this big house, they could very much have use for a male guardian. Someone big."

It took him a while to realize who she was talking about.

"Me?"

"Although I have to insist you stop dieting before there's nothing left of you. You're getting far too attractive. I don't want the girls falling in love with you."

He was always a sucker for compliments.

"Ah, shucks." He blushed. " But I really got to tell you …"

"Yes?"

"Well, you probably noticed already, but I'm an American."

"I do know that."

"Then, how can I stay in Laos …after all that's happened? You know?"

"The war, you mean? As far as I know, the war's over. Isn't that right, Soup?"

"I believe so. We Laos don't hold grudges, Waldo. If you go to Vientiane, you'll notice that your consulate is still open. We haven't thrown them out."

"You mean … I can stay here? Do you think you can get me a visa?" Saifon slapped him on the back of the head.

"Waldo. He's the goddamned president. He could make you minister of pool or something if he wanted."

"Hell."

-o-

So that's how Saifon and Waldo got to stay in Laos even through the tough times. They was real happy there and they lived happily ever after, till they died. So, I guess the only mystery that's left is who the hell I am. You know what? I decided that ain't none of your business so I ain't gonna tell you.

70

The end

No, I'm only kidding you. I'll tell you. My name's Bounlahn. I was one of them lucky kids what got sent to the Raindrop House.

Saifon didn't never get married. She was still working her butt off for the girls there. Nit and Pop, not to no one's surprise got wed as soon as they was of legal age. Man, we had some party that day.

Laos is still socialist although Soup and Mrs. P are long gone. Old Soup still found time for the odd game with Waldo even when he was retired and real old. Laos is a different kind of communist now. A lot of folks that split in 75 have come back and they're allowed to be capitalists again, so long as they share the profits with the government. People is people, right?

Saifon's restaurant's doing good again now there's money to spend. That's how come we had enough to come back with Waldo. Yeah, that's right. Ninety five years old and he was still kicking around at the house, still teaching us girls English. If it weren't for Waldo, my English wouldn't be as great as it is. There's a lot of us in Laos talk just like him and Saifon.

We didn't think he was ever gonna die. He was fit as a fiddle. Then, one day he comes into the social room and he says,

"Girls, I gotta go home."

"You are home," we say.

"No. I mean home where I was borne. It's time to be with Aretha."

It's funny how he knew. He must of got a fax from heaven or something. He'd made his peace with Aretha long before. I guess she'd forgive him for terminating her cat and she wanted him back.

Saifon knew there wasn't no point in arguing with him. She went out and bought three tickets. Two was for her and Waldo, of course. But when she told me I'd be going with 'em, I almost fell in the frigging Mekhong. Me? I was the nastiest bitch they'd ever seen at the Raindrop. I stole. I lied my butt off. I went with boys, and men. I treated Saifon like shit. But no matter how hard I tried, I couldn't never get her to hate me. I guess I was testing how deep they loved me. I never hit the bottom.

After I got over the shock I was scared to death. I'd never flown before less you count the time I fell out the upstairs window, drunk. I was sure they'd wait till we was flying over something hard and they'd open the door and throw me out. I deserved it. But they didn't. You know what they did instead? They told me a story. This story.

They sat on either side of me and it was like that stereophonic sound at the movies. One in each ear. Both of 'em filling in the gaps, laughing, and crying. Waldo tells one bit. Saifon tells another. And it's true, Waldo's memory was going towards the end, and it was like he was hearing his own story for the first time.

It was the most magic time I'd ever knew in my short life. I was pissed when they wanted to go to sleep. I didn't want it to end. Even in the rental car out to Mattfield they was still telling it.

They must of been disappointed when they saw the place. The land was sliding so bad after the rains of 78 that the government moved the last residents out and destroyed all the buildings for safety sake. They couldn't build nothing new there. We was sitting in the rubble where Roundley's used to be when they got to the end of the story, at least we thought it was the end. Tears was streaming down our faces. I ain't sure what kind of tears they was.

Waldo picked up a rock that was probably a bit of wall once, and he looked at it like it was one of them crystal balls. Then in his crunchy old voice he told us the missing part.

"I did all my chores in the chapel that morning and before the preacher was up and dressed I went to have a word with the Lord. I told the Lord what I had in mind and I waited for an answer. Nothing come, so I took that as a sign of permission.

"I walked down the main street. Being Sunday there weren't a lot of folk up. Old Mr. What's-his-name was just arriving to open up his deli so folks could get their milk to go with Sendrine's Sunday pastries. There was baking smells floating in the air. I noticed how the birds was being particular friendly. I guessed they was thanking me for not smiling in the mornings. Even the dogs bothered to look up when I walked past.

The factory was still asleep. I don't reckon it even noticed me unlock the outhouse and take out the gas tanks."

A smile come on Saifon's face like a spotlight.

" I put down a layer of petroleum all around and used my old lighter to get the fire going. Mrs. Zucherman walked past with that sick-looking dog of hers and she says, 'Morning, Waldo. You setting fire to Roundley's there?' And I says, 'Reckon I am, Mrs. Zucherman.' And she says, 'Good on you, Waldo.' And she walks on by.

Must of been another three people saw me on the walk back up the hill to the chapel. That's why I was real surprised when no one told the cops they'd seen me. I guess they was happy to watch the place go up in smoke. I didn't lie when the cops asked me. I just told 'em I didn't have no good reason for doing it. And I don't reckon I did. I just did it cause I felt like it."

He layed himself back down in amongst the rubble and he laughed and looked up at the sky. Saifon laughed too and she went over and give him a kiss on the forehead.

We all lay there for a time enjoying the fresh air and the view of heaven. And I guess Waldo liked the view so much he decided not to wait. The laughing tears was dried and powdery on his cheeks and his mouth was open.

I went to pieces. But Saifon had just this one slow tear rolling down her face. She weren't making no noise, but. She put her jacket over Waldo's head and called the police on her mobile phone. Saifon always knew what to do in emergencies.

The coroner and the hearse come out and took poor dead Waldo off to St. Dominic's funeral home and cemetery. Saifon being his only surviving kin, she give instructions to the funeral director and we camped out at the motel. Me crying most of the time, Saifon sleeping like nothing had happened.

There was only me and her at the service. We was standing beside the hole that was reserved next to Aretha. It was so close they could of reached out and held hands. The preacher played a Jelly Roll Morton tape like Saifon asked him. She only said one thing when it was her turn.

"Dear Waldo, my dad. You're the only man I ever loved."

She threw some dirt in the hole and I held on to her hand and balled my frigging eyes out.

-o-

I started writing this book just after that. Saifon bought a load of flower seeds and we took 'em back out to Roundley's to brighten up the spot where Waldo breathed his last breath. I knew I was gonna write, and I bought me some of them writing books and a pencil. I figured Roundley's would be a fitting place to start the story.

Saifon left me there for a while. She wandered off across the fields and was gone for a couple of hours. She said she was just sightseeing, but I knew she wanted time to go off and cry on her own so I couldn't see. I understand that. She was okay when she got back 'cept suddenly she didn't have no makeup on no more. We drove into South Bend and stopped by a hardware store to look at the paint charts and see what color I was. I'm 'dark coral' That sounds pretty don't it?

-o-

And that's it. This is the only book I ever writ. I writ it for an ex-fat guy who never wished no harm to nobody. He thought his life was over, but then he found it was just starting. He wasn't the smartest man that ever lived but he understood people, and that's more important far as I'm concerned. If they asked me if I'd sooner be Waldo or that Einstein guy, I know which one I'd chose. I bet Einstein never beat no president at pool.

And I writ it for a woman who had a shitty first half of her life and give up the rest of it to make sure other kids like me got a better start. I appreciate that now. I think I've got a handle on what love's all about.

Author's Note

The character; Wilbur was based on a real-life hero who was stationed in Lao during the secret war. Whatever criticisms we may have about the wisdom or ethics of America's involvement there, the fact remains that many brave people on both sides lost their lives fighting for what they believed was right.

One of those was Major Wilbur M Greene. His role in Laos was pretty much as I've described it. The thoughts and beliefs attributed to Wilbur in this book belong entirely to the fictional character. Yet I hope I haven't betrayed his spirit by painting him with humour.

Will Greene died of hepatitis in Udon in April 1972. He was loved by the men he served with, and respected as a soldier and field officer.

I hope his children enjoy his appearance in this book.

-o-

Over one and three quarter million people died from the fighting in Indochina between 1965 and 1975. Most of these were civilians.

War and violence are not the last resort of conflict. They are merely the evidence that man is not intelligent enough to solve his problems any other way.

Made in the USA
San Bernardino, CA
10 September 2014